MO
JAMES ~~GARDNER'S~~
DARK CONTINENT
CHRONICLES

"I highly recommend The Lion Killer. *I have seldom come across such fine descriptive writing in a thriller."*

—James Patterson,
America's Best-Selling author

"A riveting thriller with twists and turns galore."

—Robert Halmi, Jr., Emmy and Golden
Globe Award winner,
Executive Producer of *"Lonesome Dove"*

"Few really good books come out of Africa, but James Gardner's 'The Lion Killer' is one of those few. It's easy to see that Gardner has been there and that he understood what he saw. His powerful writing illuminates the Dark Continent."

—Nelson DeMille,
New York Times Best-Selling author

"James Gardner has done it again and more so! His first thriller was captivating. This one is riveting. An excellent read!"

—Charles and Barbara Whitfield,
Best-Selling authors, Muse House Press

THE ZAMBEZI VENDETTA

THE DARK CONTINENT SERIES BOOK II

JAMES GARDNER

PENNINGTON PUBLISHERS

PENNINGTON PUBLISHERS
ISBN 978-1-935827-04-7
Trade Paperback
© Copyright 2011 James Gardner
All Rights Reserved

Requests for information should be addressed to:
Pennington Publishers, Inc. at the following email
address or websites:

sales@thelionkiller.net
www.TheLionKiller.net
www.PenningtonPublishers.com

Pennington Publishers and the Pennington logo
are imprints of Pennington Publishers, Inc.

Cover design: Donald Brennan / YakRider Media
Interior design: Donald Brennan / YakRider Media

Printed in the U.S.A.

FOR JENNIFER

ACKNOWLEDGEMENTS

I would like to thank my editors: Barbara Gardner, Lynn Denney and Nan Britt.

I owe special gratitude to some friends who have been very supportive: William Flaherty, Robert Barrett, Robert Halmi Jr., John Jolley, Tad Knutsen and Eileen and Joe Cornacchia, and my art and production director, Donald Brennan.

My special thanks to Charles Whitfield, MD and his wife Barbara of Muse House Press, for their ongoing encouragement.

My appreciation to my agents, Marianne Strong and Diana Oswald of The Strong Literary Agency.

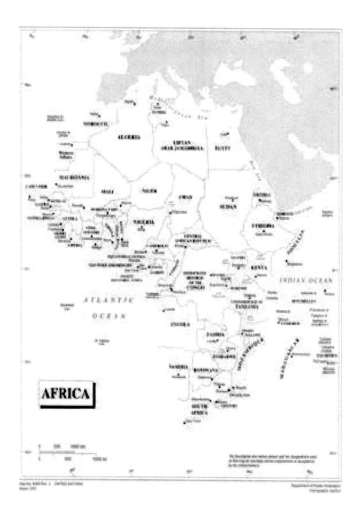

AFRICA

The Zambezi River
Zimbabwe

The mighty Zambezi was dazzling in full-flood; its headwaters, born in the Congo Basin, snaked for a thousand kilometers before cascading over Victoria Falls. A spine-tingling roar rumbled from the cataract. The sun, filtered by mist, spawned a perpetual rainbow above the falls. That same mist cooled the crowd gathered behind the old Victoria Falls Hotel overlooking the gorge. The crowd had gathered to hear the new President of Zimbabwe in what was, for them, a glorious time. Many had suffered unimaginable hardships, yet they sought no reprisals. This was a time for healing.

Steven Mabota defogged his sunglasses and scanned the sea of black faces intermingled by a few white ones. Women paddled the air with fans. Men loosened their ties. Rigby Croxford sat in the front row between the

Flaxneys and Colin White. Steven smiled, watching Rigby squirm in his outdated business suit.

A sense of pride overwhelmed Rigby as he studied Steven. Sweat and mist made Steven's face shine. My wife was right; he is the best-looking man in this country, black or white. As he listened to the speeches, he thought about Steven's fathers. What a pity they didn't live to see their son's political ambitions realized.

There were uninvited guests in attendance that day; they were the resident baboons who rummaged the hotel's garbage cans. After the security guards chased them away, the apes observed the proceedings from the safety of a wild fig tree. A violent squabble erupted within the troop. Limbs shook and leaves fell as the baboons chased each other. The troop's antics evoked muffled laughter from the crowd.

Steven and Rigby locked eyes, and in that split second their thoughts were the same; they were thinking about that day in Hwange prison.

*   *   *

1

Hwange Prison
Two years earlier

A bull baboon leaned back on his haunches as he waited for his troop. When he swaggered away, the other baboons followed him single-file down a razor-wired fence; it was the eastern wall of Zimbabwe's infamous Hwange prison. Beyond the barbwire there were rows of unpainted barracks roofed in corrugated tin. Everything was caked in dust including the sparse grass around the prison guards' mud-walled rondavels. The apes moved in and out of the crooked shadows cast by some leafless trees. Their scavenging led them into the prison's cemetery. A straggler, with her infant perched on her back like a jockey, stopped to sift handfuls of sand looking for seeds. Other baboons, some with pink rumps, dug hopefully for roots. The troop avoided a freshly dug grave and entered the prison's latrine where they separated piles of feces looking for beetles.

Sub-Saharan Africa was held captive by the dry season. All living things were suffering. The baboons' ribs were showing. The troop's hunger caused violent flare-ups, but fatigue shortened their squabbles.

As the troop fanned out to browse the hillside, an adolescent male harassed his sister by pulling on her tail. His pencil-thin penis grew stiff. His sister was so exhausted all she could muster was a half-hearted snarl. The young male's advances were not missed by the troop leader. He gave chase, but it ended when the transgressor grabbed a mother's baby and pretended to groom the infant. When the big male turned away, he tossed the baby aside and resumed his attention on his sister.

As the sun slipped beneath the horizon, the dominant baboon picked up the pace. He needed to get his troop into their new sleeping tree before sundown. Three nights ago, a leopard had come in the night killing a troop member. The tree smelled of death, which made moving necessary.

Their new sleeping tree was a flat-topped acacia near the prison wall. The troop leader waited at the top of the hill. He flashed his eyelids and yawned a warning. His thunderous bark scattered the howling baboons. The females scooped their skeletal babies underneath their bellies and loped up the hill. The lesser males recoiled as the big ape sauntered between them. They offered their asses to their leader, which calmed him. When they reached the base of the acacia, the violent eruption ended as abruptly as it had started.

Jan "Dutchy" Bosshart's arms quivered. He blew sweat from his upper lip as he stretched a rubber tire tube fastened between two iron bars in their cell window. Rigby Croxford leaned over Dutchy's shoulder to help him aim. Steven Mabota peeked over the top of Rigby's head. Fearing a ricochet, their cellmates cowered behind each other. Their target was the bull baboon. Rigby nicknamed the ape "Bob" after the resident of Zimbabwe, Robert Mugabe. Every morning, from the safety of his tree, Bob hurled his turds at the inmates. Their purpose was not revenge; their intention was to eat the baboon. The prisoners were starving.

"Hold steady, mate," Rigby said, checking Dutchy's alignment. "Aim just above the lowest branch. That's the one. Now, fire when you're ready."

"Is the stone big enough to kill him? The baboon weighs more than I do," Steven asked. Two years in Hwange Prison had whittled Steven into a living corpse.

"My friend, this could kill a rhino," Rigby said, hefting the stone. "Remember what David did to Goliath. Don't worry, if we wound him, his buddies will finish him."

The unrelenting heat sapped Rigby's energy. He sat down and fanned himself with a brimless hat. Steven slid down the wall next to him. As he studied Steven, he reminisced about the boy's father, Sam. They had served together in the war. Your father's the only reason I'm still alive, well only just alive, he thought, glancing at his surroundings. He winced when he patted Steven on the shoulder. You're nothing but skin and bones.

After the Rhodesian Bush War ended, Rigby put down his weapon and returned to farming. He gave a section of his best farmland to Steven's father. Life was good for the Croxfords and the Mabotas in the early post-war years.

Sam's son, Steven, and Rigby's daughter, Christine, played together as young children, but their friendship was suspended as they entered puberty, which was a social dictate of post-colonial Africa. When Steven and Christine attended the university in Harare and were no longer under the scrutiny of their parents, they renewed their friendship. After graduating, Christine Croxford moved to South Africa to enter medical school. Steven enrolled in law school in Harare.

Zimbabweans were hopeful when Robert Mugabe became their president. His inaugural speech emphasized reconciliation, but Zimbabwe's prosperity was short-lived. The centerpiece of Mugabe's presidency became the confiscation of the white-owned farms, which ruined the most productive economy in Africa. Faced with the confiscation of his own farm, Rigby was forced into professional hunting. Steven's father, Sam, worked for Rigby as his game-tracker. Sam's accidental death on a lion hunt in Mozambique had strained Rigby and Steven's relationship. Fate had reunited them.

"Quiet please. Our guest of honor has arrived," Rigby whispered, pressing his finger to his lips. "Steady mate, don't fire until you've got him dead in your sights. A headshot would be lovely."

Bob waited for his archrival. When the ape moved too slowly to suit him, he false-mounted the baboon and delivered a savage bite that sent his challenger scurrying up the tree.

Dutchy's first shot ricocheted wood shrapnel into the bull baboon's belly. The troop leader shrieked and bit at the wound. Dutchy reloaded and fired again. This time the stone struck the ape's leg. The ape tried to climb up the tree, but his leg appeared boneless and wouldn't support him. The baboon hit the ground with a dusty thud.

"Nice shot!" Rigby yelled. The other inmates pushed forward for access to the window.

It was pandemonium. Trapezing apes snapped off branches to vent their fury. Their howling was punctuated by ear-piercing barks. The troop rallied to their crippled leader, but instead of mounting a defense, they mauled him. The old male may have been injured, but he was still dangerous. He crushed two aggressors' skulls with ferocious head bites. The younger attackers used the distraction to savage the big male. They pressed in, bobbing and weaving and smacking their jaws. As Bob's counter-charges became feeble, the apes mangled him again and again. In the end, his eyes glazed over and his mouth fell open. Satisfied of the old baboon's death, the troop scrambled down and raced off behind their new leader in search of another sleeping tree.

A prison guard tested the dead baboons by touching each one with the barrel of his Kalashnikov. He dragged the dead apes by their tails through the gate and yelled for a trustee to fetch them.

Steven turned to face Rigby. "How did you know the other baboons would kill him?"

"Baboons have long memories. They're just settling old scores. I'm somewhat of an expert at hunting baboons, I'm embarrassed to admit. One of my few talents in life. Baboons are like African politicians. When they see their leader buggered, they usually finish the job. Steven, you need to remember this little demonstration."

"Not all politicians are bad. What about Mandela?" Steven asked.

"Point noted. Anyway, we've got baboon stew on the menu." Rigby finished in a buck-toothed Oxford accent, asking Dutchy, "I say, old chum, will you take your baboon sautéed or poached?"

"I prefer mine steamed in a buttery Chardonnay and smothered in white truffles." Then Dutchy added as an afterthought, "Although, I *have* heard boiling kills the parasites."

Rigby was smiling when he spoke. "Don't ruin Steven's appetite. I hate to think about how many baboons your father and I ate during the War. We used to call them our 'hairy eating experiences.' It's a wonder we didn't grow tails. That reminds me of—" A wailing siren signaling lockdown stopped him.

*   *   *

Hwange Prison was built to house three hundred convicts. The prison population had swelled to one thousand black inmates and two white ones, Rigby Croxford and Dutchy Bosshart. Their communal cell measured ten meters by five. It would have been cramped for twenty prisoners; it was claustrophobic for fifty. There was only enough space for the inmates to sleep on their sides. They wedged themselves in, head to feet, like English biscuits in a box. Every hour on cue, they reversed their sleeping positions to lessen the numbness. At one end of the barracks there were three buckets for shitting. Men suffering from dysentery were given priority sleeping positions for quicker access. Plump green-headed flies covered the walls. Disturbed, the insects would drone up into a buzzing cloud. The stench became more sickening as the evening breeze abated. The sobbing of some younger inmates punctuated by rattling coughs scored a symphony of misery.

Rigby lay with his back pressed against the wall. It had been four months since his wife's last visit. He was afraid for Helen to see him. When he looked in a mirror, he hardly recognized himself. Deep parentheses outlined his mouth. New wrinkles and streaks of gray hair appeared overnight. So this is what it's like to be starved to death, he thought. He remembered seeing the fear in his wife's face at his sentencing.

He tried to dream about pleasant things, but his thinking returned to why he was sent to prison. It started the day they tried to take his farm. The Croxford farm had been in his family for a hundred years. To Rigby, the land was sacred as it bore the graves of both his parents and grandparents. To give up his farm without a fight was never an option.

He remembered watching the vehicles drive up. Helen, Dutchy Bosshart and his wife, Sadie, stood next to him on the veranda. When he recognized Ian Rhodes's vehicle, he felt his pulse rate quicken.

Rhodes had started his military career as an advisor on loan from the South African Army. He was suspected of spying during the Rhodesian Bush War. The speculation got legs after Mugabe gave Rhodes two confiscated farms. Rigby was convinced that Rhodes's espionage was responsible for the death of his best friend. Rhodes's nickname in Shona was "*Magondo*," which means hyena. Africans believe the hyena is a despicable creature because the animal is a desecrator of graves.

Rhodes's cheeks were pockmarked. His neck was covered by black-heads and pimples, which he picked at incessantly. He hid his Roquefort outlined teeth behind a bushy moustache. His smiling suggested cruelty.

He walked up to the veranda, took his hat off and slapped it against his thigh to knock out the road dust. His bald head was speckled with beads of sweat. His smugness revealed there was pleasure in what he was about to say.

"Mr. Croxford, Mr. Bosshart, ladies," said Rhodes. He attempted unsuccessfully to shake hands with Dutchy and then Rigby.

"What are you waiting for, Rhodes, a roll of the drums?"

"I guess you know why I'm here?" said Rhodes at last, twirling a tip of his spiked mustache. His eyes were rippled with malice. He shifted his weight from one foot to the other as he spanked more dust from his pants.

"Why I haven't the slightest," said Rigby.

"This isn't my idea. I'm just following orders."

"Did you hear that, Dutchy? The man says— he's just following orders. Rhodes, you're a liar. Your mates in Harare told us our farm wasn't targeted for confiscation. My wife's the only doctor within a hundred kilometers. This country needs doctors. So you see— I'm not buying your bullshit. This is your work."

"Croxford, you're finished here." Rhodes walked back to his truck. Rigby recognized some of the men as his wife's patients. They looked shamefaced.

Rhodes got into a heated argument with one of his men that ended with his slapping the man. He walked back to the edge of the veranda and just stood there. Neither man spoke as they assessed each other.

Rhodes spoke first, "Croxford, I've tried to be civil with you, but you want this the hard way. I'm giving you *one last chance* to vacate this property. If you don't leave— I'll be obliged to use force. One way or another— you're leaving this farm today. Do I make myself clear?"

"Abundantly. Now, I'm giving you one last chance to *sod off*." Without warning, Rigby grabbed a soldier's rifle and jerked it free. He calmly walked over and smashed the wooden stock over a stone fence reducing it to splinters.

"Get them, you idiots," Rhodes screamed at his men. When he shoved them forward, they resisted like he was trying to push them over a cliff. Dutchy grabbed two soldiers and smacked their heads together; they dropped like coils of fallen rope. Rigby leaped at Rhodes, but Rhodes jumped in behind his men. Rigby caught one man flush on the jaw with a straight right sending him to the ground. A soldier pinned Rigby's legs together and two more grabbed his arms. Rhodes stepped forward and sucker-punched him. Rigby and Dutchy managed to wrestle free, but they ended up underneath the pile of soldiers. Both men were pummeled with hard kicks and flying fists.

"It's a good scrap— like the bar fights we had in the old days. Do you think they're getting tired?" Dutchy yelled with his face pushed against Rigby's. His grin was interrupted by a grunt. "Ouch! That one bites like a mongoose."

Rigby's voice was stifled by the weight of the mob. "I'm bloody sure their feet must be getting sore. For Christ's sake, do something before they kill us."

Dutchy bellowed like a rogue elephant. He stood up with Africans hanging on him like leeches. He wobbled one soldier with a head-slap that short-circuited the man's equilibrium dropping him to his knees. When Dutchy feigned a charge, the other soldiers cowered. "You dung-eaters fight like old women," he roared.

Rigby used the distraction to go for Rhodes, but Rhodes saw it coming and bolted. Rigby managed to latch on to Rhodes's trousers. When he tripped he pulled Rhodes's pants down around his ankles. They went down in a twisted knot like fighting cobras. Rigby managed to roll Rhodes over on his stomach. Then he took off his belt and walloped Rhodes's exposed ass turning it scarlet. Curiously, the soldiers made no effort to intervene. Dutchy engulfed Rigby in a bear hug and pulled him off. Sickened by the violence, Helen and Sadie walked back into the house. The soldiers tried to help Rhodes to his feet, but he pushed them away.

"Get away from me!" he yelled, straightening himself.

"Croxford, you think you've won, but you're wrong. Just you wait and see."

As they watched the convoy drive away, Rigby and Dutchy patted each other on the back. It was a small win, but a triumph nonetheless. They fought together in the war thirty years ago and had suffered a humiliating defeat. Now their country was being ruined by an inept tyrant. Their victories had been few and far between.

* * *

[12]

After they were alone, Helen confronted her husband. "I think we should move into the clinic. Let Rhodes have the damn farm. It's not worth getting killed over."

"If I leave, it'll have to be horizontally. He'll never get this land."

"Sometimes, your reasoning escapes me."

"This land has been in my family for over a hundred years. My parents and their parents are buried here, for Christ's sake. I fought a war for this country. It may say Zimbabwean on your passport, but you weren't born here. I can't expect you to feel the same way."

She got out of bed and walked over to a window. She thought for a moment and then she said, "So, we're back to the old— you have to be born here to really understand nonsense. You may have fought in one war, but I fight wars everyday trying to save lives."

" I love you," he said, placing his hand on her arm.

"If you love me, don't get yourself killed over this farm."

"Are those the doctor's orders?"

"You bet."

*   *   *

Two weeks later, Ian Rhodes armed with arrest warrants and accompanied by twenty Zimbabwean soldiers arrived in the middle of the night.

Rigby and Dutchy spent the next two weeks in jail waiting for a trial that lasted only fifteen minutes.

An African judge wearing a white curly wig looked over the top of his metal-rimmed bifocals at the accused and scolded them before even hearing the charges. When he closed his eyes and then reopened them slowly, Rigby had an image of a black bullfrog swallowing two bugs.

Rigby tried to absolve Dutchy of any blame, but when the judge started drumming his fingers, he whispered, "Sorry Dutchy, I'm afraid we're both stuffed."

Rhodes testified they tried to kill him. Rhodes refused to sit in the witness box, saying his injuries made it too painful. Their appointed barrister asked Rhodes to show the court the extent of his injuries; the judge denied the motion. The sentence was six months in Hwange prison, or a $5000.00 fine. They opted for the prison time. Rhodes sneered at them as they were led shuffling from the courtroom in shackles.

THE ZAMBEZI VENDETTA

2

And so, they waited in Hwange prison. As their release date got closer, time seemed to slowdown, but that day passed like any other day.

Rigby's daydream was suspended by the camp's whistle. Each ear-splitting toot was shriller than the one before it. It signaled the start of another day.

A guard unlocked their barracks' padlock. The inmates shuffled out like zombies; sleeping on the stone floor had stiffened their joints. After inspecting the building for sick or dead inmates, the guard blew his whistle giving a trustee the go-ahead to hose down the barracks.

Rigby Croxford stretched his arms and rolled his neck to work out the stiffness. Losing twenty kilos had carved his body into a sinewy tangle of muscles. A wind shift gave him a lethal whiff from the latrines. He held his breath and moved upwind to a water barrel. After submerging his head, he flung his soppy hair back and wiped away the vestiges of sleep. "Dutchy, what's on today's agenda?"

"The usual complaints — stealing food and unwanted advances by sissies." Dutchy beckoned to an inmate standing at the head of the line.

"Just another day in paradise," said Rigby, yawning.

"So, what's your problem? Well, speak up, man."

Rigby didn't seek the role of prison boss— it was forced on him. Every prison has a bully— Hwange's was a mean-spirited Shona with no neck and bulging biceps. His hair was twisted in tight springs, making him look like he had a giant tarantula draped on his head. Hardly a day passed without the bully savaging another inmate. His victims were always smaller members of the Matabele tribe. The guards refused to discipline their fellow tribesman; they saw the violence as a reprieve from their boredom.

The Shona bully's string of victories spawned cockiness. When he first laid eyes on Rigby, he knew they would eventually lock horns. There were casual bumps followed by snide remarks. Finally one day, Rigby mentioned to Dutchy, "The Shona wants a piece of me. I can't see why I shouldn't oblige him."

"He's half your age and five stones heavier. What do you want me to tell your wife if he kills you?"

"Oh, ye of little faith. No matter what happens, you stay out of this. Just make sure I don't kill the son-of-a-bitch. No sense making this shit-hole my permanent residence. Besides, I've had about all of you I can tolerate." He tugged on Dutchy's beard playfully.

Later that day, with the sun at his back, Rigby raced across the prison yard like a charging lion. His muscles stiffened for impact. Strangely, the inmates standing around the bully didn't warn him. A second before contact, the man turned to investigate, but the sun blurred his vision. Rigby launched himself into a human missile and hit the man with a flying forearm to the face. The sound of the collision was a bone-crushing wallop. The man would have fallen no faster if he'd been pole-axed. The commotion attracted most of the prison population including the warden, who watched from his office window. Some of the onlookers encouraged the bully to get up, but he didn't move a muscle.

"I think you killed him," said Dutchy, scratching his beard. When he nudged the Shona with his foot, the man groaned.

"He'll recover, but he's gonna be uglier than three shades of shit," Rigby said, massaging his forearm.

"No more bullying for this Shona," said Dutchy.

Steven dumped a bucket of water in the man's face. His incisors had severed a perfect V-shaped wedge into his upper lip. Bloody spit-bubbles inflated from his new harelip. The man's mouth resembled a rabbit's. After the fight, the inmates nicknamed the bully, "*Tsuro*," which means hare in Shona.

That fight made Rigby Croxford the new boss of Hwange prison. It was an odd arrangement as Rigby and Dutchy were the only white inmates.

Prison conditions worsened as Zimbabwe fell into economic ruin. Smuggling was tolerated as long as the prison guards got bribes. Prisoners could get palm wine and marijuana, but food was getting scarce.

[18]

There had always been bad blood between the Matabele and Shona tribes. Living in the cramped quarters added to the tension. Prisoners segregated according to their tribal lineages. Members of the Shona tribe congregated under some leafless ebony trees near the barracks. The Matabele preferred an area next to the perimeter fencing. Rigby moved easily between the two groups, which made him an ideal arbitrator.

Rigby dipped a cup of boiling water from a heated drum for his morning bush tea and said to Dutchy, "I'd sell you into slavery for a tin of milk."

"Bon appétit," Dutchy said, pointing at a man skinning a baboon. Another inmate severed the tails; without them the hairless corpses looked like human cadavers. The man dumped the baboons into a drum of boiling water. His helper added some small wrinkled potatoes and onions to the pot. The vegetables had been picked too early. Harvesting early was a necessity as both baboons and villagers had been raiding the prison garden.

"Looking at you scares the shit out of me," Rigby said, studying Dutchy. He knew if they weren't released soon, they would have to try to escape. Malnourishment was robbing their stamina. He told Dutchy and his young friend, Steven Mabota, "It's a bloody long march to the border. I hope we're fit enough to make it." Steven had already served two years, and, as such, he would be the weakest link in an escape attempt.

Rigby wandered over to inspect the cooking pot. A gray froth of waxy bubbles gurgled on top of the stew. A bow-legged African stirred the boiling mixture with a crooked stick. His assistant was a black scarecrow of a man. After sniffing, Rigby jerked his head back and held his nose. At least they're floating face down, he thought.

"*Mangwanani, Baba,*" the Shona said to Rigby, using the respectful salutation.

"Good morning to you too, my friend," Rigby answered.

"What's the Shona word for baboon?" Rigby asked.

"*Mbombo,*" the old man replied. "Why would you ask such a question? You speak Shona better than I do."

Rigby ignored him and asked another question, "How many baboons have you cooked?"

The cook's face registered a mild surprise. "This is my first, but we must eat something."

"My thoughts, precisely. Can I help you?"

"Sure, you can bring me two hundred kilos of cornmeal," the old Shona cackled through a toothless grin.

"You're a cook, and a comedian. Care for a smoke?" Rigby extended his tobacco pouch and some newspaper. The man's face was centered by a flattened nose with flared nostrils. One of his eyes had turned milky. His left hand had only part of a thumb and his pointing finger remaining. "What's your name?"

"Ezekiel."

"Ezekiel, did a puff adder take your hand?"

" It wasn't a snake. It was a bullet."

"Where?"

"In Mozambique, during the war."

"Did you lose your eye in the war?"

"It was a different kind of a war. One of my wives threw lime in my face."

"Why would she do such a thing?"

"Sometimes women do crazy things."

"What happened to her?"

"I killed her."

[20]

"Is that why you're in prison?"

"No. I got caught stealing food for my children."

Rigby considered the man's answer in silence as he rolled his own cigarette. Nothing like African justice, he thought. A man kills his wife and goes scot-free. He steals a little food for his starving kids and he winds up in prison.

"How many wives do you have?"

"Four."

"A man with four wives should understand women."

"I was always good at marrying women, but I can't say I know much about them. You don't remember me, do you?"

The man's inquiry made Rigby grin. I shouldn't think I'd forget a man with one eye and one hand, he thought. "Have we met before?"

"On the *Nyadzonya* River in Mozambique."

Rigby remembered a military operation in Mozambique. Fifty Rhodesians, posing as enemy soldiers, ambushed a large terrorist training camp. They gunned down fifteen hundred insurgents in what was the most successful raid of the war.

"The war was a long time ago," he said, attempting to change the subject.

"You had a great victory that day." There was admiration in Ezekiel's voice. His smile broadened.

"Was the war worth fighting?" When Rigby didn't get an answer, he asked the question yet another way, "Are your people prospering?"

"You know we are all suffering."

Rigby poured more salt on the wound by stating, "But Mugabe says life is better for most Zimbabweans."

"Maybe Mugabe's life is better, but mine is shit." To illustrate his predicament he spat productively in the dirt and pulled out his empty pockets.

"They say the war made you free," Rigby said, pressing the issue.

"Freedom on an empty belly has a sour taste."

"Not only are you a cook and a comedian, but you're also a bloody philosopher." He handed the cook his tobacco pouch. "Here, have another smoke."

Ezekiel acknowledged the compliment by raising his stirring stick. He sprinkled some of the tobacco on a piece of newspaper, licked the edge, twisted it and tucked it neatly behind his ear. "You and a tall Matabele captured me and another freedom fighter that day. He wanted to kill us, but you let us go. Whatever happened to the Matabele?"

"His name was Sam Mabota. That's his son," he said, pointing at his friend, Steven. "Sam was killed by a lion, actually. We were hunting down in Mozambique. Now, I remember you. Were you as frightened as you looked?"

The cook answered the question indirectly, "You had guns and our only weapons were knobkerries." The old man amended the cooking fire with another log as he pondered Sam Mabota's death. He continued talking with his back turned. "Did you know the other man you spared that day is the warden?"

"I had no idea."

"Someone high in the government ordered the warden to have his guards beat you. At the risk of losing his job, he disobeyed the order. You should be grateful."

"Indeed, I am grateful. You seem to know a lot about what goes on in here."

"I overhear things while I'm cleaning the warden's office."

"Since you have such big ears, any idea when I'm supposed to be released?"

The old man shook his head no. He slumped and looked down as he spoke. "I never thought I would die in prison." The cook's remark was so depressing, Rigby walked away without uttering another word.

*   *   *

Dutchy joked that the baboon dinner was the highlight of Hwange Prison's social season. The prison's spirit medium came dressed in his finest regalia, which included a cape fashioned from one of the baboon's skins. He was also the prison's self-appointed dentist. Rigby named the sorcerer/dentist "Joe" after the Nazi dentist, Josef Mengele. Joe wore a necklace of human teeth around his neck. His own teeth were reduced to brown spikes, which according to Rigby, was a rather poor advertisement for his dental practice. The witch doctor bartered his multi-services under an ebony tree near the outer security fence.

If someone wanted his fortune told, Joe would shake monkey bones, crocodile teeth and other unknown objects in a gourd before tossing the contents on the ground like he was rolling dice. He clapped his hands, and then burped as if he were expelling a foul-tasting substance. His body twitched and trembled. The observers moaned fearfully and covered their mouths in awe. After analyzing the objects' pattern, he spoke in a low sonorous chant.

The music was incredibly rhythmic, given the scarcity of instruments. Men beat on cans and banged on metal paraffin drums. One man emitted piercing blasts from a whistle. Another prisoner blew on a sickle-shaped antelope's horn. The lead dancer was the cook. He stomped his bowed legs and whirled about with wild enthusiasm. As the dancers leapt higher and stamped the earth harder, dust rose from the ensemble. Inmates high on smuggled marijuana undulated to the beat; their heads bobbed on rubbery necks.

Rigby shrugged off the influence and turned to Dutchy. "Let's eat before this mumbo-jumbo gets to me."

"I'm starving," Dutchy said.

"So, what else is new?"

Rigby and Dutchy devoured their baboon stew without inspecting the contents. When Rigby finished, he lit two cigarettes and handed one to Dutchy. His face curled up in a mischievous grin when he saw Steven Mabota gag. "Be careful, don't choke on a toenail. For my part, I've always preferred the brains. What's your favorite part?" he asked Dutchy.

Dutchy picked his teeth with an acacia thorn as he pondered his response. "It would have to be the eyeballs," he replied, eyeing Steven. After inspecting a dislodged morsel, he sucked the thorn clean.

Steven's nose wrinkled. He handed his bowl to Dutchy, who drained it with one gulp and belched.

"I saved you my potatoes. Better eat fast before Dutchy gets them," Rigby said, handing his bowl to Steven.

Joe, the witch doctor, walked up behind the men. "My sons, does anyone need an extraction?"

"Not today," answered Dutchy, covering his mouth to prevent an examination.

"What about me telling your futures?" the witch doctor inquired.

"How much?"

"Only one cigarette."

"Why not," said Rigby.

Joe kneeled in the sand. He inhaled so deeply, half of his cigarette disappeared into ash. A guttural reverberation resonated from his throat as he started his exhortation. His eyes rolled back in their sockets until only the whites were showing. He exhaled smoke into the gourd and then tossed the contents high in the air. Rigby started to say something, but Joe held up his hand. His voice sounded raspy. "Be quiet my son. You're lucky I'm here to read the bones. I know you've been planning an escape. There is no need to escape." The witch doctor gathered up his telltale items and started to leave. He looked agitated.

"That's it?" asked Dutchy.

Joe looked upset. "What, you're not happy to be getting out of prison?"

"But you're not telling us how we'll get out."

"Patience, my son. In time, it will all be revealed."

"What do you expect for a lousy cigarette?" Rigby said.

His disrespect wounded Joe, and it showed. He added, "I see a black cloud covering Zimbabwe and terrible suffering ahead. Soon, this prison will be closed."

"Closed? What's he talking about?" Dutchy asked.

"I reckon, old Joe here, says Zimbabwe's headed for a rebellion," answered Rigby. "I wish I believed in his hocus-pocus. God only knows, how much I wish I believed."

Joe stood up abruptly and walked away without saying another word.

Dutchy threw up his hands in disgust. "Pissing off a witch doctor is bad luck."

"Bad luck? I can't see how our luck can get any worse. We're in prison and we just ate a baboon. If it makes you feel any better, go tell the crazy bugger, I'm sorry." Rigby walked over and slid down a wall. He took out a scrap of paper. With a stubby pencil he started writing a letter to his wife.

> Dear Helen,
> The last time you wrote, you mentioned you were coming to visit me. There's no need for you to make the trip. Everything on this end is fine. The food is horrid, but nutritious. Dutchy is bigger than ever. Steven Mabota sends his best. We're all doing our daily exercises as you recommended. Let's continue to pressure the government. Hopefully, they'll release us soon.

Steven sat down next to Rigby. He suspended his writing and stuffed the unfinished letter into his breast pocket. Steven shaded his eyes and used the angle of the sun as a calendar. "Will the rains come soon?" he asked.

"If they don't, we'll all starve to death."

"Mr. Croxford, do you believe Africans are capable of governing themselves?" Steven asked, diverting the dialogue to a familiar topic.

"African politicians are only interested in lining their pockets."

"You mean like the white colonists did for two hundred years?"

"Oh no, you don't— it's too bloody hot to discuss politics. Go bother Dutchy."

"Dutchy only wants to talk about food. I wish I could discuss politics with your daughter. We had such wonderful political debates at the university."

"My daughter suffers from the same affliction as her mother— they're insufferable liberals."

"Most great empires have been built by liberals," Steven declared.

Rigby countered by saying, "Nonsense. Empires are built by soldiers shedding blood. Liberals prefer shedding words and ink. I hate to bring this up, but you're in prison, and it was political shenanigans that put you here. I was determined not to argue with you today, but by God, you've done it again." He tugged his hat down and pretended to doze off.

Steven touched him on the shoulder. "Yesterday, you started to tell me a story about my father."

Dutchy sat down on the other side of Rigby. He looked dreamy. "When I get out of here, the first thing I'm gonna eat is a whole roast of beef. Potatoes— I want lots of potatoes smothered in brown gravy."

Rigby cocked his hat back and shook his head. "Steven, I'll tell you the story if he promises to stop talking about food."

"I promise," acknowledged Dutchy.

"Where was I? Did I tell you the part about your father carrying me piggyback for fifty kilometers?"

Steven had heard the same story many times from his father. He knew that it was Rigby who carried his wounded father. Rigby always said his father had saved

[27]

his life, but in truth it was the other way around. Growing up, when Steven felt Rigby's eyes on him he felt inadequate just to be in his presence.

"Not that story. The one about the airliner getting shot down."

"Do you mean the story about the Rhodesian airliner that was flying from Kariba to Salisbury getting shot down by a missile during the war?"

"Yes, that's the one. It was accidentally shot down by a heat seeking missile."

"It was an Air Rhodesian airliner, and yes, it was shot down by a missile, but that was no accident."

"But...," started Steven.

"There are no ifs or buts about it. The way this government's rewriting history is criminal."

Rigby described what it must have been like for the passengers on the ill-fated flight. "There were fifty-eight passengers— most of them were on holiday at the lake. A Soviet- made missile struck the port engine. The motor was blown off the wing, which compromised the controls. Survivors said the pilot struggled to maintain control. Somehow, the pilot managed to crash-land in the only maize field within ten kilometers. It was a bit of brilliant flying, but the plane hit a drainage ditch. Thirty people died on impact. Miraculously, twenty-eight passengers crawled out of the tail section. Many had horrible injuries, but they were alive. Some say, it was God's intervention that saved them. I say, it was Satan's intervention that shot them down. Uninjured passengers went for help. Those too old or too young to walk stayed behind. When the terrorists arrived at the crash scene, the survivors pleaded for their lives, but the heartless bastards hacked them to pieces."

[28]

"No sane person fires a missile at a commercial airliner. As far as the atrocities go, maybe it never happened. It could have been propaganda. You have to admit, both sides used propaganda during the war."

"Propaganda, my ass, I interrogated an eyewitness. The terrorists who killed the crash survivors— I guess that was an accident. By the way, I hate being the bearer of such startling information, but some men are insane and war triggers their psychosis."

Steven was overcome by the aching realization that Rigby's depiction of the incident was probably true. He lashed out with, "I'd like to speak to that so-called eyewitness."

Anger veins bulged on Rigby's forehead. He took a deep drag on his cigarette and then exhaled the smoke in Steven's face. "Your father and I actually fought in the war. You had the luxury of studying the war in some classroom at that den of communists you call a university."

"Mr. Croxford, you conveniently blame everything on the communists. The whites owned everything in Rhodesia, yet they were only three percent of the population. Surely, even you can see the inequity couldn't last forever. My father told us the white Europeans sent missionaries carrying bibles to Africa. They asked us to close our eyes and pray. When we opened our eyes, we had the bibles and they had our land."

"What I see is that Zimbabwe was once the richest country in Africa and now it's the poorest." When Steven didn't respond, he continued, "Joshua Nkomo was the self-described perpetrator of the senseless act— may the Devil shit on his grave. He described the passengers to a London Times reporter as legitimate military targets. Nkomo was always a stooge for the Russians. The newspapers in South Africa called the attack 'a barbarous act against all of humanity.' Of course there was no condemnation from any of the other African leaders."

"The war was a struggle for freedom," Steven stated in his usual accusatory manner. "All wars have causalities."

Rigby wasn't about to concede. "How can you defend Mugabe? By the way, I hate to keep reminding you, but you've been in this prison for two years, and he put you here."

"I'm not defending Mugabe. Look what he's done to *me*," Steven said.

"Be that as it may, look what you've done to *me*. Carrying on a conversation with you is like arguing with a stone."

"But you're the only person I can talk to," conceded Steven.

His words softened Rigby. "You really know how to get under my skin." A tiny wind stirred the sticky air. Rigby turned his face to take advantage of the breeze.

He didn't hear Steven's next remark. He was lost in the dark reaches of his memory. He thought about his childhood sweetheart. She managed to survive the crash, only to be murdered at the crash-site. He wondered what her last words were as she begged for her life. He never told anyone about her, not even his wife. Rigby stuffed a pinch of tobacco behind his lower lip. After a few seconds, he spat a brown gob onto the ground. Black ants converged on the snotty mixture but rejected it.

He regained the moment and asked, "Where was I? Oh, your father and I were deployed someplace in Mozambique. We didn't hear about the air-disaster for weeks. God knows, we'd seen our share of cruelty, but I never saw your father so incensed. Killing those civilians was a violation of everything your father stood for. It

[30]

was like Nkomo had disgraced the entire Matabele nation. The act was so bloody wicked.

"Some South Africans offered a 100,000 rand reward to anyone who could bring Nkomo to justice. Your father wasn't interested in the reward money. He volunteered to assassinate Joseph Nkomo straight away. Intelligence was briefing Sam, and then for some reason they decided to use a white. Why, I don't know. It would have been much easier for Sam to mix in with the locals. They opted to use radio-activated explosives hidden in a car. Intelligence knew where Nkomo was hiding in Zambia, but killing the bastard was like trying to shoot a running cheetah with a pistol. The old boy never slept in the same place two nights in a row. I never found out what went wrong, but they mucked it up. Anyway, the government continued to pressure the military until finally the Special Air Service decided to act. It was tricky getting into Zambia, but the operation came off without a hitch. Trouble was, when they raided his house, Nkomo managed to give them the slip again. Someone on the inside had to have warned him."

Steven interrupted him with, "Did they ever catch the spy?"

Rigby's expression hardened. He bit his lower lip. "No, but I've got a damn good idea who he was, or rather is. Someday, he'll pay for his crimes. Of that, my friend, you can be certain. Am I right, Dutchy?" Dutchy had dozed off and didn't answer. Within seconds, Steven was also asleep.

Rigby was irritated by their lack of interest in his story. He closed his eyes and remembered the day he and his friend Willie were briefed about Operation Reprisal.

3

Our commanding officer, Colonel Wells, was born of English military stock, and, as such, he was inoculated against any vestiges of self-doubt. He had a way of making the most asinine plan seem almost reasonable. Looking back, I remember feeling invincible. I'm not sure the others felt the same way.

"At ease, gentlemen. We've just received some rather alarming intelligence about this character," the colonel said, handing me a photograph. "His name's Da-beng-wa," he added, struggling with the pronunciation. "He's one of Nkomo's thugs. He was trained by the Russian military and educated in Moscow. More importantly, he's the monster responsible for shooting down the airliner. The act was applauded by Mr. Nkomo, but it was Dabengwa who ordered the actual firing of the missile. Now, we know he's been given sanctuary in Botswana. HQ's devised a plan to kidnap Dabengwa. It's all spelled out in here," he said, handing us copies. "We're calling this one, Operation Reprisal."

"Sir, just how many of these are floating around?"

"Mr. Croxford. I know where you're going with this. I share your concern for security. These are the only copies. You'll note the rather poor quality of the typing. That's because I typed them myself. Nobody, I repeat, nobody has seen this report except the prime minister. Are you satisfied?"

"Quite, sir."

"I'm pleased that you approve, Mr. Croxford. You may start reading— take your time— we've got all day." The deep lines etched in his tanned face told a story of forty years in Africa. He was old, but wiry and coiled for action. The colonel swiveled in his chair and walked over to the window. He looked out with his hands locked behind his back. It was drizzling. A fogged window blurred his view. He stood there looking at nothing for the hour it took us to read the intelligence report. Years later, I realized he was demonstrating his discipline.

"We're finished, sir."

The colonel rolled the papers up and then set fire to them over his wastebasket.

"Jolly good. Now, what's your assessment?" he asked, turning back to face us.

"Concerning feasibility or logistics?" asked Willie.

"Both, of course."

"Why not kill Dabengwa and be done with it?"

"Because, we need to put a face on this monster. We're being boycotted by every misguided country in the world. I don't have to tell you how hard it is for us to buy arms. Why, if it weren't for Israel and South Africa, we'd be in a hell of a fix. I wish we could just shoot the bastard and call it a day. We need Dabengwa alive."

"It shouldn't be too difficult."

[33]

"That's the spirit. How many men will it take?"

I looked at Willie for support. "A small mobile unit, I reckon nine should do nicely." Willie nodded in agreement.

"Let's make it an even ten."

"Why ten?" I asked.

"Because, I'm going as your tenth. For God's sake, don't look so concerned— this isn't my first war, you know. Carry on, and not a word about this to anyone. This ought to be a thrilling show, wouldn't you agree?" the colonel quipped.

I would kid Willie later saying, "Do you think he fought in the First World War or the Boer War?" If we had told our men that a geriatric colonel was leading us on a parachute jump into a hostile country at night to kidnap one man, they wouldn't have believed us.

*　　*　　*

I watched Sam stare at the colonel as he struggled to climb into the C-47. I remembered whispering, "Let's hope he doesn't break a leg— bloody hard to carry a man one hundred kilometers in soft sand."

Before the pilot started the engines, the colonel pulled me aside. "I don't expect any problems, but if I'm injured, I want you to leave me. That's an order. Do you understand what I'm saying?"

"Yes, Colonel."

"I know you'll do your duty, Croxford. Cheerio," he said, giving me thumbs up.

"Cheers to you, as well," I said in return.

*　　*　　*

THE ZAMBEZI VENDETTA

The Dakota lumbered down the runway and lifted off into the night. I felt the old bird shudder from the gear retraction. The engine whine eased as the throttles were reduced. The pilot took us high hoping we'd look like a routine commercial flight. I strained to see below, but there was only blackness.

It was a short flight to Botswana. I felt my pulse rate quicken as we started a deep spiraling descent. There wouldn't be much time to deal with a parachute malfunction, but then again we wouldn't be easy targets.

I watched to see if the colonel was nervous, but he was sleeping like a baby. The copilot walked down the aisle holding up two fingers indicating it was two minutes to the drop zone. I shook the colonel. He opened his eyes and mouthed to me "good luck."

We were on our feet shuffling and then suddenly we tumbled into space. I pulled my ripcord. The canopy make a lovely whooshing sound. I'd survived another jump. Only the stars differentiated up from down. The silence was interrupted by the decreasing drone of the C-47 and the opening cracks of the other parachutes. Without any wind or heat, I knew I would hit hard. The satchel of explosives tied to my stomach knocked the wind out of me. I jumped up gasping and ran to help the colonel. I found him standing with his hands on his hips, shaking his head.

"My God, I forgot how bloody thrilling it is to jump at night. I watched your landing, Croxford. You must remember to keep your feet closer together. All right, you two, get these chutes buried." He looked at his compass. "Mabota, take the point. The road's in that direction. Off you go, lad— double time."

THE ZAMBEZI VENDETTA

We always deferred to our African scouts to setup ambushes. Intelligence reported that Dabengwa would be traveling in a three-vehicle convoy. Our plan was to blow up the lead vehicle with a TMA-3 landmine and then rake the trailing truck with small arms fire. If we could leave the center vehicle intact it would make our escape easier.

The land was dotted with termite mounds providing good cover. The lookout's job was to make sure we ambushed the right convoy by reading the license plates. After confirming we had our man, he would radio Willie, who would detonate the landmine.

The sunrise heightened our senses. Time ticked by slowly. I glued my eyes on the road and began to wonder if we'd been compromised again. Mopani flies crawled in my ears, but I didn't move. I remember wondering if the colonel was about to call it off. I worried about the long march to the border.

Sam hit me with a pebble. He'd heard the popping sound of a backfiring engine. An ancient truck came down the road sputtering and coughing up white smoke. The truck stalled right in front of us. Trouble was, it wasn't our man. Two men and a huge woman climbed out. She began berating the driver as he tinkered with the engine. Dabengwa was due any minute and there was nothing we could do. Without warning, the fat woman started walking towards the termite mound that I was hiding behind. When she moved to the left, I crawled to the right. Sam, realizing my predicament imitated a male lion snorting. The noise froze the woman, but she was so desperate, she pulled down her pants and squatted a few meters from me. Her grunting produced a prodigious fart. After relieving herself, she waddled back to the truck. I bit my lip to keep from laughing. The colonel shook his head and eyed me with disgust. The driver finally started the truck. To our relief, the Africans jumped in and drove away leaving a pall of blue smoke.

A few minutes later, two green Land Rovers sandwiching a Toyota truck came around a bend in the road. Willie set off the explosive device perfectly; it lifted the lead Land Rover on its nose killing the driver instantly. The other Rover slid to a stop in the middle of our crossfire. We raked the rear vehicle until all movement stopped. We spared the Toyota pinned between the Land Rovers. Two men jumped out and raised their hands.

When Willie found a briefcase filled with military intelligence we knew we had our man. We handcuffed Dabengwa and loaded him in the back of the Toyota. The other truck's windows were blown out, but it started. We jumped into the vehicles and headed for the border. I remember feeling queasy when I saw the road dust we were kicking up. Everything was running right on schedule. I checked my watch; it was two hours to the border. That's when we saw the roadblock. Our lead vehicle screeched to a stop. The colonel barked, "It looks like they're on to us, boys. Willie, drive the prisoners around to the left. We'll make a run straight at them. If they're the Botswana Defense Force, they'll high-tail it. We're an embarrassment to their national pride, but they won't hang around. Croxford, if they do open fire, hit them with the RPG."

They fired and I missed with the grenade launcher, but it was enough to end it.

In the confusion, both of our prisoners were wounded, one fatally. We dumped his body on the road without *slowing down. Dabengwa was gut shot. He pleaded with us to kill him. I wanted to oblige him, but the colonel was determined to keep our prisoner alive. We radioed ahead for a helicopter. Three hours later he was transported to the best hospital in Rhodesia. Everyone said Operation Reprisal was a success— I have my doubts.*

I was given guard duty at the hospital. Dabengwa's stomach wound resulted in peritonitis, which required surgery. At night, I listened to him cry out for his mother. I could have summoned a nurse to administer morphine, but I remember enjoying his pain. I kept thinking about the people on that airliner.

On the fourth day, the surgeon pronounced, "Dabengwa has just taken a crap. His turds are as hard as granite, but it looks like he'll make it. Why so glum, Mr. Croxford? I thought you'd be pleased."

Dabengwa was never charged. It was rumored he was too valuable as an intelligence asset. After the war, he worked for the government. I heard he lives on a confiscated farm someplace up in the northern highlands.

A wailing siren jolted Rigby from his daydreaming. It signaled the end of another day.

* * *

4

Four days later, Ian Rhodes made an unannounced visit to Hwange prison. A trustee opened the front gate letting his new Land Cruiser into the prison's car park. Rhodes followed his driver into the administration building. He was limping and used a cane to steady himself.

Warden Joseph Chitoa, Joseph "Stalin" to Rigby, jumped to attention as Rhodes entered his office. He was pressed in civility, but his voice reeked of irritation.

"What's the purpose of this visit? Why wasn't I informed?" Rhodes ignored his questions and walked over to a window where he stood staring out at the prison barracks.

"My sources tell me you failed to carry out my orders regarding a special prisoner. Maybe you're not happy with your position here at Hwange."

The warden sighed and sat down. He clutched a flyswatter. "Did your sources tell you that I haven't been paid in over six months?" He smacked a fly on his desk. The sound startled Rhodes and he spun around. When he looked at the warden's face he decided to soften his remarks. "Revolutions are never easy. In time, life will improve for all Zimbabweans."

"I pray my great grandchildren live long enough to see it. Comrade, I don't think you've come here to make a political speech. What do you want?"

"It's about one of your inmates. His name is Croxford. I gave explicit instructions concerning this prisoner. You've given him preferential treatment. You disobeyed my orders."

The warden smiled as he answered, "Did you know Croxford was a war hero? But of course you know— you fought with him— until you defected to our side." The warden's sarcasm was not missed by Rhodes. The warden continued, "When we withheld his rations, the other prisoners shared their food with him. Many of them fought against Croxford in the war, yet they help him. To my people, the Matabele— it's never about the battle— it's about honor."

"Croxford's a violent criminal," stated Rhodes.

"I'm not sure Mr. Croxford is fond of violence— I do know he was very accomplished at it."

Chitoa's defense of Croxford irritated Rhodes, and it showed. "I can have auditors go over the books here. You haven't been selling prison food on the black market, have you?"

"How dare you threaten me? What food are you speaking about? Everyone at Hwange is hungry, including the warden." To emphasize his point, he stood up and pulled his pants away from his stomach. "What would you have me do, kill the man?"

Rhodes spoke with his back turned. "He's no longer your problem, he's mine. Croxford's wife has been giving interviews to the foreign press. Great Britain has threatened to suspend its foreign aid. These are his release papers." He walked over and flipped an envelope on the warden's desk. After reading the contents, the warden slid the envelope back across the desk. "Croxford won't leave without his friend Dutchy Bosshart."

"Listen carefully, Chitoa. I don't care if you have to let all of the prisoners go, I want Croxford released today. Do we understand each other?"

"I will see to it at once."

"Good. I'll convey your efficiency to my superiors." Rhodes stormed out without saying goodbye.

Rhodes's new Land Cruiser stood out like a sore thumb. After three failed attempts with their high-powered slingshot, Dutchy managed to hit Rhodes's windscreen. The stone made a spiraled cobweb crack.

Dutchy and Rigby peeked around the corner of their barracks. At first, Rhodes didn't notice the crack, but when he did, he screamed and vaulted out of his truck. After inspecting the damage, he blamed his driver. The man was quick, but not quick enough. Rhodes whacked him on the shins with his walking stick. He howled and begged for mercy.

Dutchy and Rigby found the episode hilarious until Rigby was summoned to the warden's office. Joseph Chitoa kept his back turned with his hands clasped behind him. "You may sit down, Mr. Croxford." The warden gestured without turning around.

"*Siyabonga*," Rigby acknowledged.

"You're welcome, but you can speak English." Chitoa wore a starched khaki uniform. His head was shaved and shined like black marble. There was a portrait of President Robert Mugabe on the wall behind his desk.

"So, Mr. Croxford, what are we to do about you?" he said, shaking his bald head. Rigby started to deny breaking Rhodes's windscreen, but the warden spoke first. "It seems your wife has been stirring up the foreign press. I have good news. You and your friend Bosshart are to be released today. Your wife should be here within the hour."

His words caught Rigby off-guard. He thought for a minute and then blurted, "Why not release Steven Mabota? Oh, and I'd like to take your friend, the one-eyed man with the buggered hand. I believe his name's Ezekiel. You served with him in Mozambique. It would be two less mouths to feed."

"Ah yes, the war, you remembered. You can have the thief, Ezekiel, but Mabota was sent here for treasonous acts against the government. Releasing him is out of the question."

"Warden, we both know change is coming. Steven Mabota will have a role in the new government. I think it would be wise to release him."

An annoyed smile crept into the warden's expression.

"Do you have any other demands? Are you sure you don't want the keys to Hwange prison? Very well, you can have both of them, but you will be held accountable for their deeds. If they break any laws, you will serve out their sentences. Are those terms acceptable?"

"Quite."

"Good. Now, a bit of advice — leave Zimbabwe. There's no place for you in my country."

"How long did you study in Russia, Mr. Chitoa?"

"I studied in Moscow for two years. Why do you ask?"

"Your English has a slight Russian accent. It might surprise you to know, that despite what this country's done to me, I love Zimbabwe and I intend to die here."

The warden's grin melted into a frown. "I suspect you've done things far worse to my country than it has done to you."

"By the way, this is *our* country. I was born here."

"Get your things ready, Mr. Croxford. It's been a pleasure getting rid of you."

"The pleasure's all mine." Rigby got up to leave, but turned back to face the warden. "One more thing— I know what you did for me and for that, I'm thankful. Who knows, our paths might cross again someday and I can repay you."

The warden came around from behind his desk. After looking up and down the hall, he closed his office door and spoke in a hushed tone. "If you intend to stay in Zimbabwe, you should know you have a powerful enemy in the government. Be careful, and be well. Walk in God's shoes." Rigby started to say something, but Chitoa stopped him. "Please, don't even say his name in my presence. Now, we are even." They shook hands. The warden made a shooing motion towards the door.

*   *   *

Helen Croxford gasped when she saw her husband. There were plum-colored bruises under his eyes. Rigby may have looked gaunt and sickly, but he was grinning from ear to ear. Dutchy's wife, Sadie, put on a more stoic façade, but she was also shocked by their appearances. The men rode in the back of the truck with Steven and Ezekiel and a cool box of beer. Their wives rode upfront. The men hadn't bathed in weeks.

Rigby, Dutchy and the two Africans were dead-drunk by the time they traveled the sixty kilometers from Hwange prison to the outskirts of Victoria Falls. They dropped off Steven and Ezekiel near Chinotimba, the black township. The two Africans staggered down the dirt path to their village holding hands. (In Africa, men holding hands, does not have the same connotation as it does in most places.)

Victoria Falls, once a thriving tourist town, now looked seedy and deserted. Even the begging street urchins had abandoned the city for more lucrative hunting grounds across the Zambezi River in Zambia. To Rigby and Dutchy, it would have been no more appealing if it had been Paris, France.

Their wives had booked suites in the Victoria Falls Hotel. The only guests were freeloading civil servants and military personnel. Their longtime friend Larry Norton, the hotel manager, greeted them. He helped the women get their husbands up the stairs to their rooms. Rigby and Dutchy were singing and insisted that Norton have a drink with them, but he begged out promising to join them later.

The women came prepared. They had disinfectant soap, fungicides and antibiotics. After the men took the first of two baths, Sadie shaved their heads and beards. Finally Helen stepped back to inspect their work. "They look almost human," she said to Sadie, who nodded in agreement.

Rigby looked at Dutchy, and laughed. "You look like one of the baboons we ate in prison. Speaking of food, I could eat elephant dung." He guzzled the last of a whiskey and burped.

*   *   *

Later that night, in the privacy of their hotel room, Rigby woke up and found his wife sitting in a chair next to the bed. Her eyes were swollen and her cheeks were tear-stained. Without saying a word he motioned for her to come to him. He held her close with his head pressed against her bosom.

"What if something..." He stopped her from finishing by placing his finger to her lips.

"It's over," he whispered. "Helen, please be gentle. I'm only half the man I used to be."

"Which half?" she asked, giggling.

"Well now, I guess you'll have to be the judge of that."

*   *   *

On their second day of freedom, their friends threw a Coming-Out-of-Prison dinner party for the men. All of them had served in the Rhodesian military. Two of the women were on their second husbands, having lost their first ones in the war. After dinner, they moved the party to the patio bar. Dutchy tapped his glass with a spoon announcing a toast. "Here's to the best damn mate I ever had in prison. Cheers," he said, pointing at Rigby and raising his glass.

"Here — here," the group saluted, raising their glasses.

"Rigby, when Dutchy says *had*, exactly what does he mean?" The man asking the question snickered. The man's wife admonished him by pulling him down.

Rigby stood up and stepped behind Bosshart. "First of all, let me say, gentlemen never tell, so I promised Dutchy never to reveal the intimate nature of our relationship."

Helen tried to silence her husband with a stare. When it didn't work, she said, "You are without a doubt the grossest man I've ever known." He shrugged off her description with a grin.

The same man regained the floor. "Oh, come now, Helen, you must have known. Will we receive wedding invitations or will you two elope?"

Rigby put his hand on Dutchy's shoulder before answering, "By prior arrangement, I shall leave the details to my new fiancé."

Another man raised his hand to hush the group. "Let's hear it for the newlyweds. May they live—" His wife muffled him by sticking her napkin in his mouth.

Rigby sat at the head of the table with his back to the door. His wife was sitting at the other end. She winced when she saw Ian Rhodes accompanied by two soldiers walk into the lobby. Everyone at the table could see Rhodes, but Rigby was oblivious to what was going on behind him. When he saw who had caused the stir, he felt a familiar loathing.

"What the fuck's he doing here?" someone said.

"Ladies, gentlemen," said Rhodes, nodding. "And what might we be celebrating tonight?"

Everyone looked at each other, refusing to acknowledge him. Finally, Dutchy hiccupped and then spoke, "It's a reunion for an endangered species known as white Zimbabweans." The soldiers looked embarrassed by the remark.

"How was prison?" Rhodes directed at Rigby.

"I handled it. So, Sir *Magondo*, what brings you out tonight? Let me guess, I bet your Shona mistress ran away from your confiscated farm— again." Rigby's friends found his brassiness amusing. When a woman chuckled, her husband reprimanded her with a look.

"Croxford, your day of reckoning is coming," Rhodes said.

"I wouldn't wait too long with the way your boys in Harare are mucking it up."

"Making disparaging statements about the government is treason." Rhodes turned and walked away.

"A bloody traitor defining treason— now there's a novel twist." When Rigby jumped up, his friends restrained him.

"Let it go," someone said.

"He's not worth it," added another man.

But Rigby couldn't let it go, and he yelled, "Speaking of breaking the law, you should see about getting that cracked windscreen fixed." At first, his remark didn't register, but when it did, Rhodes spun back around and glared at him.

The confrontation poisoned the party atmosphere. When one couple decided to call it a night, the others followed suit. Awkward handshakes and hugs exposed their anxiety. Their circle of friends was dwindling. Each time they met, another family had left the country. They agreed to meet again, but it was one of those acceptable lies people tell to relieve the tension of saying goodbye.

* * *

Uncertainty descended on the Bossharts and the Croxfords as they drove home together. Seeing Ian Rhodes was a reminder of how precarious their lives had become.

The countryside was shackled by the dry season, but the baobabs were already budding in anticipation. The air was scented by the hint of rain. The African women they encountered were walking single-file with firewood and bundles of cut thatching grass balanced on their heads. The men carried nothing, which was normal. What wasn't normal was that the people seemed distant and unfriendly. Rigby sensed the change and responded.

"How long has it been like this?"
"About two months," Sadie Bosshart replied.
"Something's in the air," added Helen.

*   *   *

After dropping off the Bossharts, they left the main road and drove out across their land. While Rigby was imprisoned, he had dreamed about getting back to the farm. His face was locked in a perpetual grin.

Helen had warned him about the squatters living on their farm. When he saw them his grin disappeared. They were thugs sent by the government to intimidate the Croxfords. Their intention was to confiscate the Croxford farm, but for some unknown reason, an uneasy truce existed between the squatters and Helen Croxford. The dirt around their makeshift huts was threadbare. The raggedly dressed men hunkered around open campfires. Nearby trees had been felled and stacked for firewood.

Without warning, Rigby slammed on the brakes and jumped out. He waved for her to drive away and she did. He stood there glaring at the squatters, but he got no response. A fury raced through Rigby's heart. There was nothing he could do.

Towering jacaranda trees awash in blue flowers lined the driveway to their farmhouse. The fences on both sides of the road were covered in twisted vines of struggling red and white bougainvillea. He started to walk again, but the months in prison left him winded. He leaned against a tree to catch his breath. When he turned his face to the sun, his grin returned. A man doesn't appreciate freedom, until he loses it, he reflected.

Helen had insisted on turning the land surrounding their farmhouse into a wildlife sanctuary. Their friends said it was sinful to waste the best farmland in Zimbabwe on wild animals. He was glad his wife had prevailed.

A herd of impalas grazed on the other side of the fence. The impala ram snorted, but his females ignored the warning and continued feeding. Beyond a sea of golden grass, he saw giraffes gliding between woodland acacias. He reached down, grabbed a handful of dirt, and sprinkled it into the breeze; it had a clean earthy smell. The azure sky was clear overhead. Haze was building in the west. The rains will come in two weeks, maybe three, he thought. The far-away trumpet of an elephant gave him gooseflesh. He laughed like a lunatic. He was home at last.

*   *   *

The seasonal rains came and replenished the land. Baobabs and acacias foliated in emerald greenery and blossom buds. The grasses grew taller than men. Flowers cast aside their hibernation and opened their faces to the sun.

The Croxford farm lay fallow. Farms without crops were less likely to be confiscated by the government.

Their sandstone farmhouse was roofed in thick grass-thatch. The window and door frames were made of metal; wooden ones would have been eaten by voracious African termites. The windows were open and unscreened. The living room was scented by leather furniture and smoke from a fireplace. There were animal skin rugs on the floor. The walls were covered by over-stuffed bookshelves.

Rigby sat on his veranda with his crossed ankles supported by the wooden railing. He shaded his eyes to watch a pair of snake-eagles work the thermals. Unusual to see both of them in the spring, he thought. One should be on the nest tending the chicks. Maybe a snake or a mongoose ate their nestlings. The shadows from cotton ball clouds moved lazily across the rolling green hills. Helen was wrong— this land is worth dying for, he thought.

Helen studied her husband without his seeing her. It had been six months since his prison release. He'd regained the weight he lost and his face was sun-bronzed. He seemed normal, but she was worried. She engulfed him in a hug and whispered in his ear, "a penny for your thoughts."

"I can't see how we can make it through another year. Thanks to Rhodes, I lost my hunting season. And now we've got these wretched squatters living on our farm."

"Wow, we really are depressed, aren't we? We've been through hard times before. My practice *is* bringing in a little money."

"For God's sake, Helen, the inflation rate is a zillion percent. People are starving. The madness can't continue. Something's got to give."

"That's what we said last year, and the year before that," she reminded him.

"Maybe you should move to Cape Town. You know, just until things get sorted out here. If there's an uprising it *could* get messy. Eventually, they'll make their move," Rigby said, nodding in the direction of the squatters.

"While you were in prison, I treated two of them for malaria," she confessed.

He digested her admission and then he said, "Let me get this straight, you've been treating the squatters? The same bastards who want to take our farm?"

"What would you have me do— let them die?"

"I don't care if they die— as a matter of fact I may end up killing them myself."

"And another thing, I'm not moving in with our daughter, so you can forget it. This is her last year of residency. You know she wants to practice here. Besides, I can't leave my patients, especially now. Somehow, we'll make it work."

He looked at her and sighed. "One way or another, we always seem to hang on. You do know, one stubborn woman in a family is a bore— two are insufferable," he said and added, "Well, at least you're out of politics." He knew she was still very much involved, but he decided not to confront her, at least not at that moment.

When Helen told him that she was no longer involved in opposition politics, she wasn't telling the truth. During his prison stay, she had attended secret political meetings. Upon his return, she curtailed her involvement in politics, knowing it would only provoke him.

A giraffe moved cautiously to the edge of their veranda. After lions killed its mother, Helen was pressed into service as the giraffe's surrogate. The female splayed its legs outward and stuck her head under the veranda's thatched roof fluttering her long eyelashes. Helen offered a sugar cube in the palm of her hand. The animal curled its snake-like tongue around the cube and sucked it into her mouth.

The sun doesn't set in Africa, it drops like a cannonball and it takes the warmth with it. Helen rubbed her hands together and shivered. "Burr, it's getting chilly. I'm going in." She kissed him on the cheek.

"God knows, I love you, Helen, but you really know how to get under my skin."

"It's my only hobby," she said, grinning.

"Let me finish my cigar in peace."

She left him on the veranda.

He thought about the warden's advice. He hated to admit that Chitoa might be right. Maybe there wasn't a place for him in Zimbabwe. Africa for only black Africans could be the future. The thought was depressing.

Out of the night came a series of high-pitched whistles rising in sequence. The mating call of the pearl spotted owl ended in a wheeoo-wheeoo cry. He took one last deep drag, flicked the butt into the darkness and walked back into the house.

*   *   *

The next day, their Rhodesian ridgebacks heard a vehicle and bolted out of the house. The Croxfords joined their dogs on the veranda as a truck drove up. It was pulling a trailer crammed with furniture. There was a mattress lashed to the vehicle's roof.

Africa can suck the life out of women, especially white women, and it had wreaked havoc on Margaret Martin. She looked as brittle as a twig with spider-thin limbs. Witchy grey hair gave her a premature wizened look.

Her husband, Matthew, was barrel-chested with a ruddy face encircled by a confusion of red hair and matching beard. He had a lazy eye that would gaze off in a direction contrary to his wishes.

"Nice to see you, Matthew," said Rigby, trying to locate his good eye. "I guess this means you're running?"

"I see the squatters have taken over your farm as well. You could say we're running, but what choice do we have? They pinched our farm two days ago. What you see on this truck, is all we were allowed to take. We're bloody lucky to be alive. Scared the hell out of poor Mags," he explained, putting his arm around his wife. She struggled to smile. "I had to put my hunting dogs down. It broke my heart, but what else could I do?"

"Where will you go? What will you do?" Helen asked, leading them into their living room.

"We're headed to Johannesburg, and then on to England. Her brother's offered me a job as a plumber's assistant. It's not much, but beggars can't be choosers." His wife acknowledged him with a pitiful nod.

As Croxford listened, he saw the precariousness of his own life. The idea of leaving Africa sickened him. He jumped to his feet and hugged the Martins. He knew he would never see them again. "You can come back, after things get sorted out. We were just talking about how it can't get any worse. Weren't we, Helen?"

"It'll never happen, not at our age. No, we've seen the best of Africa. At least we'll be close to our kids. They live in Ireland, you know. Speaking of kids— how's your daughter?"

"She's in Cape Town. This is her last year of internship," Helen answered.

"Christine's smart, like her mother," Martin said, winking at Rigby. "Say, I almost forgot, how was prison?"

"It was wonderful— gourmet food— interesting people— a real holiday spot."

"I'll bet. Giving Rhodes that beating was priceless. I reckon you're every Rhodesian's hero. That one's a real bastard, all right."

"I apologize for my husband's foul mouth." Martin's wife spoke with her lips pressed together like she'd sucked on a lemon.

"I've heard worse. Anyway, of course you'll spend the night," said Helen.

"You're very kind. Leaving our friends is the hardest thing we've ever done." Mrs. Martin dabbed her nose with a hanky. " 'It's a brave flea that eats his dinner on the lip of a lion.' That's Proverbs, you know. You're both so courageous. I wish we could..." she started to say something, but hesitated.

Martin put his arm around his wife and said, "Mother, we've gone over this a hundred times. There's no turning back for us now."

*   *   *

[54]

After dinner, the men retired to the porch to smoke and sip brandy. The crickets were quieted by the same hooting owl. Martin spoke first. "I can't put a good face on this. God knows, we'll miss Africa. If it was just me, I'd stay, but my wife's gone mental on me. She never stops quoting the bible. She's driving me over the edge. That's enough about our problems. Rigby, we stopped by for two reasons. Of course, we wanted to say goodbye, but I've got a sweet opportunity for you."

"If this has anything to do with toilets and what goes in them, you can forget it."

"My, aren't we the fussy one? I didn't know you were related to the DeBeers. And you with no prospects until next hunting season. I'll have you know, this has nothing to do with plumbing. I was supposed to guide a photographic safari in three weeks. Her brother's expecting us in two. How about stepping in for me?"

"I'm a farmer, not a bloody chauffeur."

"Hmm, and I thought you were a professional hunter."

"Not by choice."

"It pays five thousand dollars, plus all of your expenses and they'll shell out for your staff."

"I'll take it."

"Don't you want to hear the particulars?"

"Not really. I can't believe anyone's dumb enough to holiday in Zim. This country's a powder keg about to explode."

"Mate, the safari's not here, it's in Namibia. Have you been there?"

"Only once. It was during the war. I can't remember much, except rather unpleasant chaps shooting at me."

"That was years ago. Namibia's as docile as a lamb. Besides, all African countries have their little squabbles, now and again."

"So, you're saying our problem here is a 'squabble'. If that's true, why are you packing it in?"

Martin pretended not to hear his comeback and continued, "No sir, you'll love Namibia, especially the Skeleton Coast. Why, this'll be like a paid vacation for you, old boy. Cheers," Martin said, peering at him with his good eye. Rigby gave up trying to maintain eye contact and concentrated on looking at Martin's bulbous nose.

Helen received the news about her husband's taking over Martin's photo safari with mixed emotions. They could certainly use the money, but the idea of separation made her squeamish.

The next morning, the women cried when they said goodbye. They made plans for a homecoming party when the Martins returned to Zimbabwe, but they all knew they would never see each other again.

The next two weeks passed quickly. On the morning her husband drove away, Helen thought about other times they'd said goodbye. There was something different about this time.

*   *   *

5

Rigby drove his safari truck to Victoria Falls. His partner, Dutchy, followed him in a geriatric Land Rover.

They hired Steven Mabota and Ezekiel, the one-eyed Shona, as their cook. Rigby wasn't about to leave Mabota and Ezekiel to their own devices, not after he agreed to finish their prison sentences if they broke any laws. Their efforts to buy supplies were unsuccessful. The shelves at the local food shop and butchery were picked clean. Zimbabwe's economy was catatonic. Everything was in short supply. They decided to make the sixty kilometer trip to Botswana to purchase provisions.

The town of Kasane is like the hub of a wheel with four countries and two major rivers as its spokes. It was a prosperous village, by African standards. The shops were jam-packed with merchandise. The black market was booming, thanks to the economic turmoil in neighboring Zimbabwe. The men spent three days servicing the vehicles and buying supplies.

The nights were reserved for drinking and the exaggerated retelling of old war stories. Some parties lasted until daybreak.   Unable to endure another hangover or listen to their commiserating expatriated friends, they left Kasane. The plan was to collect their American clients at the airport in Namibia's capitol, Windhoek.

Part of the 1500 kilometer drive included running a gauntlet through a long panhandled sliver of land known as the Caprivi Strip. Steven thumbed through a travel guide until he came to Caprivi. He read the following:

> " 'In 1890 Germany traded its interest in Zanzibar to the British for the marshy land, known as Caprivi. The German Chancellor at the time was Leo Graf von Caprivi, hence the name, and the inclusion in what was then, German Southwest Africa and is now Namibia. European colonizers divvied up Africa without considering tribal diversity. Kagikili is an island in the middle of the Chobe River, which dissects Caprivi. For years Namibia and Botswana have been threatening each other over the rightful ownership to the island.   The Lozi people, the dominant tribe in Caprivi, are caught in the middle. Families ended up in different countries. They're forbidden to move their cattle to the seasonal grazing islands. It is not a safe place to travel, especially at night. Rebels are known to prey on travelers venturing into Caprivi'."

He closed the book and waited for Rigby's comment.

Rigby explained, "The Lozis have been properly screwed by two countries for fifty years. No wonder they're taking potshots at passing vehicles. We're not even slowing down to take a piss."

The tarmac road to Namibia was as straight as a stretched rope. It bore on endlessly through the parched brown bush veldt. Rising heat waves distorted what they saw. The road was dissected by a few villages. Children with extended bellies played soccer on barren fields picked clean by goats and scrawny chickens.

Africans can hardly feed themselves, yet they always seem so content. Zimbabweans used to be happy like these people. Pitiful, what's happened, Rigby thought. He decided not to discuss the matter with Steven. He was too hung-over to argue politics.

Rigby couldn't keep his eyes open, so he let Steven drive. He winced from the metallic clunk of gnashing gears as Steven fumbled with the shift-lever. After accelerating to the verge of exploding the engine, Steven skipped second and third and shifted into fourth gear, which caused the truck to jerk and sputter. "Jesus Christ, man, I thought you said you could drive."

"I've been in prison for two years. How about giving me a chance?"

"C'mon man, engage the clutch first, and then shift gears, not the other way around. That's the way. Now, you've got it. Please try not to hit anything big. I need a snooze."

Rigby leaned his head against the window and started to snore.

THE ZAMBEZI VENDETTA

6

Traveling in the Caprivi triggered Rigby's memories about a clandestine incursion into Botswana during the war. Willie van Piet and Steven's father, Sam, were with him. Their mission was to either assassinate a tribal chief giving sanctuary to saboteurs or turn him into a double agent. He remembered the intelligence briefing. The colonel was like an old cavalry stallion pawing the ground at the sound of the battle bugle.

"Gentlemen, before I get into the details, I need to make one thing clear. This one is off the record. In other words, if you're captured, the Rhodesian government won't even acknowledge your existence. I suspect you'd be labeled mercenaries— as such you'll face a firing squad. Invading a neutral country can be dicey. I'm giving it to you straight. Any questions?" the colonel asked.

When we didn't respond, he went on, "Very good. This rather disagreeable chap is your target. His name's Obert Sibanda." He pushed a photograph of the man across his desk. "He's a chief of the Lozi tribe. My late brother, may God rest his soul, was a missionary in Botswana. He said the Lozis are a proud, elegant people afflicted by only two minor shortcomings. They are habitual liars and incurable thieves. Sibanda's both, and he's stirring up trouble. He's very rich. Has all of the usual trappings— lots of cattle, wives and whatnot. Supporting terrorists has been his modus operandi. More importantly, the old boy's acquired a rather large weapons cache, including an assortment of landmines. There's no need to tell you how many innocents have been crippled by mines. I aim to put an end to his misbehavior. Normally, I'd have you shoot the bastard straight-away and pinch those weapons. I'm afraid if we do kill him, another thug will take his place. Please excuse the pun, but I see this as an opportunity to kill two turds with one stone." The colonel's chuckling dislodged his false teeth. We stifled our smiles.

"Our best-case scenario is to make Sibanda a double agent. Get him working for our side. Of course, the final decision is in your hands. If you feel you can't turn him, well, you'll know what to do. Do you have any final questions?

"All right then. The moon's full in ten days. You'll need the light to navigate the Zambezi. Unfortunately, you'll be visible from the shorelines. I wish there were another way, but I see this as an opportunity to take the fight to the enemy."

He stood up and shook hands with each of us. "Carry on. And may God protect you both, and save Rhodesia."

Ten days later, we were in a rubber boat on the Zambezi River heading into Botswana. We were all dressed in camouflage. The night was painted with strokes of jagged lightning. Towering rain clouds shone distantly on the horizon. The wind turned the night air from damp to

[62]

cold. The air was charged with a smoky smell. Low rumbling thunder disguised the whine of our outboard. The river looked like polished black marble. Willie steered a course in the middle where there was less chance of hitting hippos. We heard their hissing exhales and occasionally an old bull warned us by wheeze-honking. I hunkered in behind Willie, trying to stay dry.

After a few hours, Willie cut the outboard and let the boat nudge up against the shoreline. We pushed and pulled our boat into some bulrushes and veiled it with reeds. Sam set out into the darkness. The rest of us followed him like blind men. Our imaginations gave frightening forms to the trees lining the native path. Sam stopped every few minutes to listen. The buzzing sound of nightjars made him pause. I remember hearing the haunting yelps of a scavenging jackal. When we got closer to the village, Sam made us crawl. The village looked exactly like our intelligence briefing had described it. The chief's hut was where it was supposed to be. It was connected to smaller hutments occupied by his four wives. It was a shell game trying to guess which one he might be sleeping in.

Sam's first undertaking was to poison the watch dogs. The occasional pop and crackle of cooking fires were the only sounds. We crawled in behind Sibanda's house. The backdoor was open. Two of us slipped in and waited to see if anyone stirred. The night-fire burning in the hearth illuminated the walls. By chance, Sibanda was sleeping in his own hut. He was snoring peacefully.

Willie stuffed a gag in his mouth and blindfolded him. He struggled at first, but gave up easily. Sibanda sobbed when we tied a rope around his neck. Sam jerked our man to his feet, and led him out the backdoor. The rain was

[63]

falling steadily as we slipped into the night. The raindrops fizzed in the campfires.

After walking a short distance, Sam made Sibanda squat. Willie spoke to him in fluent Lozi, "Comrade, we're here to settle old scores. We were told you have been disloyal to our freedom fighters operating in Rhodesia. We heard you told our sworn enemies, the Rhodesians, about the place where we hide our landmines."

"It's not true. They're lying. I have always supported the freedom fighters," he said, moving nervously against his bindings.

Willie muttered a favorite revolutionary slogan, "Amberi ne hondo"— forward with the war. We hear other rumors about you helping the Rhodesians," Willie accused.

"Me? I would never help the white devils. I've fed your fighters. Why, I've even given them money. The Rhodesian Security Forces have arrested and tortured me many times, but I never betrayed your cause." He spit in the dirt to emphasize the hideousness of the charge. "I hate the Rhodesians," he added.

I sensed Sam's agitation. He had seen children left legless by exploding landmines. Some of those landmines were buried by the same men Sibanda was sponsoring. Willie pushed Sam's rifle barrel downward. "No, my friend— we have our orders." We encircled Sibanda, and Willie spoke, "We believe you, comrade. But you see— we do have a small problem."

"Just tell me what you want me to do? I will do anything to help you kill the Rhodesians," said the old man. He giggled nervously.

"You old fool. We're the true freedom fighters, we're the Rhodesians. What's more, I'm not an African," said Willie.

"You can't be a European. You speak Lozi better than I do. You must be a sorcerer. This is black-magic. You're a witch casting a spell on me."

Willie made sure his face was only a few centimeters from Sibanda's. He yanked off the old man's blindfold. A flash of lightning illuminated Willie's face, which was streaked in camouflage paint. Sibanda's eyes almost popped out of their sockets as he looked into Willie's face. He screamed and fell forward, hitting the ground with a thump.

"Fuck! Now you've done it. He's had a bloody heart attack," I said.

Sam rolled Sibanda over and sat down on his chest. He slipped his army knife from its sheath and laid the cold blade on the old man's lips. "Let me cut this Lozi dog's tool off and feed it to the hyenas." Sibanda's eyes opened. He trembled uncontrollably. His pleading became disjointed. Willie helped him up into a sitting position and refitted his blindfold.

"We have a job for you, old man," Willie whispered in the chief's ear. "We want you to take us to the terrorist's weapons cache— to the place where you hide the landmines."

He answered too quickly, "I will do as you wish."

"You were right about me, I am a sorcerer. I can look into your head and I can see your thoughts. I know you plan to lead us into an ambush."

"No, no, I would never do such a terrible thing." The old man's cracking voice lacked conviction.

Willie spoke into Sibanda's ear, "Shut up! Hear me— I know many things about you. I have told these things to my friends in the Rhodesian Military. God forbid, if something should happen to one of us, I have told them about your many fine cattle and your new Toyota truck. I know you have four wives. Your youngest wife is sleek and lovely. The older wife is mad because you spend too much time in your young wife's bed. I know you have many sons. They are clever and doing well in school. You must be very proud."

The old man's head sagged and his shoulders slumped with each bit of damning intelligence. He sighed, and closed his eyes.

"If we are ambushed, I have instructed my friends to slaughter your cattle and burn your truck. They will come here and kill your wives, starting with the youngest one. Then they will kill your sons, one at a time. When it's finished, they will kill you. Do you understand me?" The old man was speechless, but he nodded his head indicating that he understood.

"How many terrorists are in this area?" He didn't answer, but held up eight fingers. "Good. Now, I want you to go to them. Tell them you will help them setup an ambush for us at this very spot. When you reach this place you must tell them you have to shit. Leave this path and you'll be spared." Willie placed his hands on the old man's head. "I'm reading your thoughts and I don't like what I see."

"But, I have no thoughts, except that I am a rabbit hiding from a hungry honey-badger."

"Yes, but I see the thoughts you might have in the future. For instance, you might deceive us. You might seek protection with the terrorists in the future. Here, sign this piece of paper."

"What is this?" he asked, scribbling his name on the paper.

"A receipt for the five hundred pounds I'm depositing in your bank account in Maun."

"Why would you give me money?"

"It shows you've received a bribe from the Rhodesian military. If you ever betray us, I can assure you, this receipt will be sent to individuals who would do you great harm," Willie said, holding up the signed paper. "Congratulations, now you're one of us."

Sibanda cried out, "I've been tricked by a sorcerer. They will come for me. I'm a dead man." Sam started to kick the man, but I stopped him.

Willie kneeled down and spoke to Sibanda, "We know the game you've been playing here. Lucky for you, no one else knows. If you carry out our orders, you'll never see us again— if you double-cross us, we will destroy everything you cherish in ways you could never imagine."

We released the old chief and watched him walk dejectedly down the path to his village.

"Willie, you missed your calling. You should have been in the movies," I said.

Ten more Rhodesian soldiers walked out of the darkness. The men were our reinforcements. The plan was to setup a cone-shaped ambush funneling the terrorists into a killing zone. If Sibanda deceived us we knew the terrorists would never come marching down the path single file, instead they would try to outflank us. Soldiers hiding at the far edges would pick up flankers or men attempting to escape.

The trap was set. We concealed ourselves in thick mopani scrub and settled in for the night. The rain added to our misery of lying motionless. Whining mosquitoes filled my nostrils and ears. Stinging Matabele ants bit my legs. I fought to stay awake. Snoring could get a man killed.

THE ZAMBEZI VENDETTA

The night went slowly. A lion roaring followed by deep resonating snorts sharpened our wits. Soon the quiet returned. The low rain clouds dissipated taking the wind. Countless stars and a slivered moon provided better light; it was both a blessing and a curse. When I could no longer hold my water, I urinated in my pants— an additional discomfort. Any movement could be fatal. I hated the gut-wrenching fear. I remember wondering if the other men were as frightened as I was.

I thought I heard something move. I lay motionless for a long time. My nerves were raw. I wanted to run. The snapping of a twig made my heart race. I fumbled with my weapon's safety. So this is how it will end, I thought. What was near me was coming quickly, and then it stopped. Again there was only silence. I flattened myself and tried to see. The thing was breathing heavily. It moved slowly at first, and then much faster. The beast stomped so close to me, I could smell it. It was a hippo returning to the river after a night of foraging. I exhaled and wiped the stinging sweat from my eyes.

Cooing ring-necked doves announced the coming dawn. The morning came and went. Sibanda didn't show up. The blistering sun stifled the air, making it hard to breathe. We heard the alarm calls of chirping guinea fowl, which suspended the cicadas' screeching. The stillness returned. Within seconds, Sibanda came walking down the path leading the terrorists. Three of them had satchels slung over their shoulders. All of them had AKs, except one man carrying a grenade launcher.

They stopped marching at the prearranged spot. Right on cue Sibanda faked his need to crap, which caused an argument with the man carrying the RGP. Willie was the first one to fire. He shot the man quarreling with Sibanda. Sibanda screamed and hit the ground. The nonstop firing dropped two more with head shots. One man carrying a satchel bolted back down the path. He got sprayed by automatic fire, which set off the explosives. The blast killed two men running behind him. It was over in seconds. Two distant shots rang out as soldiers protecting our flanks killed two more trying to escape.

The dust settled. We gathered around Sibanda. He was sitting in the dirt. His incoherent chattering was punctuated with sobbing. The chief's face was covered in bloody bits of white and blue brain tissue. None of the gore was his, but he thought it was. Sam slapped him to stop his weeping.

The body count came up one short. We were about to panic when Sam walked out of the bushes with the last one in tow. The terrorist was limping badly. He collapsed at our feet. Sam propped up his chin with his rifle barrel. He was only a boy. I stooped down to examine his wound. There was a small purple hole on each side of his thigh. The exit wound was the same size, indicating the bullet hadn't hit bone. The boy winced from my touch.

"Baba, let me finish this pup," Sam said, slapping the boy's face.

"We're not killing children. This one's not worthy of a bullet." I handed my weapon to Sam. "I'll carry him." I hoisted the boy over my shoulder and started toward the river. The jostling made the boy cry out for his mother.

I remember overhearing a soldier say, "I'm fighting for people who don't have the stomachs for victory." He was right, the war ended two months later and we had lost.

* * *

Half of the sun showed above the horizon. Steven left the highway and pulled off onto a washboard road. The bone-jarring corrugations bumped Rigby out of his nap. He yawned and rolled his neck to work out the stiffness.

"I've heard horror stories about driving through the Caprivi. I was dreaming about your father and the war. We were given orders to capture a terrorist sympathizer not far from here. The chief's name was Sibanda. We talked him into spying for us."

"How did you turn him?"

"We threatened to kill his family."

"Were you serious?"

"He thought we were. War unlocks the most hideous behavior in men. I'm sure the old fella must be dead by now. I remember your father spared a boy."

"Whatever happened him?" Steven asked.

Rigby cupped his hands around a match as he struggled to light a cigarette in the wind. His answer was delayed by picking a piece of tobacco from his lip. "I heard the terrorists became suspicious about his surviving that ambush. They severed both of his Achilles— it was one of their calling cards. I heard he learned to walk on his knees."

*   *   *

They camped under a camel-thorn acacia. The atmosphere around the campfire was tempered by their lingering hangovers. Rigby stared at the fire, deep in thought, but looked up sharply at the one-eyed cook who also seemed mesmerized by the flames.

"Ezekiel, weren't you a cop in Victoria Falls?"

"I was a policeman there for twenty years."

[70]

"I'm surprised a man of your status ended up in prison," said Rigby.

"I was also surprised," said Ezekiel. He didn't elaborate, but his eyes said he was troubled.

"What do you know about Ian Rhodes? Some of us believe Rhodes spied for the Russians during the war," Rigby asked.

Ezekiel stared into the flames as he spoke. It was obvious that he was considering his reply carefully. "The war was a long time ago. I don't like talking about the war."

"The best times in my life were in that war, and some of the worst. I have reason to believe the man I mentioned is responsible for the death of my best friend."

The cook's smile evaporated into a frown. He hawkered fruitfully into the fire— the spittle fizzed. "We know Rhodes as the *Magondo*. To name him after the hyena dishonors the animal. You're suspicions are well-founded— he did work for the Russians."

"I'm not surprised," said Rigby, also hacking into the fire.

"Did you know he paid us to bring him the ears of the whites we killed?"

"And did you?" Rigby leaned forward anticipating his answer.

"I would never do such a thing. For me, the war brings back bad memories."

"I thought you said the war was a long time ago."

"For the *Magondo*, the war has never ended," said the cook.

"My war with Rhodes has never ended," added Rigby.

Rigby stared at the glowing embers as he remembered a military operation that backfired. His best friend, Willie van Piet, was killed. He found Willie's mutilated body hanging from a tree. His ears were missing. Rigby got up and headed for his tent, but turned back when the cook spoke.

"*Baba*, I think someday you will kill this man."

"What, in God's name, makes you say that?"

"I saw it in one of my dreams."

"Funny— I've had that same dream many times," Rigby yelled over his shoulder.

*   *   *

It took three days to reach Windhoek. On the morning of the fourth day, Rigby led his two truck convoy into the car park at the Windhoek airport.

Dutchy and Rigby waited outside of the Namibian Customs office as the passengers on flight 214 from Johannesburg, South Africa filed past them. "Shit, maybe they missed their connection. You check with South African Airlines. I'll wait here in case they slipped by us," Rigby said to Dutchy.

Rigby found a seat in the terminal. He sat down and reopened his newspaper. There were five teenagers sitting across from him. They must be Americans, Rigby reasoned. One boy with pink frosted hair fiddled with a laptop and gyrated to music. The two other boys wore baseball caps backwards. Their hair was trussed in ponytails and one had an eyebrow pierced with an earring. He wore his pants so low, his ass crack showed. The girl in the group was black. Her hair was braided in cornrows. She sat alone reading a book. A blond muscular boy sat apart from the others. Their clothes selection indicated they might be colorblind. Rigby was so disgusted he decided to change seats. As he was looking for a place to sit, he ran into Dutchy.

"You won't believe what I just saw. The most God-awful bunch of brats you could ever imagine. They had tattoos and earrings. One of them had pink hair. What they need is a damn good beating and I'm just the one to…" He turned to point at the teenagers, but stopped his tirade when he saw Dutchy roll his eyes.

"You must be Croxford, I'm Agnes Flaherty," the large woman said, stepping around Dutchy to shake hands. "I've heard so much about you, Mr. Croxford." Her handshake was as unyielding as her manner. "I can't believe we missed each other," she continued. "Now then, let me round up my students."

To describe Agnes as big-boned would have been understated. Everything about her was oversized, especially her buttocks. She wore a ridiculous looking safari pith-helmet. Her horn-rimmed spectacles teetered on the tip of her pug nose; the glasses were insured by a cord around her neck.

She stopped in front of the teenagers. Rigby was flabbergasted. "There must be a mistake. I was told there would be only *six* clients," said Rigby, counting heads.

"Come now, Mr. Croxford, I may teach English, but I can count. There *are* only six of us," she said. She stood there with her fists on her hips waiting for his reply. She fell silent, took off her glasses and scrutinized a foreign speck on one lens. She raised her eyebrows and waited for his response.

"But where are their parents?" he inquired, looking very perplexed.

"Why, back in the United States, I would imagine. Listen up, students. This is Mr. Croxford and Mr.

Bosshart." Rigby stepped forward to shake hands and was unsuccessful. The boys nodded indifferently. The girl stood up and shook hands.

"Follow me, students. I'm sure these fine gentlemen can handle our luggage." Agnes marched off with her students following close behind.

The men needed two pull carts for the suitcases. "Dutchy, I've got a bad feeling about this safari. I've got half a mind to hijack a jet, fly to England and drown Martin in one of his fucking loos. That, that...crossed-eyed hyena. I wondered why he was so damned eager to give me this safari."

As they were loading, Rigby heard one of the kids make a snide remark about the condition of his trucks.

They drove away with the luggage lashed to the roofs. Dutchy said they looked like Gypsies.

Agnes rode upfront with Rigby. An hour into the six hour drive Rigby bridged the prickly silence. "Is it Mrs. or Miss Flaherty?

"It's Agnes, thank you. Do you know the name of that tree?" She pointed at a tree growing on a hilltop.

"It's an umbrella acacia, ma'am."

"*Acacia tortillis* is the proper botanical name," said Agnes.

"So I take it, you've been to Africa before?"

"This is my first visit. You see, I read books, Mr. Croxford."

Her sarcasm made him feel like he was a student and he'd failed an examination. He changed the subject by asking, "Did you enjoy your flight over?"

She punched him playfully on the shoulder. He was shocked by the severity of the blow, but hid his discomfort. "That's very funny. Forcing someone my size to sit in an airline seat should be against the Geneva Convention. There's something troubling me."

"And what might that be?" he asked.

"I wasn't prepared for the poverty I saw in Johannesburg. I thought South Africa was supposed to be a wealthy country."

"It's the richest country in all of Africa. You should see my country, Zimbabwe, if you want to see real poverty. Life expectancy for a woman is down to thirty-seven years.

She shook her head and sighed. "It's very sad, isn't it?"

"It is indeed," he agreed.

"Seeing Africa has always been my dream. And by God, I finally made it. If you'll excuse me, I think I'll catch a few winks." She removed her glasses and leaned her head against the window.

"Sorry about the confusion at the airport, I wasn't expecting children."

"Life's full of surprises, Mr. Croxford. I'm sure it'll all work out," she said. "The travel agent said you're married to an American."

"Yes ma'am. My wife's a medical doctor. You mentioned you were a teacher. The school I attended would never allow us to dress like that," he said, glancing back at the teenagers. He shook his head in disgust.

"I agree wholeheartedly, but you see, this is a new age we live in. The look on your face was priceless." Her hearty laughter evaporated into a low chuckle and within seconds, she was snoring.

As Rigby studied the woman, he realized she wasn't fat; she was just big all over. I shall name you, Madam Buffalo. And the proper zoological name is *Syncerus caffer,* he thought, glancing at the woman. He smiled imagining Dutchy's reaction to his joke.

7

It was mid-afternoon when they arrived at the cutoff road to the Shumba Safari Lodge. Outside of the lodge's security fence, there were several thatched-covered lean-tos. A family of Bushmen gathered under an anemic teak tree near the huts. Two pot-bellied boys played with an emaciated dog. Other children suspended their soccer game, picked up the curios and ran towards Rigby's caravan. The Bushmen have no artistic abilities; their elephant carvings could have been mistaken for pigs.

"They're San, or Bushmen, as you know them," explained Rigby. "I reckon they're our ancestors. Scientists claim they were the first humans. Bloody fine game trackers, I might add."

"Students, did you hear Mr. Croxford? Those people are relatives of the first hominids to walk on the earth. How utterly fascinating." Her students glanced apathetically at the waving villagers.

The Zambezi Vendetta

Shumba Lodge was nestled on the edge of the *Ongava* game reserve. It was a grass-roofed structure surrounded by tented chalets. Two bleached white elephant skulls marked the entrance of the walkway to the lodge.

The camp manager, Harry Flaxney, was a freckle-faced, bow-legged pipsqueak of an Englishman with a heavily wrinkled face and a gravelly voice realized from a lifetime of smoking. He was born on the eastside of London, fifty-something years ago. No one knew Harry's story. Some people said it was illegal mischief that put him in Africa. He had managed a safari camp in Zimbabwe before immigrating to Namibia. From sunrise to sunset, Harry was never without a beer in his hand and his pet monkey on his shoulder. The monkey's name was Wanker, which is English slang for masturbator. There was never a more appropriate name for an animal.

Harry's deficiency or virtue, depending upon one's point of view, was his fragile stomach and the prodigious amounts of gas it produced. His friends called him Flatty, which was short for flatulence, not Flaxney, as one might expect. They said he could play his hemorrhoids like the reeds in a finely tuned French horn. Harry was not shy about his affliction, or gift, again depending upon one's opinion. If he attended a wedding or a funeral, Harry could store and then release a noxious screecher at the most critical moment in the proceedings. His male friends found his wind-breaking talent hilarious, but the ladies scorned him like he was a leper. For obvious reasons, Harry had not been with a woman in over twenty years. He told his friends he rather enjoyed the bachelor's life — all of that changed the day Agnes Flaherty arrived at Shumba.

*   *   *

Red Kalahari dust engulfed Rigby's motorcade. The teenagers looked miserable as they milled around the vehicles.

"We're here. Sorry to wake you," Rigby said, turning off the ignition and lightly touching Agnes on the shoulder.

"Isn't this charming," said Agnes, squinting over the top of her half-moons.

Harry handed his beer to a servant and stepped forward to greet them. A camp-boy handed out glasses of pulpy paw-paw juice. After the welcoming introductions, Harry escorted them to their respective tents.

Rigby stopped in front of Agnes's tent. "Ma'am, there's no need to rush. I thought a short afternoon game drive might be nice. Let's say, we meet at four o'clock. Nothing happens during the hottest part of the day. The animals become more active in the afternoon."

"It sounds marvelous. We'll be ready to leave at four," she yelled back.

It sounds marvelous, Rigby thought to himself, mimicking her in silence.

Harry pulled Rigby aside. "It's great to see you, mite. I 'ear Zimbabwe's still a fucking mess." He took a long swig of beer. "I 'eard about your prison experience. 'Ow bad *was* it? You look a bit thinner, but Dutchy looks as big as ever."

"I can't say I'd recommend Hwange for a holiday spa. We survived it. So, Flatty, do you like it here?"

Harry leaned over on the side of his buttocks, and strained so hard his face became pleated in grimace creases. Relieved, his redness disappeared and he straightened himself. "I don't miss Zim, if that's what you mean. I love it 'ere, all right. I can't believe you 'aven't called it quits by now."

"I'll never leave Zimbabwe. At least not alive," said Rigby, holding his breath.

"Yikes, it's bad luck to talk like that. Say, what about your clients? They look bloody awful— like fucking circus freaks."

"Christ, I almost fainted at the airport. They seem harmless enough. The woman's a bit stodgy. I better check out my vehicles. We'll catch up on the gossip later," he said, raising his glass.

Harry leaned over on the other side of his buttocks and grimaced again. His face screwed up in pain, and then relaxed. "Say, Rigby, we've got nice white rhino and elephant using a waterhole not far from 'ear. I'll 'ave my 'ead tracker tell you 'ow to find it. Before I forget— these desert elephants can get testy in the breeding season. A German tourist was killed not far from 'ere. Be careful. We don't want an accident."

"Cheers, Flatty. Thanks for the warning."

"Pleasure," said Harry, raising his beer mug.

*   *   *

Every summer, Agnes Flaherty organized an overseas trip for some of her students. As the fieldtrip coordinator, her expenses were paid by the travel agent. It was an affordable way for Agnes to see the world. During her travels she fantasized about lurid affairs with the various men she met. Sadly, none of her fantasies ever materialized. Few people see themselves as others do, but deep down, Agnes knew she repulsed men. Her mother told her on more than one occasion, "Aggie, I'm afraid some girls aren't suitable for men. You'll have to find a life on your own."

She put her book down, and closed her eyes. She thought about the only man she had ever known intimately. It was years ago, but constant dreaming kept the affair vivid in her imagination. He was the headmaster at the school where she taught English. For six months he came to her room in the middle of night. After he was finished with her, he would leave without uttering a word. When she met him in the halls at school, he acted like the encounters never happened. And then without warning, he stopped coming. She was terrified to confront him. He *was* married, and he *was* her superior. Any confrontation might lead to her dismissal. More importantly, she hoped that someday he might come back to her. But the weeks stretched into months and finally into years and he never did.

*　　*　　*

Rigby smiled, watching Agnes walk towards him. She discreetly tugged her underwear from her rear convexity, unruffled her skirt and straightened the binoculars hanging from her neck. She had a copy of *The Birds of Southern Africa* tucked under her arm.

"Mr. Croxford, are we ready to go?" she asked, leveling her pith-helmet.

"Yes ma'am. Where are the others?" he asked, looking behind her.

"They're resting." She fogged her eyeglasses, polished them with a hanky and then held them up to the sunlight for inspection.

"Resting from what?"

"I told them we were leaving. They said they weren't interested. End of story."

"I thought people come to Africa to see the wildlife."

"Mr. Croxford, I'm not going to force anybody to do anything. I offered— they declined. Now, can we go?"

"Let me see if I can change their minds." He walked over to a tent, folded back the flap and announced, "If anyone's interested in this game drive, we're leaving."

The two boys huddling over a laptop computer didn't respond. "We'll catch you next time," one boy said.

"Namibia has brilliant game viewing. I wouldn't want you to miss anything."

"Why don't you take some photos for us?" the boy said, smirking.

"Mr. Bosshart will stay behind in case any of you change your minds."

As soon as Rigby was gone one of the boys said, "Dudes, let's not encourage this guy. This country's a fucking dump. If I had my way, I'd check into a hotel and stay put for the entire three weeks. Hey, this stupid safari wasn't my idea."

"Right on, brother," another one added.

* * *

Agnes was waiting for Rigby in the truck. "Any luck, Mr. Croxford?"

"Not really."

"I'm not surprised. I did think Latisha might be interested."

"Too much peer pressure," Rigby offered.

"It's always a problem," Agnes agreed, sighing.

On the short drive to the waterhole, Rigby outlined the safari for Agnes. They were scheduled to leave the

[82]

Ongava Reserve in two days and travel to the Etosha Pan where they would camp overlooking one of the waterholes. From Etosha they would cross the desert to the coastal town of Walvis Bay. The plan was to drive the Skeleton Coast north to the Angolan border where they would spend eight days camping on the Kunene River.

"I should have you back in Windhoek in three weeks," he told her.

Rigby hid his safari truck in a thicket of mopani trees overlooking a waterhole. Just before dusk, a cowherd of elephants lumbered in for their afternoon watering. A herd of gemsbok antelope timidly approached the water. The bull tilted back his black and white face to taste the air for danger. The setting orange sun served as a backdrop for a massive cloud of red-billed quelea swarming in to drink. The birds were no bigger than a man's thumb, but their numbers darkened the sky and eclipsed the sun like locusts. The hum of the birds was so loud, the elephants and gemsbok conceded the waterhole to the birds. Yellow-billed kites swooped in to feed on the tiny birds. One quelea covey replaced another like giant incoming waves rolling on a beach. Finally the birds lifted off and it was quiet again. Agnes watched the birds disappear into a pink and scarlet streaked sunset.

"My God, that was incredible. I could stay here for the rest of my life," she gushed.

"It *was* lovely, wasn't it? Too bad the others missed it." He started the engine and slowly backed out of the trees. "Agnes, tell me about your students."

"They're really not bad kids. My school's expensive— as you might expect. They all come from wealthy families, except the blond boy, he's on an athletic scholarship.

Some have had substance-abuse problems. I wouldn't characterize them as delinquents. The school's a place for kids to get help."

"Help from what?"

"Oh, I don't know, just life in general."

"I'm sorry, but I live in a part of the world where getting something to eat is an issue— everything else is secondary."

Agnes nodded her agreement and offered no rebuttal. She opened her birder's diary and recorded the species she'd seen. When she finished, she asked, "The booking agent said you were a professional hunter. Please tell me you haven't killed any elephants."

He took his time in answering. "I'm afraid I've killed about everything in Africa that you could imagine, including Africans, I'm embarrassed to admit."

She gave him a disapproving glance over the top of her glasses. "Oscar Wilde described safari hunting as the unspeakable in search of the uneatable."

"It's like it says in the Bible, 'Rise, Peter, kill and eat.'"

"But Peter refused," she retorted.

"I reckon Peter wasn't starving."

"Killing animals needlessly is a sin, Mr. Croxford. Killing another human is a mortal sin."

"No species goes unchallenged in Africa, including humans. If someone's keen on shooting you, and you don't shoot back, I reckon it's the same as killing yourself."

"Life is precious. It doesn't sound like you value human life as much as I do."

"We — by we, I mean us Africans— view death differently. Mortality has a seat at every man's table. You westerners are possessed by the fear of dying. You lie about your age, as if you could somehow cheat the inevitable. We don't view death as spectators— we see it every day. We accept our fate in the scheme of things. We're all perishable."

"I could never kill another human, Mr. Croxford."

"Yes, ma'am. That's what I said, a long time ago."

*   *   *

Before dinner Rigby recorded the following note in his safari log:

> Aug. 20th Departed Kasane before succumbing to severe alcohol poisoning. Drive through Caprivi uneventful. Left Windhoek after collecting clients. Bit of a shock. Clients are American teenagers and their female chaperone. The woman is bigger than Dutchy. Kids have tattoos, earrings etc. Spending two days at Flatty's camp. He says we look like a traveling Russian circus. The chaperone is their teacher at some fancy school in the States. I think the school might be a mental hospital. If I ever see Martin again, I'll get even. Have the feeling this will be the safari from hell.

The camp's cook rang a cowbell announcing dinner. An assortment of guests filed into the mess tent. Rigby's group sat together at one end of the table. Harry sat at the head of the table with Wanker perched on his shoulder. The monkey kept pestering Harry until he gave him a sip of his beer. As soon as everyone was seated, Wanker walked up and down the table panhandling. A camp-boy used a broom to chase the monkey up into the rafters above the table. As soon as the man turned his back, the monkey climbed back down and resumed his begging.

"Get, you filthy bugger," Harry yelled, throwing a spoon at Wanker.

"He's so cute. How can you be so mean to him?" asked a guest.

"He's not brothering anyone," another guest interjected. A woman shared her gin and tonic with the monkey. Wanker finished the drink with one convulsive gulp. He reached for a glass of Chardonnay, but the owner shooed him away.

"I love 'im like 'e was me own flesh and blood. I just wish 'e was more of a finicky eater, but 'e's uncommonly partial to baboon turds. I'm afraid 'e eats them like they were gumdrops. It makes 'im a rather poor dinner guest, wouldn't you agree?"

A woman's scream sent the monkey scrambling up into the rafters. From the safety of his perch, and glowing from the crowd's attention, Wanker began to masturbate. The students giggled, but Agnes was outraged. When Harry caught her glaring at him, his grin faded into a scowl.

"Mr. Flaxney, isn't there something you can do to make him stop?"

"No ma'am. I'm afraid that's another one of 'is bad 'abits. Pay no attention to 'im. 'E'll be done with 'is business soon enough. Would you be so kind as to pass me the sweet potatoes?"

*   *   *

Early the next morning Rigby shared the campfire with Harry. Harry looked different. His hair bore the tooth marks of a comb and he was clean shaven. He didn't have a beer in his hand or his monkey on his shoulder. Something's not right here, Rigby thought.

"Where's your friend, Wanker?"

"Resting after last night's stunning performance," Harry said, wetting his fingers with saliva and slicking back his eyebrows. "The woman asked me to take 'er birding. Would you mind?"

"Not at all— she's all yours. Say, you wouldn't have something else in mind?"

"With 'er? She's a wee bit too big, wouldn't you say?"

Rigby thought for a moment, and then he replied, "Hmm, if you say so, Flatty."

One hour later, Harry drove Agnes out of camp heading for the marshes where he hoped they would see nesting crimson shrikes. Before they reached the edge of the swamp, he stopped to smoke a cigarette. As soon as he lit it, Agnes plucked it out of his mouth and smashed it with her boot heel. "Mr. Flaxney, you're too intelligent to smoke."

"Yes ma'am. Lord knows, I've been meanin' to quit. I think it's the loneliness of living in the bush."

"That's a ridiculous...." He raised his hand to stop her reprimand. The distant trumpeting of elephants and the sound of clashing ivory had caught his attention. "Ma'am, if you'd agree to suspend our birding— I could show you something special. It sounds like two bull elephants are 'aving a 'ell of a tussle."

"By all means, Mr. Flaxney, lead the way."

Harry grabbed his rifle by the barrel and slung it over his shoulder. He marched off with Agnes striding close behind. As they walked she had time to study him. Harry was thin without being scrawny, more lean than boney. She noticed his fingernails were trimmed and clean, a novelty she hadn't witnessed in the other men. Naturally, his freckled complexion had been etched by the equatorial sun. Despite his physical flaws there was something very appealing about Flaxney. Agnes brushed aside her melancholy and concentrated on not getting entangled in the hook-thorn bushes.

He stopped her with a hand signal and made her crouch next to him to prevent his voice from carrying. "The elephants are at the bottom of a river bed up ahead," he whispered, pointing with his rifle. "Chances are these old boys are in musk and there's probably a breeding cow nearby. We need to keep as quiet as church mice or they'll charge us straight away. Ma'am, a bull elephant in musk is an unpredictable devil. You need to stay close."

"Mr. Flaxney, I shall stay so close, you'll think we're Siamese twins."

They came to a cliff overlooking a dried-up river bottom. Ten meters below them, two bull elephants faced off like dueling fencers. The bulls swung their heads from side to side and spread their ears to make themselves appear bigger. They were evenly matched in size. One bull was missing a tusk. The dark stains below the temporal glands behind their blood-red eyes showed both bulls were rutting. The elephants curled back their trunks as they false-charged. They circled each other waiting for an opening. Their mouths lay open from exhaustion. When one bull lunged, the other bull gave ground until madness overtook them and they collided with a meaty thump. The collision yielded the clatter of ivory. A hanging dust cloud engulfed them.

Three female elephants stood silently under a sycamore tree. The smell of one cow's urine had attracted the bulls. The younger female had come into season. The bulls would kill for the right to cover her. Without warning the one-tusked bull lost his nerve and turned away from the fight. After chasing the squealing loser for a short distance, the victor stopped and shook his head like a dog emerging from water.

Having prevailed, the winner turned his attention to the female. When he raised his trunk to taste the air, his organ lengthened until it touched the ground. The young female had to be coaxed out of the shadows by the older cows. The bull made a low rumbling gurgle to reassure her. At first, the smaller cow spun away from him, but he turned her gently with his trunk. The cow rose her tail invitingly, spread her legs and he mounted her. His organ seemed to come alive as it sought refuge in her. She yelped from its entry, but squealed from his spastic thrusts.

Agnes had seen enough. She grabbed Harry by the arm and pulled him away. As she matched his footsteps on the walk back to the truck, she tried to divert her thinking away from what she had just witnessed. Her lips were dry and beads of perspiration dotted her forehead. She blushed from her thoughts and the wetness it caused. When they arrived back at the vehicle, Harry lit another cigarette. Her stare was enough to make him extinguish it after one puff.

"That was thrilling, Mr. Flaxney. I wish we could have missed the ending."

"But ma'am, I reckon it's just God's way." His voice had a dispirited tone about it.

"I found it quite disgusting. Now, I'd like to see about those birds."

Agnes climbed into the backseat. Harry pulled himself up into the front. He mimicked her disappointment in an inaudible mumble to himself. "I found it quite disgusting." He lit another cigarette and this time he blew the smoke in her direction.

She pretended not to hear him but she did. Agnes covered her nose with a hanky and then used it to daub her tears. She had recently turned fifty and as such, hot-flashes and spontaneous crying were not uncommon. Why did I say those things, she asked herself, biting her lip. She touched him on the shoulder. "Could you pull over? I really need to use the restroom."

"Yes, ma'am. And don't you worry yourself about snikes. It 'asn't rined in months. Too bloody 'ot for snikes this time of year."

"The proper pronunciation is *snakes,* Mr. Flaxney."

"Yes, ma'am. I reckon the sifest plice would be behind that old baobab tree yonder."

Hidden from view, Agnes squatted against a clay-colored termite mound next to the baobab. She looked up through the crisp indigo sky at a soaring Bateleur eagle riding the heat thermals. The sun warmed her with intermittent sunrays filtered by the baobab's branches. The untamed enormity of Africa made her feel alive and free from her usual misgivings.

On the walk back to the truck she met Harry. "Sorry ma'am, I was startin' to fret."

"I'm flattered. Tell me about yourself and what brought you to Africa?" she asked him as they walked together.

"Me? There ain't much to tell, really. My mum left me in a shoebox on the doorstep of a Catholic parish in east London. Nuns rised me until I was old enough to go to sea. I ended up on a tramp steamer working the Congo River. That's 'ow I come to Southern Africa."

"Do you have a family?" she inquired, testing the waters.

"Nah. To tell you the truth, I 'avn't stiyed in one place long enough. Anywye, what about you, ma'am?"

"I'm single, all right. I'm afraid my life's been a real bore."

Harry's bushy eyebrows narrowed. "It's mind-boggling to think you ain't married— you being so lovely and all. Pardon me, ma'am, but I swear I'm only telling the truth as I sees it."

She searched for a clever rejoinder, but before she could find one, she blurted out, "Mr. Flaxney, that's the nicest thing anyone's ever said to me."

"So help me, God, I meant every word of it." Harry cocked his head and grinned. His expression revealed a man unencumbered by complex thinking. Agnes studied him to see if there was a speck of sincerity in his compliment— when she found it, she blushed and fanned herself with her pith helmet. The tears came and she turned away to hide them. She felt an unexpected flicker of attraction between them, but she dismissed it as she had always done.

"We better see to our birding, Mr. Flaxney."

"Yes ma'am, Right away ma'am. Say, why don't you ride upfront with me?"

They rode in silence. Agnes couldn't stop thinking about Harry and the possibilities. She avoided looking at him, but when she did, they locked eyes and both of them looked away. When he shifted gears his hand brushed

[91]

against her thigh. As a test, she moved her leg back. He touched her a second time. Agnes felt possessed by a strange calmness she had never known. She was alone with a man, and for the first time in her life she wasn't terrified of rejection. Her hands trembled as she unbuttoned her blouse.

"Why don't you pull over, Harry." She touched him on the shoulder and raised an eyebrow flirtatiously.

Harry was so preoccupied with not driving over some hook thorn bushes he missed her coquetry. He stopped and when he looked over at her he gasped. "Miss Flaherty, what's come over you? I reckon its sunstroke—but then again it might be malaria."

She placed her fingers tenderly over his lips to stop him from speaking. She popped open the last button on her blouse and shrugged it off. Her massive breasts normally sagged, but now they defied gravity.

"Good God in heaven, help me. I...I 'avn't done this in a long time," he stammered. His face turned tomato-red as he fumbled to undo his pants.

His actions were the encouragement she needed. She grabbed his safari jacket and jerked him down on top of her. Agnes was too large for the confines of the front seat. She kicked the door open and extended her legs. Their coupling wedged his face between her breasts. She kissed the top of his head as he cooed and suckled her. Harry made love to Agnes like he was afraid there might be another twenty years of celibacy in his future.

Her limited sexual experiences with the headmaster had been too swift to be fulfilling. This was different. And then what she had only read about in books, happened. The unbearable tingling started in her toes and then buzzed into every part of her body ending in an explosive release that left her breathless.

After taking a moment to regain her composure, she pulled Harry up and kissed him hard on the lips. Her sobbing shocked him. His hands shook as he wiped away her tears. His expression pinched into a mask of embarrassment as he lit another cigarette.

"Ma'am, I...I don't know what got into me. I'm sorry, I really am."

Her face was alive with pleasure. She stopped him from speaking by kissing him deeply. "Harry, I think under the circumstances you better call me Aggie." She plucked the cigarette out of his mouth, but this time she took a puff and handed it back to him. "Let's rest for a few minutes and see if whatever got into you can happen again."

"Aggie, I reckon this is the best dye in my life." He slid down and plopped one of her nipples into his mouth. He moaned softly as she raked his hair with her fingers.

They made love until they were too exhausted to continue. With twenty-years of lust satisfied, they talked openly to each other. Agnes told Harry things about herself that she'd never told a living soul. In return, she listened to Harry's life stories with glowing attention. Without warning, she broke out laughing.

"What's so funny, love?"

"Oh, it's nothing, really— I'm just so happy." She blushed, knowing that she would never dream about the headmaster again.

They delayed driving back to camp until the last minute. Harry whistled tunelessly as they drove on the edge of a great salt plain that was once an ocean. The sunset was as colorful as a peacock's tail. Agnes couldn't keep her hands off of him and Harry couldn't stop smiling.

"Aggie, maybe we should keep this quiet until I break the news to Rigby. You know, I mean about us." He patted her knee.

"Anything you say, darling," she said, leaning her head on his shoulder. "On second thought, I should be the one to tell him."

"You're the boss," he answered, tunneling his hand into her blouse.

"Are you sure you want me?" she asked.

"You bet, Aggie. Why I've never been surer about anything in my life."

*　　*　　*

Rigby and his men were up before dawn reloading the trucks. He was surprised to see Agnes in a bathrobe and sleepy-eyed. There's something definitely different about her, he thought. I wonder if Flatty? No way. As she got closer, he did a double-take. Her cheeks were rosy and she wore lipstick. Without those old granny glasses and the stupid hat, you're damn decent, he thought, shaking his head.

"Good morning. I hate to rush you, but it's a long drive to where we're going."

"Mr. Croxford, we need to talk." She grabbed his hand and led him to the campfire. "I'll get right to the point. I'm quitting."

"Teaching pimply-faced teenagers has got to be bloody awful. I can't say I blame you much."

"No, I mean I'm quitting the safari."

"But why?"

"Mr. Croxford, do you know what it's like not to have been touched by a man in twenty years?"

"That's a loaded question for a man who just got out of prison."

"Pardon me?"

"Please excuse the one-liner— it's an *inside* joke. Is it something I've done or said? Whatever it is, I know we can work it out."

"This has nothing to do with you. I'm getting married."

"Congratulations. But what's the rush— you'll be home in three weeks?"

"Mr. Croxford, I'm marrying Harry."

"Harry who?"

"That one," she said, pointing at Harry's tent.

"You're marrying Flatty? Sorry, I meant to say Harry. But you only met him two days ago. Please tell me this is a joke."

"I can assure you— this is no joke. You're an intelligent man. Look at me for a second. How many marriage proposals do you think someone like me gets in a lifetime?"

"Ma'am, I took this safari job as a favor."

Agnes acted like she was lost in a trance. "I always thought happiness was for other people. Quite frankly, I've been searching for a reason to go on living and I found it."

"With Harry?" he asked.

"Yes. If our marriage works for one day, at least I can say there was one man in the world willing to marry me."

When he looked into her eyes he knew there was nothing he could say that would change her mind. He turned his back to her and opened his hands to warm them over the campfire. He shook his head. "Well now, isn't this a lovely cock-up? What the hell am I suppose to do with these kids?"

"Finish the safari with them, I would imagine. Look, you don't need me. I hoped you'd be more understanding."

"Won't the school dismiss you?"

"I'm resigning anyway. They can't take my pension. And I have a small inheritance. Harry and I will do just fine, thank you. As for my students, they'll be elated to hear I'm leaving. They're not so bad, considering their circumstances."

He turned around and tossed her a grin. "I guess I'll manage. Cheers. The very best to you and Harry," he said, raising his tea mug.

After they concluded their small talk, she handed him some papers. "I scribbled a few notes about my students. I thought they might come in handy."

"Thanks for this. I'll do my best," he said, holding up the notes.

"I'm sure you'll do just fine. Goodbye, Mr. Croxford."

*   *   *

From the privacy of her tent, Latisha read the following note Agnes had given her:

Dearest Tish,

I apologize for my abrupt departure. I hope you never have to experience the terrible loneliness I have endured during my life. Maybe it was by divine intervention, but I have met the man of my dreams. I have set off on a new chapter in my life with a sense of joy I have never known.

Be assured, I have left you in very capable hands. The travel agency described Mr. Croxford as the quintessential safari guide.

A few words about Croxford: He was born in what was Rhodesia and is now Zimbabwe. He is a decorated war hero and a professional hunter. His father went so far as to name his four sons after firearms companies. Someplace in Africa there is a Smith, a Wesson, a Browning and we know the Rigby. As I said, Croxford has a long history in Africa.

I'm not sure he has the patience to deal with the boys' childish antics. Latisha, you are more mature than the boys. You may have to intercede as a peacemaker.

As I expected, Africa is truly a magical place. I'm sure, if you give it a chance, you will enjoy your African experience as much as I know I will. God bless you and the boys.

Agnes Flaherty

After rereading the letter, Latisha closed her eyes. She wished she had confided in Agnes Flaherty. They had more in common than they both realized. Now, I really am alone, she thought.

*　　*　　*

Rigby was deep in thought as he stared at the dying embers. He looked up when Harry approached. Harry waited, gathering courage, before he spoke. "I guess she told you," he said in a reserved whisper.

"Flatty, you fucking weasel— you screwed me good and proper."

"Don't be like that. I'm sorry Rigby, but I love 'er. You wouldn't stand between a man and his future wife, would you?"

"I hope your marriage lasts longer than the courtship."

"'Ard to believe Aggie would give someone like me a second glance. I mean 'er being such a lady and all."

"'Ard to believe you'd marry 'er after only two fucking days," said Rigby, mimicking Harry's cockney accent. "No *double entendre* intended."

"So help me, God, I love Aggie, and that's that."

Rigby smiled. He was thinking about how many second glances Agnes and Harry would get as a couple. "Say, you wouldn't be using Agnes as your ticket out of Africa?"

"Now lookee 'ere. I can't believe you'd say such a terrible thing. And I thought you were my mite." Harry looked mortally wounded.

"Jesus, Flatty, I'm only joking. Seriously— here's to you and the future Mrs. Flaxney." They clicked tea mugs.

"I guess this ain't the best time to be asking for favors, but I need one. After we get 'itched, we're driving back to Zimbabwe to collect my personals. After that, we're flying to the States. I can't take my monkey over the border. Besides, 'ee doesn't seem to get on too well with Aggie. Could you look after Wanker? I need time to find 'im a proper 'ome. I promise I'll catch up with you at the end of your safari."

"Flatty, you've got balls asking for favors."

"If I leave the little bugger, the munts will kill 'im straight away. Please mite, Wanker means a lot to me, 'ee really does."

"All right, I'll take him. Wouldn't want the munts to flog him. Besides, he's a perfect fit for *this* three-ring circus. Before we hit the road, Sir Harry, is there anything else I can do for you?" Rigby asked.

"Croxford, I owe you one."

"You're damn right you do. Good luck, Flatty. I better see you in Windhoek in three weeks."

"I'll be there."

As Rigby drove away, he saw Harry and Agnes standing together holding hands in the rearview mirror. Harry disappeared in the orange dust, but Agnes's head appeared above the hanging cloud. There they are, David and his fiancée, Godzilla. Only in Africa, he thought. He laughed out loud and pounded the steering wheel. His passengers looked at each other and shook their heads.

8

Binga, Zimbabwe

Ian Rhodes patted his sidearm for reassurance as he climbed out of the flatbed truck. His driver was a moon-faced surly African, known to the villagers of Binga as "*Hungubwe*," which means jackal in Shona. Both men waded into the group of natives congregating near the rear entrance of the local gin-mill. The monotonous beat of African rap music pulsated from the open windows. The air was fused with the gagging aroma of urine pitted against the sweet smell of ganja. Rhodes covered his nose with a handkerchief and followed his driver through the backdoor. Everyone in the nightclub stared at Rhodes as he walked in. The chattering stopped, leaving only the music and the clicking of glasses. The bartender approached Rhodes, but Rhodes waved him off.

A man sitting at the bar whispered to the other patrons, "Be careful ladies, the white *Magondo* is hunting tonight."

Black prostitutes were Rhodes's usual quarry in Binga. The man's remark made a woman giggle. She was sloppy drunk and wore a blond wig and pointy high heels. The woman left the bar and saddled up to Rhodes. She seemed to know him, but he ignored her. When she put her arms around him he wiggled free. She pouted and cursed Rhodes playfully. A friend hushed her and pulled her back into the crowd.

"Who wants to make some easy money?" Rhodes asked. Those sober enough to hear the question raised their hands.

The crowd followed Rhodes outside. He culled the group by picking the soberest among them. When he described the job to be done, some of them walked away.

The volunteers helped each other up onto the back of the truck. One man fell off as they drove away. They left him lying in the road.

*   *   *

After driving for four hours, Rhodes directed his driver to turn onto a gravel road running uphill to a dimly lit farmhouse. He ordered the man to park the truck behind some abandoned huts at the base of the hill.

In the pre-dawn darkness, the Africans gathered around Rhodes. He shined a flashlight in each man's face searching for those who could to be trusted with rifles—he found none and handed out machetes.

Leon Campbell was a feisty Scotsman who'd bought his dairy farm from his father-in-law thirty years ago.

Leon and his wife, Eileen, eked out a living on the rock-strewn land. Ten African families lived on and worked at the farm. The Mugabe regime had sent his thugs to evict the Campbells before, but despite the odds, they managed to hold out. Rhodes had been sent to finish the job, once and for all.

"Pay attention, you drunken sots," Rhodes yelled, waving his sidearm. "You men there, your job is to surround the main house." He singled out three more. "I want you three to burn the huts. The rest of you, stay here with me. Listen up. You're free to kill the white pig and his sow, but don't you dare touch their daughter—she's mine and mine alone. After I'm finished, you can do as you like with her. Wait until you hear my pistol shot. Does everyone understand me?" When he shined his flashlight in their faces they shielded their eyes and nodded that they understood.

"Everyone get into position and wait for my signal."

The farmhouse and barns were illuminated by dull security lights. Farm workers were busy herding cows into the milking shed. One man baled hay while another man shoveled cattle feed into an ox drawn wagon. Two other farmhands raked manure out of the holding pens.

The invaders' dark silhouettes appeared intermittently between some racing clouds. They slithered in the dewy grass to the edge of the light and waited for Rhodes's gunshot.

Eileen Campbell was rail thin. Her fingers looked like bird bones covered in onion skins. Her face was lined with deep wrinkles and her blue eyes looked dull and distracted. The worry of living in Africa had eroded her

[102]

looks much faster than aging. She squinted from an annoying wisp of cigarette smoke as she turned scrambled eggs with a wooden spoon.

Her husband sipped his morning tea and scanned a week old newspaper. "It says here the unemployment rate has topped ninety percent."

"Have you thought about Emma?" she asked, changing the subject.

"Concerning?" Leon folded his newspaper and used it to obstruct her glare.

"About our daughter moving to Australia."

"Damn it, Eileen, don't start in on me this early in the morning. This economy can't go much lower. Why leave now, when everything's about to turn for the better."

"Listen to you— the eternal optimist. You're the only person in this God forsaken country who sees things on the mend. We should have left here years ago. Now, all of our friends are gone to God-knows-where." She wiped a moist sniffle on the back of her wrist. Her hands shook so violently she had trouble extinguishing a cigarette and lighting another one. "How many attacks will it take before you throw in the towel?"

"Whining won't make it better." He pushed away his plate of unfinished toast. "That's enough. We'll discuss it tonight."

Eileen wanted to argue, but she lost her train of thought. She stared out of the kitchen window and considered her maid's warning. The woman had said there were rumors about men coming to burn them out. There had been so many warnings it was hard to take them seriously. She thought she saw something move in the darkness, but after blinking, whatever she thought she saw was gone. A dog's whimper made her swing the

[103]

kitchen window open. "Better check on the dogs. Something's got their dander up."

"Bloody hyenas, I reckon. It might be a lion. I'll see to it." He groaned, pushed back from the table, grabbed his shotgun and headed for the front door.

His Irish setter, Zulu, lay still on the front steps. The dog's backbone had been severed. The gash was too clean not to have been delivered by a machete or an ax.

"Fucking munts!" he screamed, slamming the door shut. He secured the deadbolt and squinted though the peephole. "Eileen, the bastards have come for us again. Better bolt the windows. Move woman— before they get in."

He crawled across the kitchen floor, inched up the wall and flipped on two switches. One switch illuminated the floodlights— the other one signaled a neighbor that he was under attack. Instantly, the surrounding yard was bathed in a sea of light. No longer hidden, Rhodes's men stood up and closed in on the farmhouse.

The burning milking barn turned the night sky from black to orange. The smoke terrorized the livestock. When Leon Campbell heard his animals braying, he stuck his fingers in his ears and screamed.

Rhodes stood in the back of his truck directing the assault. He shined his light on a girl hiding in the grass. Her tiny breasts showed that she hadn't reached puberty. "Don't let that one get away," he yelled. One of his men ran into the grass and hacked her with his machete. Rhodes's face twisted into a sadistic grin.

The farm workers, both men and women, tried to defend the Campbells, but they were old and outnumbered. The attackers chanted as they bludgeoned them without pity. Their victims' screams for mercy fell on deaf ears. Eileen heard their shrieks and cried out for them. After the killing stopped, an evil calm settled over the farm. The Campbells could hear Rhodes barking orders.

Leon felt the heat and knew they had set fire to his thatched roof. Smoke was already filtering down through the teak rafters. He heard something and spun around. It was his daughter; she was standing in a growing pool of her urine. Tears glistened on her cheeks. "Emma, damn you, get down," he yelled, running to her. The sound of shattering glass forced him to leave her and crawl back under the broken window. He pushed the safety off and held his 12 gauge tight to his chest. The attacker worked pieces of broken glass loose and stuck his head though the opening. The shotgun blast severed the man's head as cleanly as a guillotine.

"Take that, you bloody bastards," he shouted, firing aimlessly into the night. "Rhodes, I know you're out there. The name *Magondo* is too fucking good for you— you filthy murdering bastard."

"I wonder if it's good enough for that fine daughter of yours," Rhodes yelled back. His laughter was accompanied by the hoots of the men around him.

Campbell used the lull to reload his shotgun. Something made him turn around. "For the love of God, don't do it," he pleaded.

"I love you," his wife mumbled.

He ran to her, but not soon enough. Eileen fired a pistol shot into her daughter's temple, stuck the barrel in her own mouth and pulled the trigger. Pieces of burning thatch fell on Leon Campbell, but he refused to leave them. Within seconds the house was a burning inferno.

It was dawn when a neighboring farmer arrived at the Campbell farmstead. He found bloated human corpses and butchered dairy cows. He fired a warning shot to scatter some cawing magpies.

It took years to build the Campbell dairy, but only minutes to reduce it to a few crumbling sandstone walls. A pile of charred bones marked the spot where the Campbell family had died. The farmer picked up a seared wooden spoon, examined it and then tossed it onto a smoldering fire. High above the scorched land a spiral of white-backed vultures surveyed the carnage.

* * *

9

The Rhodesian ridgeback ran outside and growled at a truck struggling up the steep incline. Helen Croxford closed her book, *Epidemiology in Southern Africa,* and walked barefooted to the porch railing. She turned down the volume on Mendelssohn's Violin Concerto. Her house servants came out to investigate the disturbance. When she recognized the man driving, she admonished her dog. Her servants went back inside. The ridgeback raced out to meet the man exiting a Land Rover.

Tim Brooks was a retired game warden living on an adjoining farm. Like many Rhodesian war veterans, a landmine had cost him a leg and his hearing. What remained of his body was burly. The African sun had etched deep fissures in his face. He had the yellowed fingers of a lifelong smoker and when he coughed, mucus rattled from the depths of his lungs.

He cursed his prosthetic leg as he struggled to climb the stairs. "Bend, damn you. Bloody shame another part of my anatomy isn't as stiff," he muttered under his breath.

"My, aren't we the grumpy one this morning. How about a cup of tea?" Helen asked.

"A spot of tea would be lovely. Have you heard from your husband?"

"Just a note telling me he's not having the best of times," she said, handing him the cup.

"Guess you heard about the Campbells? The barbarity was beyond belief."

Her expression revealed that she hadn't heard. Tim looked down and sighed. "God knows, I hate being a Grim Reaper. They were massacred last night in an ambush— burned alive, actually."

"Not the entire family?"

"I'm afraid so. May their souls rest in peace."

"The insanity's unbelievable, even for Africa. Are you positive?"

"Quite. Heard it on the BBC and then confirmed it with an Afro friend. Helen, listen to me for once. This country's close to anarchy. If you're too damn pigheaded to leave, at least move to Bulawayo."

"We Americans are a stubborn lot— if you don't believe me, just ask my husband."

"But you live in Africa. You're a political activist, which makes you a convenient target."

"If I leave, what happens to my patients?"

"My dear, you can't treat them if you get yourself killed. There's not a kernel of corn left in Zim. People are starving. When it comes, it'll be neighbor killing neighbor. Believe me, Helen, it won't be pretty. This isn't my first rebellion, you know." A shrill buzzing sound from his hearing aid caused him to fiddle with the volume control. He held up his hand to stop her from speaking as he made the adjustment. "That's better. You were saying?"

"My patients will look after me," she replied, belatedly.

"I have to say, your naiveté scares me. I lived through the Mau-Mau rebellion in Kenya and I witnessed the Hutu-Tutsi barbarity in Rwanda. What can I say to make you change your mind?"

Helen refused to answer, preferring to ask her own question. "Are you running?"

Tim took out a pocketknife and began to whittle a barnacled growth on his knuckle as he considered his response. "At my age — no way. Besides, I can't run fast enough on this bum wheel." He knocked on the plastic leg with his knife. His smile curled down into a concerned frown. "Please tell me you'll be careful. If something should happen to you, I'd never forgive myself."

"Don't cut yourself with that filthy knife. If you want me to burn that off, I will."

"I wish I had a shilling for each one of these beauties I've sliced off," he said, admiring his splotchy hands.

Her scolding was interrupted by four men who walked out of the underbrush. One man was limping and used a crooked stick for a crutch. Another man's head was wrapped in a dirty rag. After she restrained her dog, the men warily approached the porch. Tim greeted them in Shona. The men clasped their hands together as a sign of respect.

"Solomon, bring my medical kit," Helen yelled to her houseboy.

Africans arrived at her farm every day seeking medical attention. Many of their injuries were incurred at political rallies, or political riots, as Tim called them. Tim listened to one man's description of the events that led to their injuries. When Tim cursed the perpetrators, the Africans nodded their heads in agreement.

"Enough of the chit-chat, I could use some help."
"I'm coming," he said, shuffling back up the stairs.

Tim unraveled a blood-soaked rag from the old man's head. The severity of the wound made him wince.

There was nothing Helen could do but clean the wound. Tim rewrapped the man's head in a fresh bandage. "I've done everything I can for you, my father. You must rest in a quiet place. Now, we must ask God to do his work," she said softly to the injured man.

The man took her hands to his face and sobbed, "Bless you, *Amai.*"

Tim studied the man as he walked away. He rubbed his chin stubble, shook his head in disbelief and said, "Only an African could survive a head injury like that."

"I've seen worse. What did he say?"

"It's just like I said, the country's about to explode. Men came to their village looking for food. When they didn't get what they wanted, they turned savage. This wasn't the usual tribal tit-for-tat— it was rape and pillage and the devil's work. Tell me you'll leave with me this very second."

"I'm not going anywhere."

"Then by God, neither am I. Let's see how long you can stand having me under foot." He stood up defiantly and thumped his cane on the wooden floor.

"I'm glad that's settled. You'll have to earn your keep around here. Go wash your hands. You'll be the only one-legged nurse in Zimbabwe."

Tim struggled up the steps, but swung back around to face her. "Say, I almost forgot. I picked up your mail in town," he said, retrieving a thin stack of letters from his back pocket and handing them to her. Helen scanned them and when she found one from her husband she sat down to read it.

> Dear Helen,
>
> I tried to phone you from Walvis Bay. As usual, the telephone system is buggered. This safari has gone from very bad to bloody awful. We lost our woman chaperone in charge of these horrid American brats. It seems Flatty married her. And no, I'm not making it up. He said it was love at first sight. I think he saw her as a replacement for his monkey, Wanker, which I might add he has abandoned to my care. Wanker has become very depressed over the divorce. He's either crapping on us or living up to his well-deserved name.

Helen stopped reading and laughed. "Tim, you must read Rigby's letter. Flatty's gotten himself a wife." She reopened the letter and continued reading.

On a more pleasant note, we had fabulous game viewing at Etosha. Saw lots of black and white rhino. Good desert elephant and three prides of lion. These kids can't wait to leave Africa, which is a shame. Nothing seems to interest them. I've almost given up. All they do is play with their computers and listen to music. The plan is to put them on a plane back to the States in two weeks. Dutchy and yours truly will have a few drinks on that day, I can assure you. We leave tomorrow for the drive up the Skeleton Coast. You would love Namibia. I would like to bring you here one day.

All my love,
Rigby

p.s. Will phone you from Windhoek.

*   *   *

10

Tim Brooks's prophecy about Zimbabwe was not exaggerated. Looting in the big cities was rampant. Within days, lawlessness spread from the cities to the rural areas. Roadblocks manned by thugs made travel impossible. The schools closed, because the teachers' salaries weren't enough to pay for their daily transportation costs. Without medicines or food, the hospitals closed. Thousands died from cholera and were buried in mass graves. Open-air food markets were emptied by hoarders. Tribal hatred exploded with mobs of club-wielding Shona swarming into Matabele villages wreaking havoc, which resulted in revenge raids. Just as Brooks had predicted, neighbor turned against neighbor and the country succumbed to mayhem.

Helen's medical clinic was overwhelmed. Some patients were forced to sleep in the open at night. Medical supplies, already in short supply, were used up in three days. There were no bandages or ointments or even surgical tape. Nothing was left but Helen Croxford's determination.

Every morning, her staff used pushcarts to haul away the dead bodies to a communal grave. There were too many corpses to adhere to burial customs. Blowflies descended on the clinic like a black curtain. The stench of death clung to the land and everything on it.

In desperation, she enlisted the help of the local witch doctor. Samuel Humba arrived one afternoon riding an emaciated donkey with his five wives walking dutifully behind him. Two of his wives balanced large goat-skinned water bags on their heads. The other three had babies lashed to their backs. Humba wore sunglasses and a brimless top hat decorated with ivory beads and cowry-shells. A leopard skin covered his shoulders. His massive belly jiggled as he dismounted. Tim remarked that Humba must be the only obese person left in all of Zimbabwe.

After greeting Helen with the skepticism of a professional for an amateur, Humba went to work boiling an undisclosed oily liquid in a black iron pot. He explained his medical hypothesis to Tim, who translated it for Helen. The mainstay of his medical theory was that all of the major diseases could be cured by administering a massive enema or by consuming his secret potion, which caused explosive diarrhea. Helen prevented Humba from treating patients suffering from dysentery as she knew it would be their death sentences.

She gave up shadowing the witch doctor as he made his morning rounds, preferring to watch him from the veranda. Tim struggled to sit down next to her. He lit a

[114]

cigarette and blew a smoke ring. "I think he's making quite a difference. I know it's psychosomatic, but who cares."

"Don't tell me you believe in his rubbish?" Her tone was testy.

Tim's response was delayed by the launch of a gooey hawker over the railing. "Not entirely, but I've seen things no doctor in the world can explain." He picked something from his lip and smeared whatever it was on his shirt.

"How often do you see a local bush doctor?"

"I don't see one. Well, not regularly. Helen, why do I sense you're about to take me behind the woodshed for a spanking. Although I must admit, the thought does have some   appeal."

"You're a dirty old man. And you say *I'm* stubborn. Why are you still smoking?"

"You had to mention my smoking, didn't you? Why haven't you convinced your husband to quit?"

"You're not getting off that easy."

"Bloody hell, I'm eighty and I've buried two ex-wives. I've lived so long, I've worn out three of these," he said, knocking on his prosthesis. He frowned and sucked one final lungful of smoke before flipping the butt over the railing.

"I thought you divorced those women. Or was it the other way around?"

"Now, why would you ruin a first-class yarn with a few nasty facts? I've survived four wars and—" A noise interrupted him. He stood up to investigate. It was a mob of Africans marching up the road towards the clinic. They were singing and toy-toying. Soon their antics spread through the clinic. The patients started chanting political slogans. Tim hobbled down to meet them. After talking with an old woman, he limped back to the porch.

[115]

"What's happened?" Helen asked.

His answer was delayed by a coughing jag that ended with a sneeze. "It seems the beast has fled his lair. Mugabe's left the country in his fucking private Boeing, please excuse my French. He's gone to Switzerland or wherever he's stashed his millions. It was a military coup. Helen, our nightmare's over. I can't believe he's gone," he said, before blowing his nose.

Helen grabbed Tim and they danced a jig. The nurses joined their celebration. Tim's emphysema curtailed his dancing. He bent over gasping for air. Helen started to sob. "Let it go, Helen. God knows, you've earned a good cry," he wheezed.

"I just wish Rigby was here," she said, wiping away her tears.

*   *   *

The next day Helen was faced with the reality that despite the departure of Robert Mugabe, her clinic was still besieged with patients. Most of the food was gone. The electricity hadn't been on in two weeks. The emergency generator's petrol tank was almost empty. Lights were reserved for emergencies.

"I think we should drive to Binga," she suggested.

"I'm not so sure that's such a good idea. You can bet the natives are restless. We need to let this thing run its course. What difference will a couple of days make?"

"That's absolute crap," she snapped. "I've got patients who need drugs. We might find those drugs in Binga. Be a dear, and bring your truck around front. I'll just be a minute."

"Now I remember why I got divorced."

"And put out that cigarette."

"Are there any other orders?"

"I think that just about covers it," she replied, grinning.

The road to Binga was devoid of people. Helen said it was because they were recovering from their hangovers, but Tim wasn't buying her explanation.

"Helen, I don't like this. There should be people on this road. There's something not right here. We should turn around, before it's too late."

"Keep driving," she insisted.

"All right, but remember, this is your idea. I've witnessed a dozen coups in my life. Most of them were beastly. I'm not about to drive in to Binga unannounced. Let's stop and get our bearings."

Tim parked on the side of the road. He grabbed his rifle and led her to a vantage point on a knoll. Below them lay the smoldering ruins of what used to be Binga. Lake Kariba served as backdrop for the carnage. Most of the native huts were smoldering. Through his binoculars he saw soldiers milling around dead bodies. There were barricades at both ends of the village. He beat on his hollow leg and cursed, "Shit, I knew it was too good to be true." She followed him back to the truck. They sat there without speaking.

"I think we should drive down and question those soldiers," she said.

He snapped out of his spell and glared at her. "Helen, God knows, I love you, but please shut-up." He spun his Land Rover around, and headed back towards the clinic. She wanted to say something, but before she could, he broke the silence. "I had such hope, and now this."

"What're we gonna do?" she asked.

"I wish I knew."

On the road they met Sam Humba riding his donkey in the opposite direction. The witch doctor gave Helen a rotten-toothed smile and tipped his hat. His entourage stopped and swung down their portages. The women used the break to suckle their babies. Tim walked across the road to talk with him. Helen stayed in the truck.

"*Makadini, Baba Gosorwa?*" Joe the witch doctor asked.

Tim was shocked to be addressed by his African nickname, "coughing man." He flipped his cigarette butt on the ground and smashed it with his heel. "I'm doing just fine, Fatso," said Tim. Unable to understand English, Humba smiled. They carried on a conversation interrupted by Tim's hacking. When they finished speaking, they shook hands. Tim walked back to the truck. Humba's wives rebalanced their loads on top of their heads and followed him down the road.

Helen studied Tim as they drove away. "What's wrong?"

"Let's find a safe place. I need time to think." He pulled off the road. He started to say something, but stopped.

"Well, what did he say?" she asked, again.

"The beast has fled his lair, all right. Trouble is, the man who replaced Mugabe is even worse, if that's possible. The head of Mugabe's secret police is now the new president of Zimbabwe."

"Not Jeremiah Seke?" Helen cried out.

"That's Jeremiah *Hitler* Seke. And if things weren't bad enough, Ian Rhodes supported the coup. The military junta made Rhodes the new commissioner of Matabeleland. We are now under his absolute authority.

[118]

Damn it, only in Africa could something like this get so buggered up."

"Nothing could be as bad as Mugabe."

"Seke didn't change his middle name to Hitler to inspire people. Odds are— he's just another crook."

She screwed her eyes into him, and threw her hands up. "Lots of freedom fighters changed their names during the war. For the love of God, you could describe a rose as something as ugly as a toad."

"Maybe he's another Nelson Mandela or Margaret Thatcher. Jesus, Helen, don't you get it? It's always the same in Africa— the thug with the most guns always wins. I hate it, but it's true."

"I'd like to go back to my clinic," she said, folding her arms and staring straight ahead.

"I'm afraid that's impossible. I have more bad news. "

When he told her the medical clinic had been firebombed, she gasped. Her face hardened when she learned Rhodes was responsible.

He decided not to tell her about Humba's warning. You've got enough on your plate, he thought. Humba's vision revealed that Helen and Rigby would be in great danger. Their daughter would also be in peril. Christ, maybe she's right. I *have been* in the bush too long. Their daughter doesn't even live in Zimbabwe. Bloody superstitious munts, he thought with disgust.

"Let's drive to my farm," said Helen.

"Not an option. Rhodes is waiting for us."

"Rhodes has taken everything. There's something about this that doesn't make sense. Why does he hate my husband so much?" She bit her lip and looked at the empty road ahead.

"I'll get to the why, in a minute. I remember you mentioned that your husband had devised an emergency plan in case the government collapsed. By the way, we're driving to my houseboat on Kariba, unless you have a better suggestion."

"Promise me you won't get mad. I know it's out of our way, but I can't leave Sadie Bosshart and her kids."

"If we run into soldiers, they'll shoot us straight away. It's like I said before, this isn't my first insurrection. God only knows how many innocent people have already died."

"You can't ask me to leave them," said Helen.

"All right, we'll take them. Now, let's hear about this so-called emergency plan," he demanded as he started the engine.

Tim smiled as he listened to Rigby's plan. After the Rhodesian Bush War, the government gave amnesty to those combatants willing to hand over their weapons. Those veterans who defied the order were executed. Rigby decided to hide his weapons in an adjoining country. As a professional hunter, he was allowed to keep one bolt action rifle and a limited amount of ammunition. His holidays were always involved around fishing expeditions on the Zambezi River. Each trip ended on Livingstone Island, which was a part of Zambia. Any leftover ammunition from his hunting safaris was always buried under the same abandoned shack. After twenty years of stockpiling, his weapons cache was large enough to arm an insurrection.

"You're sure no one knows about this place?" asked Tim.

"Just our daughter knows."

"I must say, I'm disappointed that your husband didn't confide in me. He must have had his reasons. It's a brilliant piece of planning. I can't believe I didn't think of something like this myself." Helen held the steering wheel as Tim struggled to light another cigarette. He shook his head as if something bothered him.

"What's wrong?"

"My fishing boat will take us down the Zambezi. When Rigby hears about Mugabe's departure, he'll make straight for his farm. Somehow, we need to warn him."

"Do you think Rhodes will be waiting for him?"

"I don't think— I *know* he'll be waiting."

"Tim, get back to the reason why Rhodes hates my husband?"

He took her back thirty years to the war in Rhodesia. "In the end, we all knew we were losing the war, but like idiots we fought on to the bitter end." He went on to say that military intelligence was always suspicious about a spy working inside the Rhodesian military. Too many clandestine operations were compromised not to be wary. When Tim reminded her about her husband's friend Willie van Piet getting killed in an ambush, a light of recognition switched on. She knew her husband thought that Rhodes was responsible for Willie's death. Now it all makes sense, she thought.

"The first time I met Rigby was at Willie's farm on New Year's Eve. He never got over Willie's death."

Tim went on to say, "After the war ended, lots of veterans immigrated to South Africa. Years later, when we compared notes, we realized it had to be Rhodes who sold us out. When he received the confiscated farm from Mugabe, we had all of the confirmation we needed. We knew he was most definitely the mole working for the Russians."

"You still haven't told me why he hates my husband."

Tim cracked his window open to allow cigarette smoke to escape. His face tightened into a mask of seriousness. "I don't think Rhodes hates Rigby as much as he fears him. Do you remember the war veterans' reunion in Cape Town?" When she nodded yes, he continued, "Five men took an oath at that meeting. When the Mugabe government fell, one of the five would sort out Ian Rhodes."

"When you say, sort out — you mean kill, don't you?"

"That's precisely what I mean."

Helen stared at the passing landscape for a long time before speaking. "As I remember, you were all dead drunk for the entire ten days. Was my husband one of the five men who took the oath?"

"Yes. Remember, it wasn't just Willie who got killed. Rhodes was responsible for the deaths of lots of innocent women and children."

"Regrettably, Ian Rhodes is not on trial here. I'm sick of your stupid war. It ended thirty years ago, for Christ's sake. I've watched my husband wake up in cold sweats, and for what?"

"We Rhodesians have long memories. In our defense, we did lose our country."

"I suppose Leon Campbell was one of the five men who signed this so-called pact?"

"Yes. Campbell was the fourth to die. Your husband is the only one still alive. I wanted to be one of them, but they said I was too old. Seems like we were all too old."

"What do you want me to do, admire your bravura? Four million years of human evolution, and nothing's changed. You men fascinate me, you really do."

Tim tried to think of a clever answer, but stopped himself. There was too much bitterness in Helen not to give her the last word. One minute they were celebrating, and the next minute there was only despair. Africa really is the land of false hopes, he mused.

*   *   *

They drove on a seldom-used road to the Bosshart homestead. Dutchy and his wife, Sadie, had turned the little shack into a friendly home for their children. Whitewashed window boxes were filled with struggling African daisies. A curl of cooking smoke billowed from the chimney. Sadie stood on her porch shading her eyes as they drove up.

"This isn't a social visit, is it?" she asked. Her children hid behind her. She ushered them back into the house and stepped forward. Her smile soured when she heard Tim's plan to move her and her children to his houseboat on Lake Kariba. She turned her back to them before answering. "We lost our last farm. I promised Dutchy to stay put. I'm not running."

"Sadie, don't do this to your kids."

"Helen, my farmhands are like family to me. They'll look after us. We're safe here. Really we are."

"Tell her about the Campbells," Helen demanded.

As Sadie listened to his description of the massacre, her expression amended from apprehension to revulsion. She walked back inside without saying a word. Tim and Helen followed her into the house. She disappeared and then spoke to them from the kitchen. "I went to school with Eileen Campbell. I've known her my whole life. How can they be so cruel?" When Tim heard Sadie crying, he nodded for Helen to do something.

[123]

"Sadie, we haven't got much time. Just grab your kids and some clothes," Helen shouted from the living room.

"I have to say goodbye to..." Her words were choked off by a sob. When she reappeared she had her own two children and two black ones. "Their mother left them in my care. I'm not leaving them."

"Jesus, Sadie, I don't think..." Before Tim could finish, Helen swept the African children up in her arms and carried them to the truck.

The farmhands waved frantically as they drove away. Sadie couldn't look at them. Helen tried to engage the children with small talk, but they were too upset to respond. The adults lapsed into their private thoughts and the children slept.

Twice, they passed military vehicles driving in the opposite direction. Tim watched them apprehensively in the rearview mirror until they disappeared from view. His fidgeting made Helen and Sadie tense. The women were relieved when he turned off onto a side road. A sign marking the turnoff read: Lake Kariba-- 50 kilometers.

The driving was slowed by ruts from last season's downpours and the onset of darkness.

It was midnight when they reached the lake. The waters of Lake Kariba shimmered like black porcelain under a bright crescent moon. Halfway down the steep incline to the shoreline, they met a tall raggedly dressed African blocking the road. The man carried a stubby knobkerrie, which doubled as a walking stick.

The old Tonga's nickname was "Davy Crockett." His fur hat was fashioned from a honey badger's pelt; its tail dangled between his eyes.

In the foreground, the Rover's headlamps illuminated a listing houseboat moored to a makeshift dock. "Don't be afraid, he's an old friend. Everyone stay put. I need to sort out a few things." He got out and greeted the man. "I see you, Davy Crockett. Are you feeling well?" Tim asked.

"*Makadini, Baba*," the man replied, extending his hand. "I'm well enough. And you?"

"I am good, for an old man," Tim replied in Tongan.

"We are both old," Davy answered.

Tim whispered to Davy as he pulled him out of earshot. "Have you seen any soldiers?"

"Two days ago."

"Was it the *Magondo*?"

"*Yebo*."

"God damn it. I was afraid of that." Tim thought for awhile and then he said, "If anything happens to me, *you* must guide them downriver to Livingstone Island. Give me your word of honor that you will do this thing for me."

Davy thought for a moment and said, "Does a son need to give his word to his father?" It was clear that Davy was offended.

"Are you calling me your father? Why, you old goat, you're old enough to be my grandfather," Tim said. He tried to snatch Davy's fur hat off of his head, but Davy was as quick as a cat and danced out of his reach. Both men laughed and hugged each other.

In a few minutes they walked back together to the vehicle. The walk winded Tim. He struggled to speak. "My friend says he hasn't seen a living soul in over a week. It's safe, at least for now."

"Thank God," Helen sighed.

Tim illuminated Davy with a flashlight. The African's face was as black and wrinkled as a pitted prune. Glossy tribal scarring on his cheeks and forehead glistened in the moonlight. His earlobes had been pierced and stretched with ear-plugs until the holes were as large as English teacups.

Davy stepped forward and took Sadie's sleeping children, one in each arm and headed for the houseboat. The two black children followed him down the houseboat's rickety gangway.

After they got settled in, Davy disappeared to stand guard.

Like most Africans, the Tonga people are superstitious. Their world is one of evil spirits carrying out grudges against the living. A recent dream caused Davy to request a shaman's interpretation. The old sorcerer puffed on his dagga pipe, expelled the smoke from his pierced nostrils and dropped his eyes. He was sorry, but yes, Davy would soon join his ancestors. He accepted the shaman's verdict stoically, but when the man said Tim Brooks would also die, he was saddened.

When Davy told Tim about the incident, he scoffed at the notion of fortune telling. They had spent many nights camped in the bush where they discussed the mysteries of life and death. Tim didn't believe that when someone dies, his soul is inherited by another living person. According to the sorcerer, Tim's spirit would be lost forever, and that was troubling for Davy.

Following a dinner of pickled bream and rice, Helen, Sadie and Tim listened to a BBC newscast on his shortwave radio. The news from Zimbabwe was bad. The borders, railroad lines and airports were closed. Major cities and townships were beset by riots and looting. Sadie gasped when she heard the number of deaths attributed to the violence. When the news commentator turned to more worldly events, everyone lost interest and called it a night.

The mosquito netting draped over Helen's bunk made the air stuffy and hard to breathe. She tossed and turned in the clammy sheets. Croaking bullfrogs harmonized with a steady high-pitched chorus of smaller frogs. A reedbuck's death bellows and a hyena's giggling made her look out of a porthole. A thick blanket of night fog covered the lake. Without the moon's pollution, the night-sounds were hair-raising. She buried her face in a pillow and sobbed. Her sorrow wasn't caused by fear. She wept for the people of Zimbabwe.

"Helen, are you awake?" Tim asked, standing in the companionway.

"I am now."

"Would you like to talk?"

"Sure, why not."

He fell heavily into the wobbly chair next to her bunk and groaned from the discomfort. "God help me, for the first time in my life, I think I've lost the plot."

"You'll come around. The madness can't last. The rest of the world won't tolerate another thug raping this country."

"I'm afraid I've heard that one before. The rest of the world doesn't give a rat's ass about what happens here. Helen, I feel like I've wasted my whole life in Africa."

[127]

"Oh, come on, there must have been some good times."

"Not enough to offset the heartaches. Did I ever tell you about my first wife?" When she didn't respond, he continued, "Her name was Lynn. God, she was a lovely bird. Proper British, you know. The war was raging, but my time with her was magic. Lynn was always so frightened of Africa. It's takes a special woman to live in the bush— a woman like you, Helen."

"Sometimes I wonder. What happened to her?"

"She moved back to England, actually. I woke up one morning and she was gone. And so was what little money we'd saved. I heard she married a solicitor from Lancaster. Now my second wife was a real jewel. Hilda was uglier than a hairy wart. She made up for her homeliness by having an absolutely horrid disposition. The Africans called her "*Nyamafungu,*" which means spitting cobra in Shona. Your husband used to say she was 'scarier than three shades of shit'."

"That sounds like something Rigby would say. I'm sure you're both exaggerating. She couldn't have been *that* bad."

"You must ask Rigby about her. He'll tell you. She was a vile little creature."

"Did she leave in the middle of the night, like the first one?"

"Good Lord, I'm not that bad, am I? No, I hired out as a mercenary to get away from her. Damn near got myself killed fighting rebels in the Congo or was it Angola? No matter. Anyway, she married my friend, Colin White. Colin became a better friend after he stole my wife. I thought I was the only person in Africa dumb enough to marry that woman. He did me one hell of a favor and he never let me forget it. I must have bought him a thousand drinks."

[128]

"Any other regrets?" she asked.

"None. Well, maybe one."

After Tim's silence became uncomfortable, she asked, "Did you ever have any children?" He didn't answer so she changed the subject, "How long have you known Davy?"

"Over forty years," he said, at last. "I've never seen him without that filthy hat on his head." He slapped a mosquito on the back of his neck. The silence descended again making it even more painful. She started to say something, but he interrupted. "Helen, there's something I need to get off my chest. There was a child, a boy."

"Does he live in England?"

"He lives here in Zimbabwe."

"How come you never mentioned him?"

After dangling a cigarette in his mouth, he scratched a stick match to light it, which filled the cabin with sulfur smoke. His face was momentarily illuminated. Helen faked a cough to show her displeasure. Tim took a heavy drag, let the smoke linger and then sighed deeply through the exhaled cloud. "I've never mentioned him, because he's black."

"Why are you telling me this now?"

"Because I'm dying, and I had to tell someone."

"I'm your doctor. You're not dying."

"You're a brilliant liar. The reason I look like this is because I've drank and smoked and shagged myself to death, and I had a helluva good time doing it. I'm afraid I've worn out this old body. I know it's an old cliché, but I would have taken better care of myself if — well, you know the rest. Let's not waste time arguing. I need to get this off my chest. Please, just listen and save the wisdom."

He told her about a relationship with an African woman that ended when she got pregnant. "She was the only woman I ever loved. I swear on my mother's grave, it's the truth. A day never passes that I don't think about her."

"Why didn't you marry her?"

"What choice did I have? You know interracial mixing wasn't accepted in this country."

"So you saved your precious reputation. It all seems like such a waste. What happened to her?"

"She died three years ago."

"And your son?"

"He's a political activist for the opposition party. He just served two years in Hwange prison. Falsely put there by our illustrious president, I might add."

"Does he know you're his father?"

"No. An African married the woman before he was born. I've left the boy everything I own. It's spelled out in my will. There's quite a bit, you know. Savings accounts in South Africa, my guns and my farm. I can tell you're disappointed in me."

"Of course I'm disappointed, but not for the reasons you might think. All of you, including my husband, proclaimed Rhodesia to be this oasis of racial equality, which is an absolute farce. Do you think your generosity will wash away your sins?"

"I guess I was hoping the boy won't hate me. Look, I'm not proud of this."

"What about the man who raised the boy, is he alive?" Helen asked.

"No."

"Tim, is Steven Mabota your son?" She heard him move uneasily in the darkness.

"How did you know?" he said, at last.

"We all knew, or rather we suspected. I mean, just look at him. He's not much darker than my daughter. He's the best-looking man in Zimbabwe, black or white. Steven was the brightest student at Plum Tree. Many of

[130]

us thought he'd become president someday. Tim, you should be proud of your son."

He needed time to digest the term *son*. The pause ended with a question, "Did Rigby ever say anything about any of this?"

"No. Did he know?"

"Yes. He witnessed my will."

"As you know, my husband's never broken his word to anyone about anything in his life. He was close to Steven's father. He would never do anything to embarrass Sam. It's like I said before, you men fascinate me." She watched his outline move against the dull light from a cabin window. She heard his troubled breathing and a muffled cough. "Please don't judge me too harshly. I did what I thought was best for all concerned. Maybe I should have handled things differently, but what's done is done. I can't change history."

She opted not to tell him what he did was selfish. After all, he *is* dying, she thought.

"I can hardly keep my eyes open."

"Goodnight, Helen. Sorry to be such a bore. Oh, one more thing. Would you consider telling the boy about me?"

"Steven's thirty-something. He's a man, not a boy. I'll do whatever you want, but you should be the one to tell him."

"Let me sleep on it. I've always considered you my best friend. I wanted you to know before... well, you know."

"Get some sleep. And for God's sake, stop smoking."

"Yes, doctor."

He closed her cabin door softly behind him and then reopened it.

"Helen, it's you who should be president of Zimbabwe. You've made huge sacrifices for this country."

"Zimbabwean men treat women only slightly better than their donkeys. Maybe in a hundred years. Better yet, make that five hundred years for a white woman."

"You've certainly got my vote. Goodnight."

This time he closed the door for good.

Normally, waves slapping against the hull would be a lullaby, but now it was a noisy irritation. When Helen closed her eyes, she saw her husband's face. I need you beside me, she thought. Her thinking slowed down and she fell into a shallow sleep. Her dreaming took her back to another time.

She was camped with Rigby on Lake Kariba. They were both young and fearless. Native fisherman saw their cooking fire, and stopped to investigate. Rigby liked to walk the shoreline plug-casting for tigerfish. She was alone when the men came ashore. At first, they seemed friendly enough, but then they demanded money. They seemed dazed by the screaming madman who rushed out of the bushes swinging a tree limb. Within seconds, Rigby had bloodied all of them. She spent the rest of the day stitching and bandaging their wounds.

That dream was replaced by another vision. A man was warning her. He was saying something about her daughter, but the distance made his voice soundless. Before she could hear him, she felt someone shaking her.

"Helen, wake up, " Tim said. Her answer was incoherent.

"Listen to me. Davy's seen lights coming down to the lake. It might be Rhodes. You and Sadie take the children and go with Davy."

[132]

"Come with us," she pleaded, grabbing his arm.

"The boat's too small. I'll catch up with you downriver. Please hurry, Helen."

After Tim helped Sadie and the children into the skiff, he handed Davy a burlap bag of essentials. He hugged Helen and whispered, "As the Matabele say, 'Walk in God's shoes'."

The finality of his words made her shiver. She reached out to grab him, but she could only touch his fingertips. He pushed the boat away from the dock. His next words became almost indistinguishable, and then his voice faded away altogether. He blew her a kiss and disappeared behind a moonless curtain.

The outboard engine started on the second pull. The fog made the night and the lake seem like one and the same. Davy steered the boat under a star-peppered sky. He had dreamed he would see two shooting stars at once and they appeared. To the Tonga, it meant someone was about to pass to the other side. When he saw the third shooting star he knew he wouldn't die alone. It's just like the witch doctor predicted, he reflected.

Their commotion on the lake temporarily quieted the frogs, but not the mosquitoes. The burbling sound of the outboard dissolved into the insects' insidious whine. Helen covered the children with blankets and looked around; there was nothing but blackness.

*   *   *

Tim watched headlight beams dance in the treetops above the lake. The thought of Rhodes cursing the rutted road made him smile. He patted the Winchester on his

[133]

lap, and pinched his collar together to ward off the night chill.

As the first evidence of dawn appeared on Lake Kariba, Tim took up the anchor line to pull the boat away from the shoreline. He returned to the stern and waited.

Daybreak revealed men standing on his dock.

"Good morning, Mr. Brooks," yelled Rhodes. "What, might I ask, are you doing here? We're under Martial Law. I'm afraid you're breaking the law, old boy."

"I'm on a fishing holiday, actually."

"Do you always fish with your rifle?" Rhodes asked.

"I'm having problems with hyenas." The reference was not missed by Rhodes. He bristled from the insult.

"Is Helen Croxford with you?"

"She's not here. Why do you ask?"

"It's a medical matter. If she's not with you, why do you care?"

"Because I know you're a liar."

Rhodes ordered his soldiers to swim out and pull the houseboat in. When they objected, he threatened them at gunpoint. Reluctantly, two of his men waded waist-deep into the murky water.

"For God's sake, Ian, the crocs will have them before they get halfway. I'll slacken my anchor line. Have your men pull me in. I can't let you do this to them."

After his men searched the houseboat, Rhodes sat down in front of Tim. He thumped Tim's forehead with his knuckles. "Brooks, I haven't got the time or the inclination to muck around with you. The unmade bunks say that you had people onboard last night. Before things get, shall I say, unpleasant, why don't you just tell me where they're going?"

"My, aren't we the Sherlock Holmes— sod off. We both know what this is about. You killed Leon Campbell and his family, not to mention the others. Croxford won't be as easy, you know. This time you can't hide behind Mugabe. You're finished, my friend. What's it feel like being a hunted man?"

"Brooks, I've done things to men that you could never imagine. When I'm finished with you, you won't fear death, you'll pray for it."

During the Rhodesian War, Rhodes had been in charge of interrogations. His fellow officers had no stomach for torturing men, but Rhodes enjoyed the work.

"Gag and hold him." His men pounced on Tim, pinning his arms behind him. Rhodes took a soldier's machete and tested its sharpness against his thumb. He smiled as he sucked the blood from his finger. He laid the cold blade on Tim's forehead. "I'll ask you one more time. Where are they going?" Tim's coughing jag ended with him hacking in Rhodes's face. A wicked smile crossed his lips as he wiped away the spittle. He thumped the machete against Tim's prosthesis. Without warning he chopped Tim's other boot in half. The bloodcurdling moan unsettled the Africans, but not Rhodes. He reached down, picked up the boot and emptied the severed toes on the deck. "Talk to me or I'll cut off your good leg, you one-legged freak."

The soldiers suspended Tim over the gunwale. "Hold his head under," Rhodes ordered. "That's the way." As Tim's thrashing subsided, Rhodes nodded for his men to pull him up. Green bile spurted from Tim's nose and mouth. The soldiers dunked him repeatedly, until he went limp. Rhodes slapped his face to revive him. "I'm not ready for you to die just yet," he hissed in Tim's face.

Tim's thinking may have been muddled, but he knew he was dying. The old sorcerer predicted I would die soon, and by God here I am, he thought. He closed his mind to the pain and prayed for the white light. His mind's eye raced through images of his life. The last image he saw was a black woman holding a baby boy. Her smile released him from the will to live and he saw the white light.

Rhodes had seen enough men die to know Tim wouldn't survive more than a few minutes. The gray face and blue lips meant death was close at hand.

"Come, my friend, you're going for a little swim. The crocs are hungry."

The soldiers dragged Tim to the stern and suspended him by a hangman's noose over the side. Enough of his body was buoyed by the water to prevent strangulation. Rhodes leaned down to question him one last time, but he was unresponsive.

After they ransacked the houseboat, they set his body adrift.

*　　*　　*

It was his plastic leg bobbing in the bulrushes that attracted the large crocodile. The black and yellow reptile elevated itself, waddled down the bank on pigeon-toes and slid stealthily beneath the surface. An oily blood slick diverted the crocodile's attention away from the leg. The reptile made a V-ripple on the water as it zeroed in on the blood trail oozing from Tim's body. The croc's swimming was unhurried. Sensory receptors on the crocodile's jaws revealed its prey was lifeless.

[136]

*   *   *

Davy stayed offshore. From a distance, he hoped the Tonga villagers would mistake them for kapenta fishermen. The sun came up and so did the wind. The breeze furrowed choppy waves, which forced him back into the leeward protection of the shoreline. Water lapped over the boat's stern. It took continuous bailing just to stay afloat. Their presence alerted crocodiles basking on the sandbars. The larger crocs slid gracefully into the water. The smaller ones exploded off the banks. The children made a game of counting them, but the crocs were so numerous they quickly lost interest.

Just before nightfall, they came ashore on an uninhabited island near the mouth of the Zambezi River.

After slashing through thick elephant grass, Davy made a clearing and started a fire. Sadie steamed a large pot of corn porridge from the sack Tim had given them. She spiced it with dried fish and hot spices. All of them ate, except Helen.

When the children dozed off, Helen pulled them close to her and strained to see into the darkness. She saw the net fishermen's lanterns twinkling like fireflies in the distance.

Her thoughts traveled back down the roads of her life again. She was thinking about her loneliness when a movement startled her. She spun around to find Davy staring at her over the campfire. He looked down into the flames. She hoped his bloodshot eyes were caused by smoke, but she sensed they weren't.

"You startled me. Have you camped on this island before?" she asked.

"Many times, *Amai.*"

"I want you to call me Helen. The children are suffering from the mosquitoes."

"We all are suffering, *Amai.*"

"I give up. When will Tim meet us?" When Davy didn't answer, she asked the question differently. "He said he would catch up with us downriver. Did he say where he would meet us?"

"He's not coming, *Amai.*"

She challenged his abruptness from yet another angle. "I specifically heard him say he would meet us downriver."

"It saddens me to tell you our friend has cast his last shadow."

"What on earth are you talking about?"

"Baba Tim is dead. His suffering has ended," he said, averting his eyes.

"What? Why, that's ridiculous. Of course Tim's not dead. Besides, how would you know?" The tears on his leathery face glistened in the campfire light. His chilling expression made her tremble. She struggled to maintain her composure as she tucked blankets around the children. "I'm sure he'll meet us just like he said he would."

"I'm only telling you what I know to be true, *Amai.*"

"Oh, now I get it. You dreamed this silliness. But you see, I don't believe in your superstitious gobbledygook." Helen looked away and waved for him to leave her.

Her sobbing was muted, but he heard her and glanced back for a second. The whites are a curious people. They fear death much more than we do, he reflected.

THE ZAMBEZI VENDETTA

I won't let you see me cry. Damn you, Davy Crockett, and damn Africa, she thought. She tried to stop weeping, but couldn't. She knew her friend Tim was dead.

*   *   *

11

The rolling road from Victoria Falls to Botswana was littered with abandoned vehicles; the cars and trucks had run out of petrol. Some of the vehicles had been rolled over and burned and resembled charred turtles lying on their backs. Household items too heavy to carry were also left by the wayside.

The cluttered road was interrupted by the border-crossing separating Zimbabwe from Botswana. The border post was besieged by Zimbabweans attempting to flee the violence. Fearing their country would be overrun, Botswana deployed soldiers to maintain order by preventing the refugees from entering their country. The mood on the Botswana side was orderly, but tense. The mood on the Zimbabwean side was hysterical.

A tented shantytown emerged along the barbed wire fence on the Zimbabwe side. The air was permeated by smoke and the squalid stench of humans. Raggedly dressed Africans huddled around campfires. Their half-naked children played cricket on the road.

At night, Kasane villagers smuggled food and bits of gossip through the fence. They retold rumors of United Nations trucks bringing aid. The rumors never materialized.

The atmosphere in the Zimbabwean customs office was chaotic. Screaming officials threatened the people standing in line. Women held up their starving babies to illustrate their desperation. Zimbabweans pleaded for entry into Botswana, but the orders were clear; no one would be allowed to leave the country.

Sebastian Kuno had been the Chief Customs Inspector at the Kasane border post for five years. Accepting bribes from desperate Zimbabweans smuggling goods across the border was a lucrative business for Kuno. His hustle ended with the border closing. Depressed, he barricaded himself in his office and got drunk. Empty chibuku bottles littered the floor. A framed black and white photograph of President Robert Mugabe hung lopsided on the wall behind his metal desk. The glass covering the portrait was cracked.

Kuno slept with his head arched back and his bare feet propped up on the desk. His mouth was open. Pounding on his office door shook Kuno from his drunken stupor. He picked up an empty bottle and hurled it at the door. "Go away! Leave me alone!"
"Open this door at once. Do you hear me?" The shrill voice made Kuno cover his ears. He yawned, smacked his lips and rubbed his neck. His throat was raw from snoring.

"Open this door— you, you baboon." Those words were the last straw. He jumped to his feet, staggered to the door and flung it open with the intention of striking whoever was on the other side. When he saw the blond woman, he instinctively came to attention. He tried to speak, but the words lodged in his throat. He wiped the vestiges of dried vomit from his shirt and stood there with a foolish grin locked on his face.

"How dare you grin at me? Well, what have you got to say for yourself?" Christine Croxford demanded in fluent Shona.

He answered with a noncommittal shrug and then he said, "Madam, why are you screaming?" He gestured for her to sit down, but she ignored his invitation and stood there with her fists on her hips.

"Why have you closed this border?"

"It's not me— it's the government. No citizen shall be allowed to leave Zimbabwe,'" he recited the order by memory and handed her a copy. She refused to look at the paper and flung it back at him.

"You imbecile, I want to enter Zimbabwe, not leave it. I am a Zimbabwean doctor on official business," she explained.

"Only a fool would...," Kuno started and stopped his reply. He batted a fly away from his face and then picked something from his ear. Whatever it was, he flicked the object with his finger. Kuno sighed theatrically and rubbed his temples.

"This is none of your business, but if you must know, I need to see about my parents." There was exasperation in her voice and her expression.

"Name?" he asked, grabbing her passport.

"Dr. Christine Croxford. And yours?" She waved her hand to rid the air of his pungent body odor.

"I am Chief Inspector Kuno." His answer registered indignation.

She scribbled his name on a piece of paper and stuffed it in her breast pocket. "I'm reporting you to the proper authorities." Her all-knowing smile seemed to unnerve Kuno.

"Are you related to the Dr. Croxford who runs the clinic at Binga? The woman who is involved in politics," he inquired, tugging on his chin whiskers.

"She's my mother."

"And you're both *Ngangas*?"

"Yes, yes, we're both doctors," she answered impatiently. "Now, order your men to open the barricade at once!"

Kuno yelled at his assistant to come into his office. He started to make a disparaging remark about Croxford, but remembering she spoke Shona, he diverted to English. "This... lady wishes a travel permit. See to it," he ordered, handing the man Croxford's passport. "I'll have my men escort you."

"Thank you, but that won't be necessary. You don't look well. If you'll follow me outside, I have some medicine for you."

"Thank you, Doctor, I haven't been feeling well."

"I can't imagine why," she said, glancing at the empties strewn on the floor.

*   *   *

The rumor of a doctor in camp spread through the shantytown like a wildfire. Within minutes Croxford's vehicle was surrounded by sick and injured Africans. As an intern, she'd seen many of the same diseases: malaria, chronic dysentery and the number-one killer in Sub-Saharan Africa, AIDS. Her last patient had suffered a

[143]

severe beating. His face was so swollen his eyes were reduced to mere slits. He spoke in a voice muffled by missing teeth.

"I wish I could pay you, but I have no money," the man said, struggling to open his mouth.

"What's your name?" She peeled back his upper lip to examine his teeth. "I'm afraid you'll need a dentist to extract these stumps."

"Joseph Chitoa." He pulled away from her touch and held his jaw.

"Mr. Chitoa, this will hurt," she said. She stuck a hypodermic in his arm.

He flinched from the needle prick. "Ouch. I was the warden at Hwange prison."

"Who did this to you?"

"After the prison guards deserted me, the prisoners revolted. I'm lucky to be alive."

"Do you know my name?" she asked.

"Yes."

"Were you the warden when my father was in Hwange?"

"Yes, but...but...I didn't put him there," he stammered. "I have great respect for your father. He would never have allowed the other prisoners to do this to me." Chitoa made a feeble attempt to smile, but it ended in a painful grimace.

She backed away and studied the man. She remembered her mother's description of her father on the day he was released. Tears welled up in the corners of her eyes.

He sensed her anger and looked away. "Dr. Croxford, life at Hwange Prison was difficult, even for the warden.

[144]

The Zimbabwe we had all hoped for is lost. A long time ago your father spared my life. I have repaid my debt to him. *If* you ever see him again, I am confident that he will vouch for me. I am a good man and I treated your father fairly."

"What do you mean, *if* I ever see my father again?"

"Traveling in Zimbabwe has become very dangerous. Criminals are roaming about like packs of wild dogs. I'm afraid you won't get very far. I think maybe you should go home," he said, pointing in the direction of South Africa.

"But Zimbabwe *is* my home."

He picked at a scab on his lip and winced. "There is one way I can repay you." He retrieved a snub-nosed revolver from his hip pocket and handed it to her. "This saved my life. Take it."

"I could never use one of these," she said, handing the pistol back to him. "Do you know the back road to Binga?"

"I know it well."

"Joseph, could you draw me a map of that road?"

"Of course." He stared at the barricade separating Zimbabwe from Botswana. "They'll never let us leave, will they?"

"I'm afraid not. And Botswana won't accept another refugee."

"Good, then it's settled. I will show you the way to Binga."

"You seem to be having trouble taking care of yourself."

Chitoa's smile curled down into a scowl. "You'll never make it to Binga without me. Your father would tell you to trust me."

She started to argue, but hesitated. She knew getting to Binga without a guide was far-fetched. Instead of

[145]

answering, she smiled and held out her hand. I hope my instincts are right about you, she thought.

As they drove away from the camp, the refugee children ran beside their truck. Weakened by malnourishment, they gave up and gasped by the side of the road. Even the dogs gave up the chase.

Driving was like fording a human river against the current. The people they passed were all headed in the opposite direction. The evacuees gawked and scratched their heads; they seemed confused by someone driving towards the violence.

The sun dipping beneath the horizon cast deceptive shadows across the road. She strained to see, but driving on the rollercoaster road was impossible. A near-miss with a donkey cart convinced her to pull over. She stopped at a lay-by to spend the night.

At first they were alone, but soon their campfire attracted wanderers like insects drawn to a lantern. An ancient bus pulled in behind them. The bus was so overloaded the weight of the passengers almost flattened the tires. Crates, boxes, suitcases and a motorcycle were lashed to its roof. The passengers kept exiting the bus, until Christine and Joseph were completely encircled. The people offered to share what little food they had with them, which didn't surprise Christine. Africans really are a mixed bag, she thought. One minute they're killing each other, and the next minute they show incredible kindness. After declining their hospitality, Christine ate a few pieces of ostrich biltong and washed it down with hot tea. She tried to engage Joseph in conversation, but the pain pills made him woozy.

[146]

"Do you have a family?" she asked.

"I thought I would find my wife in Kasane, but I was disappointed. We were separated in the rioting. I hope to find her in Binga." His nasally voice struggled from a clumsy tongue.

"Is she your only wife?"

He nodded yes and replied, "She's a good wife." When he started to snore she left him by the campfire and climbed into the backseat of her truck.

She snuggled under the blanket and closed her eyes. Her thoughts were about her parents. There was never a doubt that she would follow in her mother's footsteps. Like her mother, doctoring the poor was her passion. She longed for her father's protection. Living in Africa *really* is a challenge. I wonder what it's like living in a normal country. Probably very boring, she thought, drifting off.

*   *   *

Ian Rhodes made himself a general. The military junta gave him absolute authority over the southern half of Zimbabwe. His first order was to place the town of Victoria Falls under Martial Law. What the looters didn't steal, the soldiers pilfered. The Victoria Falls Hotel was spared in the rioting and reopened as the Regional Military Headquarters for Matabeleland.

Rhodes was eating lunch with his junior officers when he received the telephone call from the Chief Customs Inspector at the Kasane border crossing. He learned that both Warden Joseph Chitoa and Rigby Croxford's Christine were at the same border post. He excused himself. He needed to talk to Chitoa in private.

He seemed uplifted when he returned to the table. Despite the inquisitive stares from his men, he refused to elaborate on the call.

An officer pleaded for more firing squads to deal with the ever-increasing number of looters. Rhodes nodded in agreement, but he wasn't paying attention. His mind was muddled by the news that Croxford's daughter was being delivered to him by Joseph Chitoa.

"Lieutenant, have some men move my things to the Croxford farm," Rhodes ordered.

"But General, the Croxford farm is over one hundred kilometers from here." Rhodes's stare caused the man to suspend his questioning. Rhodes dabbed his mustache with a napkin as he got up from the table. His counterfeit smile melted.

"Lieutenant, may I remind you that Croxford's a sworn enemy of this country." Before the lieutenant could apologize, Rhodes got up and left the table. He picked up his rifle, walked outside and sat down under the giant rain tree. Nesting starlings and wire-tailed swallows infested the thatched roof over the patio bar. A warthog mother and her piglets nibbled on the green lawn grass behind the hotel. Using the table as a brace, he aimed his weapon and pulled the trigger. The high-caliber bullet dropped the sow and scattered her squealing babies. The piglets returned to their mother and tried to suckle her. The rifle shot brought his men, but Rhodes waved them off. The men looked troubled by the needless violence. They left him alone.

Rhodes closed his eyes and allowed his demented fantasies to come alive. A tingling sensation made him squirm. He was rehearsing the rape of Croxford's daughter.

*   *   *

Joseph Chitoa was up before dawn. When he knocked on Christine Croxford's window she rolled it down. He handed her a cup of hot tea.

"What time is it?" She yawned and rubbed her eyes trying to focus on her wristwatch. "That was the best sleep I've had in weeks."

"Doctor, there are people waiting to see you. They say they are sick, but I think most of them are only hungry."

"Mr. Chitoa, let's leave the medical diagnosis to me. Put the people with obvious injuries at the head of the line. Tell them I'll be there in a minute."

Four hours later they drove away. It was twenty kilometers to the turnoff to Binga. The back road turned out to be nothing more than a rutted path. Two tire punctures delayed their progress. Knocked over trees reduced their speed to a crawl. The road was so overgrown by mopani shrub Christine became disoriented and held up her hands in frustration. Like most Africans, Chitoa possessed an internal compass. Certain trees were road signs to him. He led Christine on a winding route that was devoid of any signs of a road.

"Are you sure you know where you're going?" she asked.

"I've traveled on this road many times."

She was about to voice her doubts, when the road reappeared. "I'm glad you talked me into bringing you along." Chitoa's face radiated from her praise.

[149]

The road worsened. She wrestled for control in the soft sand. Joseph tried to lend her a hand, but he was too weak to help. After an hour of struggling, she gave up. "I've had quite enough of this shitty road, thank you."

They camped under a giant mimosa tree next to a rocky outcropping, known in Africa as a kopje. He gathered up some kindling and logs and got a fire going. She boiled a pot of maize and smothered it with a tin of English bully beef. When he refused to eat she sensed something was wrong. "It's your teeth, isn't it?"

He nodded yes. "I've never known such pain."

"I thought so. Let's have another look." After inspecting his teeth she stepped back and shook her head. "It's like I said before. The nerves are exposed. Those stumps will have to come out. If you want me to take them out, I'm willing to try."

"Please, *Nganga*, anything to stop the pain."

"Let me get my instruments ready. We can use my vehicle's headlamps. Go rest your head against the bush guard." She retrieved a pair of vice grips from the Rover's toolbox and carefully hid them from Chitoa. "Before we get started, I'm going to give you an injection for the pain." He looked at the syringe and shivered.

"I don't want the needle. I have my own medicine."

"Suit yourself. Now, open wide, Mr. Chitoa." She clamped down on his front tooth and started to pull, but the stump held fast. A hideous cracking sound made her stop. She reset the vice-grips, and she used a twisting motion. The broken tooth popped free from its socket. His head slumped forward. He moaned, turned his head, and spit out a mouthful of blood thickened saliva. "One down and one to go— be brave, my friend. It'll all be over soon." The second tooth was also stubborn. Again, she had to twist it free.

[150]

Under normal conditions, English was slippery on Chitoa's tongue. He tried switching to his native tongue, but the loss of his front teeth made him unintelligible. When he saw she didn't understand him, he handed her two small twigs that had been dipped in the sap from a candelabra tree. She remembered watching her mother use the sap to cauterize wounds. She carefully inserted the wooden pegs in his empty sockets, and backed away to inspect her work. Good God, you look like a giant snake, she thought.

"Mr. Chitoa, I know your bush-medicine is strong, but I insist that you take these pills." He was in too much pain to argue. He swallowed the pills. The drug knocked him for a loop. Within minutes, his eyes closed and his head slumped forward. A long string of bloody drool hung from his lower lip. She covered him with a blanket and left him by the campfire.

The front seat was too cramped for her to stretch out. Christine curled up into a fetal position. The events of the week triggered her reflections. She remembered listening to the news broadcast about Robert Mugabe's stepping down. The news from home caused great jubilation among her fellow Zimbabwean students. They partied all night. How pathetically naïve we were, she thought. Christine had promised her parents she would stay in South Africa, but the allure of seeing the rebirth of her country was too much. She rehearsed her excuse to her father over and over. You can't expect me to miss the most critical moment in my country's history!

Eventually, the censored news from Zimbabwe filtered out. The people's hopes for a new beginning were dashed. Once again an African country had succumbed to a violent coup.

Concern for her mother's safety lent a special urgency to Christine's trip home. She drove almost nonstop across South Africa. When she crossed the border she had a premonition that her mother was in great danger.

*   *   *

When Joseph Chitoa woke up, he felt feverish. He sought relief from the campfire heat by climbing to the top of the kopje. He held his forehead against the cool granite face of a boulder. A thin scum of rain clouds dulled the moon and blotted out the stars. A wood owl's hooting reassured him. When he dozed off he dreamed about his last day as the warden of Hwange prison.

There must be something wrong with the siren, he remembered thinking. Every morning the prison siren signaled the start of a new day, but not this day. He called for his guards, but none answered. He was still in his sleeping gown when he stepped out into the prison grounds. The inmates glared at him as he walked to the prison guard's barracks. He noticed the watchtowers were unmanned. The door to the barracks had been left open. The guards had abandoned their posts in the middle of the night. He was alone with hundreds of prisoners. His nonchalant walk turned into a run for his life. He made it to his office and bolted the door behind him, but the inmates were already climbing in through the windows. And then the beating started. Had it not been for the prisoners' bare feet, he would have been stomped to death; even so he was sure he was going to die. A gunshot stopped them. The last thing he remembered hearing was Ian Rhodes shouting.

A strange noise jolted Chitoa. He was sweaty from his nightmare. He strained to hear, but there was only silence.

Christine tossed and turned, but she couldn't get comfortable in the narrow seat. She felt a slight jostle. It's only the wind, she thought. She sat up and strained to see, but the campfire's dying embers provided no light. The blackness beyond the fire's glow seemed to move, but she convinced herself it was nothing. She leaned her face against the cool window and closed her eyes. Again, she heard a noise. Was it whispering? She turned on the headlamps. Instantly, the windows were filled with black faces. The African licking the windshield had a harelip and chipped teeth. She tried to lock the doors, but he jerked her out and threw her to the ground. She felt calloused hands groping her. The men laughed as they ripped her shirt to shreds. She tried to cover her breasts, but they held her arms. The reek of body-sweat made her retch.

"Chitoa, help me!" she screamed.

Chitoa looked down from his vantage point. The campfire silhouetted the men circling her. He recognized them as the prisoners who beat him. He crawled away from the edge and climbed down the other side of the kopje. He ran, but his terror made him careless; he tripped on a rock and fell. He jumped up and started to run again, but Christine's screaming stopped him dead in his tracks. The lightning came long before the thunder. An incandescent jagged flash transformed the leafless trees into ghoulish outlines. He looked up at the sky. Slanting rain pelted his face. He blinked away the raindrops and looked back over his shoulder.

*   *   *

The escaped prisoners ransacked her Land Rover. They tossed her clothes out of the windows and rifled through the medicines. They found food and gulped it down like ravenous dogs. The disfigured man grabbed Christine and pulled her next to the campfire. She struggled at first, but he was so strong she gave up. They surrounded her on the ground. She looked up through her tears at them. Their eyes were as wild as feeding hyenas. One man nudged her with his foot. Another man stroked her hair.

Thunder rumbled as Chitoa stepped from the shadows. One of the escapees shined a flashlight on him. His head had swelled to the size of a buffalo's, which reduced his eyes to reptilian slits. It was his wooden fangs that unnerved them. The plunderers stood frozen, unable to move or speak, their eyes glued on him. A man's moaning was followed by a chorus of whimpers. A bolt of white lightning snaked across the sky. The beast was outlined by the flash of light.

"Get away from the woman," Chitoa shouted. His breath was grayed from the chill of the air. His fangs distorted his words into birdlike chirping sounds.

"The sorcerer speaks like a bird, but he has the head of a snake." The man who spoke was the first one to bolt. It panicked the others; they tripped and fell over each other as they ran. One man was so eager to escape, he ran headlong into a darkened tree. Dazed, he scrambled to his feet and staggered after the others.

The man with the harelip didn't run. He shook his fist yelling, "Hear me witch— I'm not afraid of you."

"Surely the mighty *Tsuro* remembers me?" Chitoa asked.

"No man calls me a rabbit and lives to brag about it." He picked up the cold end of a burning log and lunged forward swinging it wildly. Without hesitating Chitoa fired point-blank at the man. The gunshot transfixed him momentarily, but he fell backwards and rolled into the campfire setting his hair on fire. Chitoa fired a second time without aiming and missed. Christine stepped into his line of fire to prevent him from firing a third time.

"Where were you when I needed you?" she barked. She grabbed her blanket and tossed it over the man's head.

A mask of vengeance covered Chitoa's face as he took aim. Before he could fire, she grabbed his arm. She crouched down in front of the man and gently pulled his hands away from his face. He flinched from her touch. His hair was still smoldering. The bullet had severed his right ear leaving only the hole.

"Now look what you've done. Can you hear me?" she asked him. He made no acknowledgement that he could hear.

"You're an absolute mess." She stood back to study his injuries. "Don't just stand there — give me a hand," she demanded of Chitoa.

"Please *Amai*, let me put this Shona dung-eater out of his misery."

"Put that gun away before you shoot yourself."

"But I know this man. He was a dangerous inmate at Hwange Prison."

[155]

"I don't care if you know him. Now help me collect my medical kit." Both got down on all fours and searched the ground. As an afterthought, she added, "I might remind you, my father was also an inmate at your prison."

He shook his head in disbelief. "This woman is determined to get us both killed," he said quietly to himself.

She sterilized and sutured the man's ear-hole. When she finished with the stitching, she injected him with morphine. Chitoa wanted to tie the man's hands, but she knew the drug would render him helpless. He grumbled as he struggled to climb back up to his perch. She retreated to the safety of her Rover.

The rest of the night was uneventful, but she was too keyed-up to sleep. Fear made her hear things. Each time she called out for Chitoa, he shined his flashlight to reassure her.

A light breeze signaled daylight. Chitoa climbed down from his lookout. After he stoked the campfire with fresh logs, he pushed a scorched kettle into the coals. He walked behind a tree to urinate. After he finished, he walked over and tapped on her window.

"Good morning, Mr. Chitoa, I trust you slept well. Do you know our patient's name?" she asked, rolling the window down.

"In Hwange Prison, he was known as *Tsuro*. I know him to be as untrustworthy as a jackal. I stayed awake because I was afraid he would kill us both."

She ignored him and asked, "What's his Christian name?"

"His Bible name is Moses."

[156]

"I see. And how is Moses feeling?" she inquired.

"Why do you ask? He's unworthy of living. All night I prayed he would die, but God didn't answer my prayers. Perhaps, it's because..." He didn't finish. He handed her a cup of tea. She noticed he'd removed the wooden pegs and that his swelling was almost gone.

"You seem to be doing much better." She touched her teeth as an indication of her inquiry.

"The pain has left me. There is much for you to learn about bush medicine. My people have used the remedy for many years."

So much for modern medicine, she thought. "And our friend, how did he sleep?" She used the term *friend* as an irritant. Your punishment for not showing me the slightest grain of gratitude for pulling your teeth, she thought.

"Why wouldn't he sleep? He has nothing to fear. Let me kill this dung beetle."

"Shame on you— you're an educated man. You need to elevate yourself above this... this prehistoric barbarity."

"I'm educated enough to know this man will kill us if he gets the chance."

"Why was he sent to prison? What were his crimes? The man was obviously disfigured in some sort of an accident."

"The *Tsuro* is a convicted murderer. His mistake was getting into a fight with your father." He smiled comically and then waited for her reaction.

"You expect me to believe my father did that to him?"

"Believe what you want. I was the warden at Hwange."

"How long will it take us to reach Binga?"

"If you insist on treating every sick person we meet, we may never get to Binga."

[157]

"You're impossible. Let's get going before it gets any hotter."

"What about him?" he asked, nodding at the injured man. "We should leave him."

"Put him up front with me. You can keep an eye on him."

I will never see my wife again, he thought. He walked over and kicked the man.

"I spent half the night stitching him up. Now, leave him alone," she yelled. He grumbled as he smothered the campfire with sand.

*   *   *

A relentless sun turned the morning muggy. The night rains made the road more cantankerous. She cursed each time she was forced to downshift into four-wheel-drive. Two hours into the struggle, Moses demanded that she pull over. She would have ignored him, but Chitoa backed him up. As a poacher, Moses had spent his life tracking animals. Like most bush Africans, he had the eyes of an eagle.

"What is it?" she asked.

"I'm not sure," Chitoa answered. Both men got out and walked back. In a few minutes they returned to the vehicle.

"What did you find out?"

"He saw tracks. He says they were made by soldiers. For some reason, they tried to cover their spoor. Their tricks could never fool this old poacher," Chitoa said, nodding at Moses, who tried unsuccessfully to grin.

They convinced her to take a more roundabout route to avoid what could be an ambush. The diversion delayed

[158]

their progress. It was mid-afternoon by the time they intersected the tarmac road to Binga. The people they drove past stared back at them with dazed expressions. Many of them motioned with their hands to their mouths begging for food. One group of refugees caught her attention. She pulled over and stopped.

"It's not safe to stop here," said Chitoa, looking in the side mirror.

"I know him," she claimed.

"You had better take this," he said, handing her a pistol. She shook her head no, but he forced her to take it.

"Don't worry, it's empty."

She stuck the gun in her pocket. Why would he give me a gun without bullets, she asked herself. She got out and walked back.

It was Humba, the witch doctor, and his five wives. This time he was walking. Christine learned they were forced to eat their donkey. She held her hand over her mouth in horror as he told her about the burning of her mother's medical clinic. Her face tightened when he told her Ian Rhodes was living on her parents' farm. When she walked back to the vehicle she was crying.

Chitoa eyed her with sympathy. Tears had stained her cheeks. He wanted to console her, but he didn't know what to say. When she didn't say anything, he asked, "Are we driving to your farm?"

"Why would I turn around and drive in the opposite direction? I thought you said you were born here? It doesn't make any difference which way we go. What's left of Binga is controlled by the rebels. It's not safe there, and we can't go back to my parents' farm— it's been confiscated by the government." She pounded the steering wheel in frustration. An alarm surfaced in the back of her mind, but she repressed it.

"It's far too dangerous to be traveling about. And I don't trust this one," he said, nodding at Moses.

"There is one place we can hide," she said, starting the engine.

"Where?" asked Chitoa.

"Livingstone Island," she blurted. She glanced at Moses in the rearview mirror. Their eyes met and she saw a reflection of her own misgivings. She looked over at Joseph Chitoa and cringed.

12

The Croxford farm had changed. The smell of death clung to the land. What had been alive was dead. Rhodes's first order was to cut down the surrounding jacaranda trees for firewood. White-backed vultures roosted on the stumps. His second order was to slaughter the tame animals for food. Helen Croxford's pet giraffe was killed and butchered first. Meat strips drying in the sun attracted blowflies. The sky was hazed by smoke and insects.

Fear robbed Rhodes of sleep. Drugs and whiskey made him paranoid. When he heard the wind rustle, he was sure it was Croxford. Sometimes, he fired warning shots into the night, which unsettled his men.

Christine Croxford reentering Zimbabwe was good news for Rhodes. Joseph Chitoa was bringing the young woman to him. He knew Croxford would eventually find his daughter. Assaulting Croxford's daughter would be the ultimate payback. The idea made his genitals tingle.

At dusk, the summer wind eased making the house stifling. Rhodes and his African mistress walked out on the veranda to cool off. She put her arms around him, but he twisted free. When she caught him looking at her with disgust, she left him and walked back inside.

As he watched a scarlet sun dip below the horizon, his thoughts diverted to the military takeover that had given him his command. The Chinese government panicked when their puppet, Robert Mugabe, was overthrown. They were eager to back the coup as long as they retained part of the *Marange* diamond concession. It was the world's largest diamond discovery in over a hundred years and it was right in the middle of Zimbabwe. Rhodes was delusional enough to think that his part of the spoils would make him richer than his wildest dreams. Someday, I might move to Cape Town. Why, I might buy a vineyard. Yes, a vineyard would do quite nicely. Then I could find myself a proper woman.

His mistress rejoined him. When he threatened to hit her, she left him again. He closed his eyes and smiled. His thoughts returned to Rigby. The Shona are right—vengeance is far sweeter than honey. He drained the last of his whiskey and laughed out loud. When he realized some of his men were staring at him he regained his composure.

PART TWO

Smooth seas do not make great sailors.
—An old African proverb

13

The Skeleton Coast

Bushmen refer to Namibia as "the land God made in anger." To the uninspired, it's a collage of inhospitable landscapes. To more spiritual witnesses, Namibia is a pristine wilderness. The Namibian Atlantic coast is known as the Skeleton Coast, which was named after the skeletal remains of shipwrecks half buried under the sand dunes.

After camping on the edge of the Etosha Pan for three days, they drove to the coastal town of Swakopmund. The plan was to resupply and then drive north on the ocean road.

Rigby and his men had worked tirelessly to make the teenagers' safari pleasurable, but nothing they did was good enough to please them. Only the girl seemed vaguely interested. The teenagers' grumbling was nonstop. It was too hot in the afternoons and too cold at night. They disparaged the cook's efforts. The boys even sabotaged the vehicles by letting the air out of the tires. Rigby saw them grinning as they watched Steven and Ezekiel take turns working the hand-pump to inflate the tires.

Rigby put up with their complaining, but slowly their antics began to grate on his nerves like fingernails on a blackboard. His feelings for the teenagers changed from amusement to indifference, and then finally to hostility.

*   *   *

The Benguela current moistened the air with night dew. By midmorning the fog had burned off, leaving the sky cloudless. Hell, old Martin was right— if it weren't for these spoiled brats, this *would* be paradise, thought Rigby.

As they were about to leave for the trek north to Cape Cross, Dutchy jumped out of his Land Rover and ran forward. "I've got another bloody puncture. We'll catch up with you later."

"I'll stay behind this time. Drive my vehicle. You take the girl, Ezekiel and Steven. They stay with me," he said, looking at the teenage boys. "Off you go, now."

"You sure you don't need some help?" Dutchy asked.

Rigby nodded no and said, "See you up ahead."

The boys sat in the shade listening to music while Rigby changed the tire. The desert sun was wicked. Sweat streaked Rigby's chest and disappeared into the waistband of his shorts. When he checked the tire for leaks, he found none.

He waited for the boys to climb in and then he said, "All right, get out."

"What?" Jacob asked.

"Are you deaf? All of you, out."

"Why are you doing this?" Joshua asked.

"You know why. Now, get out." He drove off and left them in the desert. He stopped six kilometers away and placed a canteen in the middle of the dirt road. He parked another six kilometers down the road and waited. Two hours later, the teenagers climbed into the truck. The boys fell asleep almost immediately.

Rigby whistled a happy tune as he drove away.

*　　*　　*

He found Dutchy and the others waiting for him at Cape Cross. "This looks like a good place to camp," he said to Dutchy.

"Wouldn't upwind be..." Dutchy's advice was stopped by Rigby's nod.

Cape Cross is the breeding grounds for thousands of fur seals. Rigby wanted to make sure the teenagers got the full effect. The men pitched the tents downwind from the seal colony. The overpowering stench was a blend of decaying dead seal carcasses, afterbirths and feces. The noise was an earsplitting cacophony of bellowing beach masters and seal-pups bleating for their mothers against a background of crashing waves and screaming seagulls.

After feeding on anchovies and squid, the mothers struggled up the sandy beach belching "ort-ort" calls for their babies. Beach masters battled for the right to breed. Some of the baby seals were squashed in the confusion, which provided food for jackals, spotted hyenas and coastal lions. Offshore, white sharks gorged on the baby seals. It was a sensory overload for even the most callous spectator, but the teenagers remained unimpressed. And *that* was the straw that almost broke the camel's back.

It didn't come to a head until their last day at Cape Cross. Dutchy and Rigby were wading in the tidal pools harvesting oysters when Joshua walked to the edge of the surf, cupped his hands and yelled, "Hey, Croxford, we need to talk." Rigby waved, but continued his rummaging under the kelp. Dutchy started to wade in, but Rigby stopped him.

"Don't pay attention to that little prick." Dutchy turned around and waded back out. The boy sat down in the sand to wait. Finally, the men came ashore dragging a gunnysack of oysters.

"Croxford, we thought Africa was supposed to be an unspoiled wilderness, not a sewage dump. Why can't we stay in town?" Joshua asked, pointing.

"You mean Swakopmund, of course?"

"Yeah, that's the one."

"Why, so you can buy more ganja from the locals?"

"That's not the only reason. Hey, I'm just kidding. Seriously, this place stinks."

"I see. Tell your buddies we'll make a new plan tonight." The boy got up and headed back towards the tents.

"What're we gonna do?" Dutchy asked Rigby.

"Kill them and bury their bodies under these dunes? Don't look so scared. I'm only kidding."

"Who's scared, I thought about killing them myself." Dutchy laughed.

The students had packed up their duffels and were standing by the vehicles when Rigby and Dutchy arrived back at the camp. Joshua stepped forward as the group's spokesman.

"Well, let's hear it," Rigby demanded.

"We've had enough of this hellhole. Our parents paid you big bucks for this stupid safari. We wanna go home. My father's a big-time attorney. You're screwing with the wrong people, pal."

Rigby threw up his hands in disbelief. "Just when I thought you were really getting into this wildlife stuff. I must warn you, you're gonna miss seeing the desert elephants. Dutchy, are you as shocked as I am?" he asked. His mouth formed a grin, but his eyes told a different story.

"I'm flabbergasted," Dutchy answered.

"Hello! You're not *listening.* Fuck the desert elephants. We want outta here. Now, crank up this wreck," Henry said, intervening.

"I suggest you start walking in that direction, because we're going the other way."

"It's over thirty miles to town."

"There's nothing like a brisk walk to heighten the senses," Rigby said, looking at Dutchy for confirmation.

"He's bluffing. He'd never leave us out here. C'mon boys, follow me," Henry said to the others. The boys followed suit. The girl stayed behind. "Aren't you coming?" Henry asked Latisha.

"I'm not so sure he's bluffing," she said.

"Leave her. She likes it here," said one boy.

"It's because she's one of them. These porch-monkeys are her long lost ancestors," added another boy. Pain flooded Latisha's face. She ran to her tent. Dutchy knew Rigby would go for the boy and he stepped in front of him to prevent it.

[168]

The boys headed down the beach. When they were far enough to feel secure, they hurled obscene gestures.

"How far will they get?" Dutchy asked Rigby.

"Not far enough. Unfortunately, I'm sure we haven't seen the last of their shining faces."

Rigby found Agnes Flaherty's letter in his vehicle's glove-box. He walked into his own tent, sat down on the edge of his cot and reread her letter.

Dear Mr. Croxford,

If you're reading this... you're probably frustrated. I can't expect you to forgive me. Harry's my chance at happiness and I had to make the best of it.

As I told you, my students have varying degrees of behavioral as well as maturity issues. I thought it might be helpful to give you a short background on each student. I hope my remarks help you to better understand them.

Joshua and Jacob Goldman: This trip is a graduation present from their father. Mr. Goldman is divorced and has recently married a woman not much older than his sons. His new wife doesn't allow the boys in her presence. They haven't been home in two years. The brothers are extremely intelligent. Both received early acceptance at Harvard. They are good kids, but unfortunately very immature.

Prone to carry out pranks. Patience is the key.

Latisha Williams: Her father's a professional athlete. She seldom mentions her mother. She's an excellent student. I wouldn't expect her to give you any problems. She's basically a loner and the best-adjusted of the lot. You have a daughter, so there's no need to elaborate on the obvious.

Billy Barrett: Billy is an exceptional student. I don't think he's ever met his father. He lives with his mother and his two older sisters. Billy has had substance-abuse problems in the past. He acts effeminate, but the school's therapist says its immature growing pains. Keep an eye on him to make sure he doesn't get his hands on any drugs or alcohol. Compassion is the key.

Henry Buford: Parents unknown. Lived with various foster families. His trip was paid for by a wealthy benefactor of the school. He is on an athletic scholarship. Henry's had problems with the law, mostly petty crimes. He has a tendency to be a bully. Vigilance is the key here.

Mr. Croxford, I know you'll get through this. Deep down, they're all good-natured kids. Please be good to them. Hope to see you again someday.

God bless and good luck,
Agnes Flaherty

[170]

He balled the letter up and tossed it on the ground. I was right— their school must be a mental hospital. Rigby, old boy, whatdaya do now, he said to himself.

*   *   *

Jacob and Joshua skipped flat stones on the backs of cresting waves. Henry pulled Billy into the surf and held him under until the other boys intervened. Soon, fatigue got the best of them. They squatted behind a sand dune to get relief from the sun.

"Look at these blisters," said Billy, carefully peeling off a sock.

With his hands on his hips, Henry spoke with an effeminate lisp, "Do your little footsies hurt? Billy, you're such a queer." Billy's face turned pink.

"Leave him alone," demanded Jacob.

"Hey, go fuck yourself, Jew-boy."

"Confucius say, 'Ignorance is the night of the mind— a night without moon or stars.' Henry, you live in perpetual darkness."

Henry's pinched brow narrowed his eyes. "I don't get it."

Frustrated, Henry slugged Jacob in the stomach. Joshua rushed to defend his brother, but Henry jumped out of the way causing Joshua to fall on top of Jacob. Henry kicked sand on the brothers and laughed. Billy started walking back to the camp.

"Where's he going? C'mon, Billy, I was only kiddin'," Henry hollered. One by one, the boys fell in behind Billy.

A few miles from camp a truck overtook them. The driver waved for them to stop. The man stuck his head out of the cab and yelled, "Are you with the Croxford safari?"

"Yeah, we're with Croxford. Why?"

"I was supposed to deliver this to Croxford— make sure he gets it." The man handed an envelope to Jacob. "*Dankie,*" the driver yelled doing a u-turn.

"Hey, no problem," Jacob shouted, holding up the letter.

"Let me see that." Henry snatched the envelope out of Jacob's hand. Instead of reading the letter, he tore it up and threw the pieces into the wind. "Fuck Croxford."

"You shouldn't have done that," said Joshua.

"Croxford looks tough enough to eat nails and shit rivets."

"I'm not scared of Croxford. Besides, he'll never find out, unless one of you assholes tells him. If you do, I'll beat the ever-loving snot out of you."

"Henry, you have such a wonderful way with words."

*   *   *

The camping gear was stowed in the vehicles. Both engines were running and the doors were open when the boys arrived back at the campsite. Billy and Latisha opted to ride with Dutchy and Ezekiel. Henry and the brothers rode with Rigby and Steven.

Rigby refused to acknowledge their failed mutiny. At that moment, he hated them and the circumstances that put him in their charge. The silence was nerve-racking. Steven, sensing Rigby's agitation, attempted to engage him in conversation, but the replies he got were one-syllable grunts.

[172]

The gravel road was dissected by an unnamed ephemeral river. Over time, rare torrential downpours had etched the desert on its way to the sea. The obstacle was a good excuse to stop driving. Rigby chose a campsite on the opposite bank under the arthritic limbs of a leafless acacia. After they unloaded the vehicles, Rigby approached the teenagers. "If anyone's interested, I'm going on a game walk."

"I wanna go," said Billy.

"Wait for me," added Tish. The others weren't interested. The threesome marched away. The men continued to pitch the tents. The brothers grumbled about the stupidity of walking in the heat of the day. Henry seemed unsettled as he watched Latisha walk out of sight.

Not far from the campsite, Rigby found a pile of elephant dung covered with yellow butterflies. He squatted down and broke up the yellowish-brown spheres, washing his hands in the sand as he spoke. "I'd never pretend to be a game tracker, but I can tell you a few things about these elephants. First of all, the more rounded tracks tell me they're cows. Bulls have more elongated footprints. This female is very old," he said, pointing at the dung. "She's probably the matriarch of the herd."

"How can you tell she's old?" Latisha asked, pinching her nose.

"Humans have two sets of teeth in a lifetime, elephants have five. This old girl's having trouble chewing her food. Her teeth are so worn down she can't chew her food. Look at the size of these undigested twigs," he explained, kicking open a dung ball. "When she wears out her last set of choppers, she'll starve to death. The wind direction's right and the spoor's fresh— if we hurry, we might catch up with them. Local herdsmen chase these desert elephants away from waterholes. Water is so precious— they don't like sharing it with wild animals. Sometimes, females with calves can get pissy. We better keep our wits about us."

"Are you sure it's safe?" Latisha asked.

"Elephants usually mock charge. Don't run unless I tell you to. Just remember to keep me between you and the elephants."

"I wish you said they *always* mock charge," she whispered.

"Well, if it's any consolation, you don't have to outrun the elephants, you just have to outrun me."

"Great. Now I feel better."

When they rounded a bend in the riverbed they found the herd of females standing next to a desert acacia stump. Dusted mud had painted the elephants ghostly white. Nearby, the matriarch used her trunk to excavate a borehole in the soft riverbed sand. She flipped the moist sand over her back. A smaller cow squealed and tried to get access to the borehole, but the big female gently pushed her away. Two adolescents took turns chasing each other. The mothering females fanned their ears to cool their calves.

They watched the elephants until Rigby motioned that it was time to leave. On the walk back he breached the silence. "Somehow, I get the feeling you two were only interested in getting away from Henry and his mates."

"I can't speak for her, but it did cross my mind."

"At least you're honest, Billy."

"What about you?" he asked, addressing the girl.

"They hate me."

"Nobody hates you," said Billy.

"Oh yeah, what about Henry?"

"Henry doesn't hate you— he's got a crush on you."

"Yuck." She pointed at her mouth and pretended to gag. "Miss Flaherty told us you used to be an ivory hunter," stated Latisha, challenging Rigby.

"Surviving in Africa hasn't been easy. Mind you, I can't say I feel good about killing elephants. I've done worse things."

"Like what, for instance?" asked Billy.

Rigby didn't answer. He stopped dead in his tracks and quieted them with a hand signal. He used his cigarette smoke to check the wind direction. "Damn it, where'd he come from? Nobody move."

The young bull elephant was the same color as his surroundings. Elephants are notoriously short-sighted, but they have remarkable senses of smell and hearing. The elephant standing in the middle of the riverbed was less than fifty meters away. He swayed uncertainly and then raised his trunk to taste the air. The smell of humans unnerved him and he whirled around and trumpeted. This bull had recently reached sexual maturity. The females no longer tolerated his presence. He could follow the herd as a sentry, but only from a distance. He shook his head and sounded a gurgling rumble to warn the females.

The elephant didn't hesitate. He came at them in a shuffling charge. Rigby grabbed Latisha and jerked her up behind a boulder. His heart fluttered when he realized Billy hadn't moved. The charging bull lowered his tusks to impale Billy, but at the last second, Rigby ran back yelling and flung his leather hat in the elephant's face. The distraction was enough to cause the bull to miss the boy by a whisker. The bull spun back around but then charged away. Rigby grabbed Billy's hand and pulled him into the rocks.

"So much for mock charges. What in God's name were you thinking, son? Why didn't you run?" He reached down, picked up his hat and knocked the dust out of it.

"I thought you said not to run."

"Yes, but..., never mind. I'll say one thing— you've got guts. Let me shake your hand, my friend. Christ, that's the second time I had to use that hat trick. The last time was..., it doesn't matter. I can't wait to tell your mates."

"Promise me, you won't tell them."

Rigby scratched his chin stubble and shook his head. "I need to settle the old nerves." He leaned against a boulder and lit another cigarette.

He picked an errant piece of tobacco from his lip before he spoke. "Billy, why do you let Henry pick on you?"

"What am I suppose to do? Henry needs someone to push around. Jacob and Joshua are glad it's not them. I guess I serve a purpose."

"It's not fair," interjected Latisha. Billy dismissed her with a look.

On the hike back to camp, Rigby saw something moving in the rocks. He walked over, picked up a dried tree limb and used it as a lever to overturn a stone. The stubby snake was as thick as a man's forearm. It coiled into a defensive ring and struck at the limb.

"Too bad Henry's not here. He's scared shitless of snakes," said Billy.

"This nasty bugger's a puff adder. These little beauties bite more natives than all of the other poisonous snakes in Africa, combined. What they lack in size they make up in meanness. The venom is cytotoxic. Turns the flesh around the wound as black as tar. Lots of Africans are missing hands and feet after being bitten by adders."

"Why don't you stop talking and kill it," demanded Latisha. She held her hands up to her mouth.

"Billy, did you just say that Henry was frightened of snakes?" asked Rigby.

"He's terrified of snakes."

"Is he now? Well, I think we're gonna have ourselves a little fun with Henry." Rigby's face curled up into a mischievous grin. He beat the snake with the limb until it stopped moving, then he cut its head off with his pocket knife.

"Let's get back to camp."

Twice, Rigby broke out laughing on the walk back to camp. Latisha and Billy looked at each other and shrugged.

*　　*　　*

Later that night, during dinner, Rigby gave a vivid dissertation about the venomous snakes of Namibia. Particular emphasis was given to the agonizing deaths of people bitten by puff adders. A typical victim would foam at mouth, roll on the ground in excruciating pain and then slip into a life-ending coma. Ezekiel, who was told to lie about the cause of his missing fingers, came forward to have his hand examined. Henry became wide-eyed and moved uneasily as he inspected Ezekiel's deformity.

"This area's infested with puff adders. If you see one, you must remain absolutely motionless. Do not disturb these snakes under any circumstances. Does everyone understand?"

"Billy, if you see a snake, whatever you do, don't cry," chided Henry. The Goldman brothers chuckled. Latisha looked exasperated. Billy's smile gave no inkling as to his thoughts.

After dinner, the teenagers retired to the tents. Dutchy and Rigby sat next to the campfire. The ocean fog rolled in, which obscured the stars and moon. They passed a bottle of whiskey back and forth to ward off the dampness.

"Here's mud in your eye, Dutchy. Just think, two more weeks of babysitting these brats. Christ, I can't wait."

"Are all of the kids in America like this bunch?"

"They can't be."

"What happened with the elephants?" Dutchy asked.

"I damn near got them killed. Flatty was right— these desert elephants *are* short-tempered. Himba herdsmen keep them agitated by chasing them off the waterholes. Can't say I wasn't warned."

"So the boy ran. I'm not surprised. He does act a bit girlish," Dutchy whispered, checking to make sure he couldn't be heard.

"It didn't happen that way. The kid never moved a muscle. Hell, I'm the one who bolted. I managed to grab the girl and pull her up into some rocks. I thought the boy was right behind me. That elephant passed so close I could smell his breath. The boy could have reached out and touched him. Getting a hunter flogged is one thing— getting a kid killed is different. Damn lucky— touch wood," he said, kicking a log into the fire.

After Dutchy took a swig of whiskey straight from the bottle, he said, "Come on, it's time to knock Henry down a peg or two."

Earlier, they hid a rope underneath the canvas floor in Henry's tent. His sleeping bag was directly over the rope. Dutchy pulled on the rope ever so slightly and nothing happened. He pulled it again. The men giggled like school girls when they heard Henry voice his concern. Dutchy pulled on the rope a third time, Henry whimpered. The fourth time he pulled until a knot passed under Henry's sleeping bag.

"Oh God, somebody help me! There's a snake in my tent. Somebody do something!" he pleaded.

"Whatever you do, don't move," Dutchy yelled back. Rigby shined a flashlight in Henry's face. "What's the problem?"

"There's a snake under my sleeping bag," Henry whispered.

"You mustn't move a muscle. It's probably a puff adder. Their bloody fangs are long enough to bite clean through the canvas. Whadaya think, Dutchy?"

"Oh, it's a puff adder all right. My best friend was bitten by an adder."

"What happened to him?" Rigby asked. He pinched himself to keep from laughing.

"His foot turned as black as coal from gangrene. In the end, he swallowed his tongue and choked to death. Poor bugger," explained Dutchy. He took a long hit of whiskey and burped.

"Don't just stand there, help me," Henry cried out. His voice trembled with fear.

"We don't wanna get bit. If you lie still, maybe it'll crawl away."

Dutchy pulled the rope out as Billy appeared from behind the tent. "I got him," he yelled, holding up the headless snake that Rigby had killed earlier. He walked over and tossed the snake in Henry's tent. Henry levitated out of his tent. He stood there shivering with his hands locked over his mouth.

"Don't worry, it's dead," said Billy.

"All right, it's over. Let's get some sleep. We've got a long drive ahead of us. Henry, maybe you should sleep in the vehicle."

"I think..." Henry's voice was so hoarse he had to clear it with a nervous cough. "I think I *will* sleep in the truck."

"Keep an eye on things." Rigby patted Billy on the back.

"Glad I could help out," Billy said.

"Think Henry will behave himself?" Dutchy asked Rigby as they walked back to the campfire.

"It'll take more than a dead puff adder."

*   *   *

Henry's embarrassment over the snake incident was short-lived. Billy *was* granted a temporary reprieve, but his taunting of Jacob and Joshua resumed the next day. Even Wanker wasn't exempt from Henry's torments. Anytime Henry got too close, the monkey jumped up on Dutchy's shoulder and clung to his neck.

That night, Rigby spoke to Jacob and Joshua about Henry. "Eventually, one of you is gonna have to stand up to Henry."

"As Jews, we try to avoid violence. Negotiation is less painful than confrontation."

Rigby thought for a second, and then replied, "After the war, I left Rhodesia and moved to Israel to work on a kibbutz. The Israelis I met weren't much interested in negotiating. I'm just curious, have either of you ever been in a fight?"

"Us? No way."

"That's what I thought."

"You're wasting your time, Mr. Croxford. We're yellow to the core."

"Bullies are usually cowards. Picking on people is their way of trying to prove they're tough. Why, if one of you were to smack Henry in the mouth, I bet he'd back down straight away."

"And if he doesn't back down?"

"One thing's for sure — he'll never bother you again."

"Now, I feel better. We get our teeth knocked out, but our dignity's restored," said Jacob.

Over the next few days, Rigby and Dutchy tried to hone the Goldmans boxing skills. The harder they worked, the more Rigby realized Joshua was right. Henry would beat the hell out of both of them.

Dutchy also realized the futility of their training. "Whatever you two become, it won't be prizefighters."

*   *   *

It took them three days to reach the Kunene River. The Himba village was located at the mouth of the inlet where the river empties into the Atlantic Ocean. The Himba people are normally nomadic, but the outpost had seduced this clan into a sedentary existence. Selling trinkets to the infrequent tourists and posing for photographs kept them there. The only other enterprise was a dirt airstrip serving as a petrol station for both airplanes and vehicles.

Rigby downshifted to start down the steep embankment to the desert floor. Below them lay a collection of beehive huts constructed of looped-over tree limbs covered in stretched animal hides. Scrawny cows and a few goats grazed hopefully on the barren ground around the huts. A weather-beaten shack, they later learned, was the home of a German missionary away on a leave-of-absence.

The villagers stared at the visitors as they got out of the trucks. The Himba men acted unapproachable. They were lean and elegantly muscled, but compared to the women they looked as common as female birds. The teenage boys gawked at the topless Himba women who covered themselves with a mixture of red-ochre and animal fat making their curvaceous bodies shimmer like varnished red mahogany. Their red hair was styled in elaborate coiled plaits. After Rigby explained that Himba women never bathe after they get married, the boys seemed to lose interest.

The older Himba children pestered the group to buy curios. Smaller children hid behind their mothers. A skinny dog barked incessantly until an old man threw a stone at the animal.

"Listen up," Rigby insisted. "We've got work to do. The Himba are a proud people. You're free to wander about, but you must treat these people with respect. If you take photographs, they expect to be paid. And make no mistake about it, you *will* pay them."

After Rigby showed a young woman written authorization to purchase petrol, Dutchy helped him hand-pump fuel into their spare Gerry cans. Ezekiel and Steven refilled the water containers.

The grumbling teenagers sought refuge from the curio sellers by staying in the vehicles. Henry resumed his taunting of Wanker until Latisha admonished him.

Rigby and Dutchy were examining a map when a Himba man approached them. Rigby folded the map and followed him into the center of the village. Rigby was fluent in Afrikaans as was the ancient matriarch sitting cross-legged on a gemsbok hide in front of her hut. Her wrinkled skin hung in layers. Her deflated breasts were reduced to leathery pouches. Her eyes had lost any hint of whiteness. What teeth she had were brown and worn. A few curly white hairs grew out of her chin. She smoked a dagga pipe with one hand, and used a cow's tail to swat flies with the other. Rigby thought the woman was about eighty, but Dutchy reminded him that guessing the age of Africans can be tricky. "The passage of time doesn't age them like it does us," Dutchy went on to say.

"Where are you from, my son?" the old woman inquired. Her boney head resembled a grinning skull.

"Zimbabwe."

"I always planned to visit Zimbabwe. Now, I'm too old to travel."

"You don't look *that* old," said Rigby.

"Are all the men from Zimbabwe liars?" She threw her head back and cackled.

"He said something about an injured woman and an infant," Rigby said, nodding at the man.

"Two days ago my youngest granddaughter and her baby were attacked by a crocodile down by the river. I'm afraid they will die. He will show you to her hut." She pointed a crooked finger at the man.

"I can have a look, but I'm no doctor."

The old woman sounded like she didn't hear him saying, "I know God will smile on you for saving their lives."

Throughout Africa it's believed that all foreigners are doctors, and that they possess lifesaving medicines.

When the headwoman asked Rigby to treat her granddaughter, he was hard-pressed to say no.

As Rigby walked with the man, he listened to the description of the crocodile attack. Himba women are expected to give birth alone, so the girl had gone down to the river to have her baby. The difficult delivery had caused excessive bleeding, which attracted a large crocodile. The croc tried to drag the girl into the river. She used the same knife she used to cut her baby's umbilical cord to gouge out the crocodile's eye. Her baby was uninjured, but the woman was badly mauled.

Rigby pulled back the animal skin covering the opening to the hut. A naked girl lay on the dirt floor. He guessed she was no more than fourteen. She was covered in flies. A baby suckled at her deflated breast. She moaned incoherently. He gently raised her arm to inspect her injuries. Milk leaking from the puncture wounds on her breast had stained her ribcage. Her skin felt white-hot. He was filling a syringe with an antibiotic, when he heard an airplane zoom overhead.

The small Cessna circled the village. After landing, the airplane spun around peppering Rigby in prop-wash sand. The pilot shut down the engine and emerged from the cloud. He was carrying a clipboard.

"Is the woman in there?" the pilot demanded, pointing at the hut.

"She is indeed. Otto Bern, you're a sight for sore eyes."

"Rigby Croxford, well, I'll be damned." They embraced each other in a back-slapping bear-hug.

"Bern, I heard a rumor that you were still running guns in the Sudan."

"I prefer to call myself an import slash export consultant. Anyway, I got tired of people shooting at me. I'm flying for a charter company here in Namibia. I do these emergency medical flights in my spare time.

"How's she doing?" Otto asked. He kneeled next to the girl and took her hand in his. "Good God, she's on fire. The baby's temperature seems normal," Otto said, placing his hand on the baby's belly.

"You'll take them with you?" Rigby asked.

"Why, yes. I just got the emergency call this morning. Is this the drug you gave her?" he asked, reading the label.

"Yes," Rigby answered.

"I forgot your wife's a quack. Say, why aren't you in Zimbabwe?"

"Because I'm trying to make a living. Wait until you see my clients. It'll give you an idea about my level of desperation."

"You don't know, do you?" Otto asked, putting his hand on Rigby's shoulder.

"Know what?"

"But you'd have to know. The messenger boy told me he gave my note to one of your clients."

"Otto, what the hell are you talking about?"

"Robert Mugabe went into exile eight days ago. I'm surprised you haven't heard about it from someone on the road. Bloody communications in this country are still in the dark ages. Before you get carried away— I'm afraid there's bad news. Military goons have taken control of the government by force. It's anarchy. God knows, I hate to be the one telling you this. For the life of me, I don't know why you didn't get my message." Otto pushed back his mop of unruly hair and shook his head.

"I've got a damn good idea," Rigby replied, glaring at the teenagers.

[185]

"Wish I had time to chat, old boy. I need to get her to the hospital in Windhoek. Can I send a plane for you?"

"No thanks. We'll need our vehicles, when and if we make it back to Zim."

"Is there anything else I can do for you? Just name it, my friend."

"Otto, I can't think of a thing."

"Help me carry her. You there, take this woman's baby to the aircraft," he yelled at the man standing outside of the hut.

After Otto strapped in the woman and her baby, he reached out of his Cessna's window to shake Rigby's hand. "Cheers. Thumbs-up for Rhodesia. Good luck, Croxford."

Rigby shouted goodbye, but his words were lost in the engine noise. As Rigby watched the Cessna liftoff, his mind went into overdrive. The first thing he needed to do was to tell his men.

He made sure the teenagers couldn't hear him as he told his men the news about Zimbabwe. Their expressions melted from elation to apprehension. The men asked questions, but he had few answers. It was 700 kilometers to the Zimbabwean border. They would travel as fast as they could to get home. Without breakdowns or roadblocks they would arrive home in two days. It would mean driving at night on unlit roads, which was dangerous in Africa.

"Okay, let's figure the quickest way home," he said, spreading out a map on the ground. He traced the route with his finger until he stopped at the border. "According to Otto, we could have trouble crossing the border."

"What are we gonna do about them?" Rigby asked Dutchy, looking at the teenagers.

"I say we leave them. We need to take care of our families."

"Dutchy, we can't leave them. Hopefully, we'll run into someone on the road to Epupa Falls. If we do, we can arrange transport back to Windhoek. Good, then it's settled."

"Ezekiel, get those last petrol cans filled. Steven, check the air pressure in the tires. Once we start driving, there's no slowing down. Dutchy, come with me. I need to tell the kids." Rigby was flushed with anger. *You better get a grip on yourself, before you do something awful,* he told himself.

He found them milling around the trucks. "All right, everyone, listen up." He waited until he had their full attention. He noticed Henry hanging back. *I was right, it was you,* he thought, glaring at Henry. "I'm sure all of you will be saddened to hear— this safari has ended." His tone was sarcastic. "We just got the news— there's an armed rebellion taking place in Zimbabwe. We need to get home as fast as possible. So, there you have it. Are there any questions?"

Jacob raised his hand before speaking. "So what happens to us? You can't leave us in the middle of this desert."

"If it was up to me, that's precisely what I would do. Fortunately for you, this man has convinced me otherwise," he said, touching Dutchy on the shoulder. "I'm trying to find transport for you back to Windhoek."

"This is bullshit, man. Nobody in his right mind abandons kids in a place like this. You can't be serious," said Henry.

"*Kids?* You're not bloody kids. That injured girl is a kid. She saved her baby by driving off a crocodile. Now,

[187]

she's fighting for her life. She's got more guts than the lot of you. I never should have taken this pitiful job in the first place. Don't look so worried. I'll get you back to Windhoek. You can check yourselves into some fancy hotel, and tell your friends back home about how you survived darkest Africa. Sorry, but our families come first."

"Rigby, you're one sick son-of-a-bitch to leave us here." It was Henry again. He slouched against a vehicle. He nervously picked a pimple on his chin. When he grinned, it triggered Rigby's response.

"What's sick is a spoiled little prick receiving a personal note, and then destroying it." Croxford's mouth grew thin and his eyes narrowed, like those of a mongoose stalking a cobra.

"I don't know..." Henry's high-pitched voice squeaked, he cleared it and tried again, "I don't know what you're talking about. You wanted to dump us from the get-go. I'm gonna make sure you don't make a nickel for this lousy safari." Henry spewed his words like bile. He flexed his muscles and spat defiantly at Rigby's feet.

Dutchy tried to restrain Rigby, but he wasn't fast enough. Rigby grabbed Henry's hair and pinned him over the truck's bonnet. Henry's struggling was as useless as Dutchy's efforts to stop Rigby. Rigby slapped Henry four or five times and then held him by the throat.

"You need to grow up. Your little prank could get innocent people killed. This isn't a game, you little shit. For starters, you will address me and the rest of the men as 'Mister'."

Henry's lips turned blue and his eyes bugged out. Rigby released him. Henry held his throat and gasped in a

[188]

raspy voice, "I'm not calling them 'Mister'." He pointed at Steven and Ezekiel.

Rigby pulled him so close, their faces almost touched. "You'll do as I say, or I'll finish what I started. Make up your mind and be quick about it." When Henry nodded submissively Rigby walked away. Henry slumped to the ground clutching his throat. Billy and Latisha tried to console him, but he pushed them away. Joshua and Jacob couldn't hide their smiles.

*   *   *

Rigby drove like a madman as he raced across the desert towards Zimbabwe. Dutchy cursed the malicious back-roads as he fought to keep up. Joshua mentioned the Himba village was looking pretty safe compared to an overland car race. Henry held on as they slid around a corner. Rigby's Rover sprayed Dutchy's truck with road gravel.

"Mr. Bosshart, I think you'd make one hell of a Nascar driver," yelled Jacob over the wind noise.

"Do you reckon?"

"Oh, there's no doubt about it."

"This is nothing. Wait until it gets dark," Dutchy yelled.

"Is it dangerous because you can't see the road?"

"No, it's dangerous because you can't see the animals," Dutchy answered. He pointed at a dust-devil touching down in the desert.

"I'm not following you, Mr. Bosshart."

"Imagine hitting a Cape buffalo or a kudu when you're traveling at over a hundred kilometers an hour. Why, I couldn't tell you how many people get killed driving at night. *Now*, do you see the problem?"

[189]

"I'm so happy you warned us."

"I'm curious. What were you and Mr. Croxford doing before you took this *pitiful* job?" asked Joshua, interrupting his brother.

"We were in prison."

"Let me guess. I bet you were both prison guards."

"We were inmates."

"Wow! That's just great. Okay, in for penny— in for a pound. Care to tell us what crime you committed?"

"Which time?"

"Well, let's start with the last time."

"Attempted murder, but we were both innocent," Dutchy said, laughing.

"Of course you were innocent. Jacob, did you hear that? They were framed."

"You wanna hear about the other times I was in prison?"

"Maybe later, that's assuming we don't hit a buffalo or that other thing you mentioned."

Jacob asked Dutchy why the Himba people kept staring at them. Dutchy said it was because they were twins. When Joshua pressed Dutchy for more information, he explained that there were no twins in that part of southern Africa. When the Goldmans challenged Dutchy, he explained that twins *were* born, but the mothers usually kill one baby, because twins are seen as bad luck. The clarification silenced them. Henry gloated.

*   *   *

They drove for thirty-six hours, stopping only to transfer petrol from the Gerry cans or to relieve themselves. Rigby noticed the land changing from raw desert to sparse woodlands. The white sun on the horizon made him squint. He pulled over and stopped.

Rigby chewed his lip reflectively as he studied the map spread out on the truck's bonnet.

"Dutchy, I must have missed the turnoff. These roads are buggered like the roads in Zim."

"Mr. Croxford, are you saying we're lost?" asked Jacob. They waited for his answer with unbelieving stares on their faces.

"I prefer to call it, temporarily misplaced."

They pushed on for another three hours. When the land grew hillier, he was sure he had crossed the unmarked border into Zimbabwe. Every mile took them further away from the possibility of finding transportation back to Windhoek for the teenagers. At midday, they came to a fork in the road.

"Shit!" Rigby yelled. He pulled over and waved to Dutchy to pull up next to him.

"What's wrong?" Joshua inquired. Rigby ignored his question and stuck his head out of the window.

"Dutchy, I've driven this way before."

"Ezekiel says we've been in Zimbabwe since daybreak. I should have said something."

"This is my fault. Let's stretch our legs. We need to make a new plan."

After conferring with Dutchy, Rigby called everyone together for a meeting. He confessed that he'd inadvertently crossed the border sometime during the night. They were now in Zimbabwe, albeit illegally. They would have to stay put until the next morning, at which time, either Rigby or Dutchy would drive them to Windhoek.

"Sorry about the screw-up. My brain must have been on holiday."

Ezekiel cooked the first dinner in two days; it consisted of heated tins of beans and boiled potatoes. The teenagers ate alone, away from the campfire. Henry hadn't uttered a word since his altercation with Rigby. He tried unsuccessfully to tune his portable radio. Billy and Latisha sat with their backs leaning against each other. Joshua and Jacob used their headlamps to read books.

"I must say, I'm relieved our ordeal's almost over. I can't wait to take a hot bath and sleep between some clean sheets. Our father will go ballistic when he hears about this fiasco," said Jacob.

"Ballistic? Our father doesn't care about us. What my brother doesn't want you to know is— our father doesn't want us anywhere near him or his new family. As a matter of fact, we haven't been home in two years. That's why we're in Africa. Right, Jacob?" His brother didn't answer. He tossed a twig into the fire and sighed.

"And I thought *I* came from a dysfunctional family. Your family makes Ozzy Osbourne's family look like the Waltons," said Latisha.

"The Goldmans are clones of the Osbournes, only without the tattoos," added Joshua.

Even Henry couldn't resist the humor— he burst out laughing, and then he said, "Why hell, back in Texas we're damned near normal compared to you nut-cases."

"So, Henry, what do you call a Texan with a sheep under each arm?" asked Joshua.

"I give up."

"A pimp."

[192]

Everyone laughed, except Henry. "That's the dumbest joke I ever heard." Henry started to punch Joshua on the shoulder, but something made him stop, instead he grabbed him in a playful headlock.

Jacob turned to his brother. "You must remind me to contact the Simon Wiesenthal Center in Germany. Adolph Hitler didn't commit suicide in that bunker in Berlin. He's working undercover as a safari guide under the assumed name of Rigby Croxford."

Everyone laughed again, including Henry, who remarked, "Croxford ain't that bad." He stood up and punted a pebble like it was a football.

"Why, Henry, you surprise me. I thought you'd still be pissed after he bitch-slapped you," said Jacob.

"I've had worse beatings from some of my foster fathers. Besides, I guess I deserved it. I'm damn sure gonna tell him I'm sorry about tearing up that note."

"Wow, this has the makings of a great short story. I think I'll title the work, 'The Rebirth of Henry Buford.' It's the story of a violent redneck reincarnated into a human being. I smell a Pulitzer, sports fans," said Jacob.

"Do all Jews talk as much as you two?" Henry asked.

"We've taken vows of silence, compared to most New York Jews."

"Guess I'll cancel my first visit to New York," Henry said, laughing.

Joshua replied, "Too bad. We were thinking about asking you to come home with us for Rosh Hashanah."

A quizzical look waxed Henry's face and his brow furrowed, always signs of unaccustomed mental exercise. "But I thought you both said your father disowned you."

Jacob and Joshua got up and walked away. Latisha and Billy followed them. "Now what did I say?" Henry said.

The Zambezi Vendetta

*   *   *

The men were up before daybreak. Dutchy added two liters of oil to both engines. Steven patched a tire. Ezekiel cleaned the windscreens.

As they were preparing to drive off in opposite directions, a Namibian Defense Force truck drove up. The hatchet-faced officer who got out of the truck wasn't smiling. "*Goeie more*," the man said, greeting them in chilly Afrikaans.

Dutchy returned his greeting in English. "Good morning."

"Papers?" the man demanded. Rigby handed him their passports, visas and a travel permit. He gave Dutchy a concerned look as the officer walked back to his truck. After talking on his shortwave radio, he came back with their papers.

"These papers are not in order— there are no exit stamps on your visas. You have crossed the border illegally."

"Look, maybe we *did* accidentally wander over the border last night. We're trying to get back to our families in Zimbabwe. I'm sure you can understand why. By the way, what are you doing in my country?"

The man puffed himself up. He thought for a moment. "We have been granted special permission by the new Government of Zimbabwe to patrol both sides of the border. Our orders are to prevent refugees from entering Namibia. You said you were driving at night. Something's not right here. We need to get your travel documents sorted out. You will follow me back to the border post. But first, we must inspect your vehicles."

"How far *is* the border post?"

"Sixty kilometers."

[194]

I haven't got time for this crap, Rigby thought.

The soldiers worked at a snail's pace searching the vehicles. After they finished, they climbed back into their truck and signaled for Rigby and Dutchy to follow them.

"All right, everyone back in the trucks. Where the hell's Henry?" Rigby asked.

"I'm here," Henry replied, from the backseat. "Mr. Croxford, I'd like to ride with you, if it's all right." Rigby glanced at him with a suspicious eye.

"That's fine, Henry, but I'm in no mood for your twaddle." He pounded the steering wheel in frustration.

"I wanted to apologize for tearing up that note," said Henry.

"Apology accepted. Now, what I need is total silence. Do we understand each other?"

"Yes, sir," Henry replied.

Rigby had trouble seeing the road through the dust kicked up by the army truck. "This can't be happening," he muttered, straining to see.

"Mr. Croxford, you're following too close. Better drop back a bit."

"Henry, what did I tell you about silence?"

"I know what you said. But something's gonna happen."

"What do you mean, something's gonna happen? What kind of mischief have you been up to?"

"I unscrewed the drain-plug in their crankcase. Look, you can see the engine oil spilling out on the road. I'm surprised the engine hasn't seized up by now."

As Henry spoke, the army truck's break lights flashed on. The truck clunked and sputtered a few times before quitting. When Rigby skidded to a stop, Dutchy almost rear-ended him. Without warning, Rigby spun around and sped off in the opposite direction. Dutchy followed suit and beeped his horn trying to find out what was going on. Rigby slowed down after hitting a hidden swale in the road. He pulled over, leaned his head on the steering wheel and groaned. *"Now* you've done it, Henry."

"But, I only wanted to help you." Henry looked so pitiful, Rigby toned down his outburst.

"Son, it's like I told you before. Innocent people could... never mind. We're in the middle of a military coup, not some Hollywood movie."

He got out and walked back to confer with Dutchy. When he returned he had everyone in tow. "Henry here, although his intentions were honorable, has buggered our chances of getting you to Windhoek." Upon hearing the news, they all groaned.

"Here's the situation, as I see it. You have two choices, both of which have risks. Unfortunately, this is as far as we can take you. You can walk back down this road and present yourselves to that army patrol or you can go on with us. I wish we had time to drive you back to the border, but we don't. Each of you must decide."

"Gee, I always wanted to be in an insurrection," said Joshua.

"Shut up, Josh. Just how safe *is* Zimbabwe, Mr. Croxford?" Jacob asked.

"To tell you the truth— I haven't a clue."

"I didn't mean to screw up. I...I... just wanted to help," stammered Henry.

"To hell with Windhoek, I say we go for it," Billy shouted. Latisha grabbed Billy's arm to show her support.

"I wouldn't want to miss another one of Ezekiel's yummy gourmet dinners," Joshua said, licking his lips.

"What my brother's trying to say is— we're for going on to Zimbabwe."

"Good. Then it's settled. We're all going to Zim," acknowledged Rigby.

14

Harry and Agnes arrived in Victoria Falls on the same day the Mugabe Government was overthrown. They were married by a minister on a cliff overlooking the waterfalls. During the marriage ceremony, a feathery mist gave birth to a double rainbow. Someone said it was a good luck omen. Most of Harry's friends had emigrated to other countries, but for those in attendance, it was an excuse to get drunk.

There was a party atmosphere in Zimbabwe. The people's suffering under a bungling incompetent had finally ended. Agnes and Harry were having so much fun they decided to extend their stay. A friend of Harry's donated his safari camp as a retreat for the honeymooners. Their thatched bungalow lay nestled in a cove on the Zambezi River. The camp had no means of communication with the outside world.

The Zimbabwe they found after eight blissful days in the bush was far different from the one they expected. On the one hundred kilometer drive back to Victoria Falls, they passed refugees walking on the road. Harry stopped and talked with an old man. Although Agnes couldn't understand their conversation, she knew something had gone terribly wrong. "Harry, what's happened?"

"Aggie, I'm afraid things have turned for the worst. This is my fault. We should 'ave 'eaded back to Windhoek sooner. Sorry, love, but I may 'ave put us in a 'ell of a pickle."

"Well, whatever happens, this has been the best week of my life," she said, putting her head on his shoulder.

"It *was* wonderful, wasn't it? Let's 'ope we make it over the border."

Victoria Falls had atrophied during their absence. Feral children ducked out of sight as they drove past them. The burned out shells of cars littered the streets. Most of the shops had been vandalized. The store windows that weren't smashed were blackened by arson fires. Vultures fed on a donkey's carcass near the railroad station. Harry raced through the city without slowing down. It looked like they might make it unscathed, but on the outskirts of town they came to a roadblock. As soon as he stopped, soldiers surrounded his truck. They looked disheveled and acted undisciplined.

"What are you doing here?" the officer in charge asked. "Victoria Falls is now under Martial Law." His eyes were hidden behind reflective sunglasses. His mouth was locked in a perpetual smirk.

"Look friend, we just got married. We've been camping in the bush. We're on our way back to Namibia."

"Get out of your vehicle." The man stuck his Kalashnikov in Harry's face.

"Now, lookee 'ere, there's no need to go barmy. I've got some nice things in the back. Take what you want. Just let us go." The man jerked the door open, and pulled Harry out. Another soldier dragged Agnes out roughly. Several soldiers pilfered the couples' personal belongings. When squabbling ensued over particular items, Harry knew they meant to take everything.

"Listen to me," Harry yelled. "This woman's an American. You're gonna find yourselves in big trouble, my friends."

The officer in charge walked over to Agnes. His look dragged lazily over her body and then he hollered, "I bet this *umfazi* has a hairy one." The other soldiers laughed.

"Hey, that's my wife you're talking about."

Harry used his head as a battering ram and charged straight into the officer. The man was knocked down and rolled on the ground gasping for air. Two soldiers restrained Harry as a third man pummeled him. His first two punches were to Harry's midsection and the next dozen were to his face. Only the soldiers' exhaustion stopped the beating. Harry collapsed at his attacker's feet. Agnes's bloodcurdling shrieks sounded like a dying animal. A soldier hit her on the back of the head with his rifle butt to shut her up. She fell to the ground in a lifeless heap next to her husband.

When Harry opened his eyes, he realized he was riding in the back of his truck. His hands were bound, but he managed to sit up straight. He found Agnes curled up next to him. Her hair was matted in coagulated blood. She'd vomited on herself.

"Aggie, open your eyes," he whispered. When he nudged her with his foot, she groaned.

"Thank God, I thought..." The words lodged in his throat. "Aggie dear, can you 'ear me?"

"I can hear you," she answered, dozily. She rolled her shoulder and winced from the pain. "Why are they doing this to us, Harry?"

"It's the old story of being in the wrong place at the wrong time, I reckon."

"Where are they taking us?"

"I'm not sure. Here, put your 'ead on my shoulder. That's better, love. Don't worry, I'll sort this out. I promise."

"Are they going to kill us?" she asked.

"There's no need to kill us." For a split second they were locked in each other's gaze, but Harry averted his eyes to keep her from discovering his thoughts.

"Harry, why doesn't it ever work out for people like us?"

"Now, don't you give up on me." He kissed her on the cheek.

*   *   *

It was drizzling when they arrived at the Croxford farm. Harry and Agnes looked miserable as they were led to the house. They were soaked and shivering. Riding in the open truck bed had stiffened their joints causing them to shuffle like much older people.

When Harry recognized Croxford's farmhouse he was hopeful, but then he saw Ian Rhodes though a window.

Rhodes sat slumped over in a chair. There was an empty whiskey bottle on the table. His watery eyes

[201]

bulged and his head drooped. His speech was slurred. "What do you want?" Rhodes hissed, trying to refocus. He regained the moment, stood up and opened the door.

"Well, now, what have we got here. Who is this... this rather immense woman?"

"She's my new wife," Harry declared, proudly.

"Is she now? Harry, my men tell me they caught you looting."

"That's a bloody lie. Your men robbed us. My wife's a yank, you know. 'Er country won't take it lightly at 'aving one of its citizens roughed up. Of course, if you could see fit to let us go, we could forget this mess ever 'appened."

"Is that right? Sergeant, come in here."

A large African with rounded shoulders pushed passed Harry and came to attention. "I'd like to question this woman in private. Please see that his Lordship here, is, shall I say, entertained. Harry, don't look so concerned. I promise I won't hurt her."

Harry saw Rhodes's lewd smile and jerked free. "Rhodes, if you 'urt 'er, you damn well better shoot me. If you don't, I'll kill you."

"Harry, I must say, your chivalry is most impressive. Sergeant, take him away."

Rhodes waited until they were alone. Her face was illuminated by the lantern on a table. As he walked behind Agnes, he visually raped her. When he touched her shoulder, she flinched, which made his genitals quiver.

He whispered in her ear, "If you cry out for Harry, I'll have my men beat him. We don't want that, do we?"

"Please don't hurt him," she sniveled.

"I've always admired devotion. It's such an endearing quality, don't you agree?" Agnes didn't respond. He helped her up and walked her over to the table. He reached around from behind her and fondled her breasts. He unbuttoned her pants and pulled them down around her ankles.

"Oh my, you have such a lovely, large ass, my lady." He gave her a playful spank and slid his fingers between her cheeks. Her blubbering caused her nose to run, but she refused to wipe it. He pushed her over the table and pressed himself against her, but his limpness prevented entry. He tried playing with himself, but that didn't work.

"I'll have you, or die trying," he gasped. He pinched her nipples. Her sobbing aroused him. His member stiffened a little, but not enough to make it functional.

Harry heard his wife whimper and cried out for her, which provoked the soldiers. When Agnes heard Harry groan she screamed, "You bastard, you promised they wouldn't hurt him!"

"Shut up and spread your legs."

Rhodes struggled to insert his bendy organ. He was so preoccupied by his failure, he didn't see her grab a metal ashtray on the table. Without hesitating, she spun around and smashed Rhodes in the mouth. He stumbled backwards and then used his hand to check for blood.

"You crazy bitch, I'll kill *you and your* husband for this."

Agnes came at him like an enraged lioness. The next blow dropped him to his knees and the final coup de grace was to his temple. He fell forward landing on his face. His eyes rolled back in his head and his body lurched and twitched.

Agnes struggled to pull up her pants as she moved briskly into an adjoining bedroom. The African woman

[203]

sitting in the bed pulled a blanket up under her chin. She blinked back tears and pointed at a rifle hanging on the wall. Agnes grabbed the rifle and left her.

Rhodes was conscious now, but his ranting was incoherent. When he saw the rifle his eyes got big. "You can't shoot me in cold blood."

Instead of answering, she placed the end of the barrel between his eyes and tried to pull the trigger, but something stopped her. She left him and walked out on the veranda.

"Get away from my husband, you filthy bastards. Now, untie him."

One soldier complied; the rest of them jumped back and raised their hands.

Harry stood up saying weakly, "Better give me the gun, Aggie."

Harry was still woozy and staggered slightly as he pried the rifle from his wife's hands. He nodded at the soldiers to go inside. Agnes walked in first. Without warning, she picked up the same metal ashtray, spun around and hit one of Harry's attackers in the face; it sent the man spinning out of control.

"Now you know what it feels like." She tried to hit him again, but Harry grabbed her arm.

"That's enough, Aggie. Go make sure the keys are in our truck."

Harry waited for his wife to leave the room. "Rhodes, you filthy bugger, you've added rape to your list of crimes." He lifted Rhodes's chin with the rifle barrel.

"I swear to God, I was only having a laugh with her."

"A laugh, was it? I 'ave every right to kill you. I wouldn't want to spoil Rigby Croxford's fun. I reckon you'll meet the Devil soon enough." Without warning, Harry kicked Rhodes in the groin so hard it lifted him off the floor. Rhodes gave a blood-curdling scream. He stayed coiled into a fetal position.

After disabling the soldiers' vehicles, they sped off into the dead of night.

After a few minutes, Harry slowed down and turned to his wife. "Aggie, you saved us. Make no mistake about it, they messed with the wrong gal, they did. The way you smacked that soldier was something. Yikes, remind me never to make you mad."

"Sweetheart, what's that button on a rifle called— the thingy that prevents it from firing?" She snuggled up to him and rested her head on his shoulder.

"It's called the safety. Why do you ask, love?"

"Croxford was right. We're all capable of killing."

"But Aggie, you didn't kill anyone."

"I sure tried. That safety thing stopped me."

15

They drove all night and well into the next day. Harry was beginning to feel like they might make it to the border when he saw two vehicles approaching from the opposite direction. It was too late to leave the main road. He accelerated and so did the trucks traveling in the opposite direction. They whizzed past each other in a blur.

"It's Miss Flaherty!" screamed Billy. Croxford stomped on the brakes and so did Harry. The vehicles reversed until they were abreast of each other.

"Doctor Livingstone, I presume," said Rigby, smiling.

"Well, I'll be damned. Never thought we'd run into you," Harry said. "I see you've taken good care of my Wanker." The monkey gawked at Harry.

"If it was a lovers' quarrel you had, it looks like Agnes won by a landslide."

"Ian Rhodes did this to me, and her. I'm afraid we've got some bad news."

"Let's get off the road. Follow me," Rigby ordered. He headed off into the bushes with Dutchy and Harry following close behind. They hid the trucks in a stand of monkey nut trees. The teenagers piled out and ran to greet Agnes. The men surrounded Harry. As Rigby listened to Harry relive their ordeal with Rhodes, he became incensed. He looked wistfully in the direction of his farm.

"I should have killed that bastard a long time ago."

"Be that as it may, what can we do about them?" Dutchy said, nodding at Agnes and the teenagers.

"I know, I know. Let me think for a minute." Rigby puffed on his cigarette and exhaled a smoke ring. "There's only one place Helen would go, and that's where we're headed. Harry, there are some very pissed-off soldiers up ahead. It would be safer to come with us. It means a bit of backtracking, but at least it'll give us some breathing room. I feel naked without my weapon."

Harry retrieved the .416 from his backseat and handed it to Rigby. "Compliments of Mr. Rhodes," he said. Rigby broke the double open, extracted the bullets and squinted down the barrels.

"Thanks Harry, but this *is* my weapon."

"I figured as much. If Aggie could have worked the safety, Ian Rhodes would be burning in 'ell."

"I bet she's had her fill of Africa," said Rigby.

Harry beamed. "I wouldn't bet too much. She's tougher than most men I've known."

"She's special all right, and too good for the likes of you, I might add. We need to get going— it's a three hour drive to the river."

*   *   *

Davy Crockett guided Helen, Sadie, and the children safely down the Zambezi. They camped near the river at nightfall. The burbling song of the Zambezi was seductive, but Davy fought to stay awake. Just before dawn he slipped out of their protective thorn-bush corral. After stripping naked, he moved as silently as a stalking lion. As he walked he heard a wood-owl hoot followed by the squeak of a dying mouse.

Davy usually spoke to his ancestors at night, but not tonight. He remembered his friend, Tim Brooks. The years he spent tracking for Tim were his best years. In the beginning, the war years were also good, but he had cast his lot with the losing side— the white Rhodesians. The post-war years were difficult. His fellow tribesmen treated him like a Judas. Even his relatives shunned him. Amputated from his tribe, he grew closer to Brooks. *Baba Gosorwa*, I will miss hearing you cough in the morning, he reflected. The memories were so depressing he dismissed them and pressed on into the night. His pace was steady. His movements were soundless.

Earlier, Davy had seen campfire smoke. He hoped to find fishermen, but he needed to make sure. Tim would want me to investigate, he thought.

The leopard-eyed moon hid behind a cloud. He froze until the moonlight improved. He heard something, but then he recognized the sound of trees moaning and he continued on. A cracking sound followed by a loud pop was made by a foraging elephant snapping off a limb. Everything was as it should be.

When Davy saw the red glow of a campfire, he crept closer and saw the outlines of men sleeping on the ground. There was a gunboat beached on the shoreline below the camp. The boat's fifty-caliber machine gun was pointed skyward. Its twin outboards had been cocked upright.

Davy waded into the icy water and lowered himself to his neck. The gunboat was held captive by a rope tied to a sapling. After cutting the rope and the fuel lines, he eased the boat out into deeper water. The fuel-slicked river mirrored the clouds and a veiled moon.

The sound of trickling water made him freeze. A soldier had come down to the river to urinate. The man stood so close, Davy saw the steam rising from his piss. He eased the boat back against the beach, and lowered his head until only his eyes showed. After the soldier left, Davy waited for a few minutes before setting the gunboat adrift. Slowly his frozen legs complied and he hobbled up the riverbank.

They were still sleeping when he returned. He shook Helen to wake her. "*Amai*, we must leave this place at once. I found a soldiers' camp not far from here." He scooped up two of the sleeping children and started running towards the river. Still groggy, the others stumbled after him.

They reached the river as the first light of dawn peeked on the horizon. Davy made the children lie down in the boat. Helen and Sadie helped him wrestle the boat into deeper water. After paddling to the other side, he let the boat drift on its own accord.

As they floated past the soldiers' camp, Helen looked over the gunwale. She saw soldiers running towards the shoreline. Their shouts were followed by rifle shots. A hail of bullets ricocheted on the water around them. One shot hit the transom. It seemed like an eternity, but within a short time, they were out of range and the bullets fell short.

When Helen saw the gunboat beached on a sandbar, she screamed. "For God's sake, Davy, start the engine."

Davy shook his head. "They'll never get to their boat, *Amai*. We must save fuel for the rapids." Earlier, the soldiers had wantonly shot a hippo and now the hippo carcass lay beached near the gunboat. Black and yellow scaled crocodiles took turns twisting off large chunks of hippo meat. The overhanging trees were decorated by vultures and marabou storks.

*   *   *

Davy used the outboard engine to stay clear of the whirlpools and to circumnavigate around partially-submerged boulders. A few times, they encountered fishermen who paddled their dugout canoes out to meet them. As they drifted together, Helen asked them about the gunboats. The fishermen were eager to provide information. They said the rogue soldiers were either demanding money or stealing fish from their nets.

Soon the sun rose towards its zenith. Without a breeze, the air seemed unbreathable. Sadie dipped water from the river to cool the children. Both women draped soaked rags over their heads. Helen constructed a makeshift sunshade out of tree limbs and a woolen blanket. Davy's head bobbed, as he fought to stay awake.

Just before dusk, their skiff nudged against something. Everyone sat up expecting to see another sandbar. What they saw were periscopic beady eyes.

They had drifted into a pod of hippos. The dominant bull's warning yawn revealed his yellowed tusks. The frantic hippo cows wagon-wheeled around their calves and then turned back to face the intruders.

Davy jerked the rope-starter, but the cranky outboard wouldn't start. The current drifted them deeper into the pod. It looked like they might escape and then without warning, the bull smashed headlong into their launch. The collision knocked the boat over on its starboard side. Sadie and her daughter were knocked overboard. Helen rushed to pull them back over the gunwale.

"Oh, God, he's coming again!" Sadie screamed.

This time his charge was more violent. The bull impaled the skiff with his razor-sharp tusks tearing a gash in the bow. The boat was tossed about like a toy boat in a bathtub. With Helen's help, Sadie and her daughter managed to scramble back onboard.

In desperation, Helen ran to the bow and smacked the hippo between his piggish eyes with an oar; it splintered like a toothpick, but the distraction was enough to stop the attack. The bull glanced over his shoulder as he water-trotted to safety.

The hippos stared at them as they were swept out of harm's way. The bull's thunderous wheeze-honking was joined by grunts from the other hippos.

Finally, the outboard sputtered and caught hold. Davy gunned the engine, but the boat was sluggish with bilge-water. They stuffed rags into the gash and bailed until the bilge was dry. After they finished the repairs, Helen examined Sadie and her daughter; both were rattled, but uninjured.

Helen spoke with exasperation, "Goddamn stupid hippos. I've had enough of this river for one day. Davy, find us a safe place to camp."

The river was studded with islands, but most were little more than barren sandbars. Davy found one with enough vegetation to camouflage the boat. Fearing the smoke might be seen, he would wait for nightfall to build a campfire.

*   *   *

16

Rigby grew up kayaking on the Zambezi. The river was an old acquaintance, albeit a fickle one. With the roads patrolled by rogue soldiers, traveling on the river made sense. His plan was to drive to a fishing camp thirty kilometers upstream from the rendezvous island. If he could find a boat, they could float downriver on the Zambian side, which would take them out of gunfire range. Dutchy said Rigby's plan had more snags than the Zambezi.

The overland drive to the river took up most of the day. With the sun setting behind them, Rigby and Dutchy lay hidden in some underbrush passing a pair of binoculars back and forth. Thin wisps of black smoke rose from the razed fishing camp. The foundations where the cabins once stood were still smoldering. The only structure intact was a ramshackle boathouse. A rubber raft and two kayaks were moored to a sagging dock nearby.

"What do you think?" Dutchy asked, handing him the field glasses.

Rigby thought for a moment and then replied, "I think a man could get himself killed waltzing in unannounced. Colin was always jumpy, especially when he's on a toot. No sense both of us getting shot. I'll sneak down and have a look-see."

After easing down the sandy riverbank, he made his way along the shoreline. As he got closer, he saw a frail white man and two Africans skinning a large crocodile hanging from a tree. Rigby ducked behind a tree to keep from being seen.

The man spoke without turning around. "So you made it, Croxford, did you? Thirty years ago I wouldn't have heard you. Now, you make more noise than a rhino in heat."

"How did you know it was me?"

"I've been expecting you. Lots of unsavory types are looking for you, not the least of which is your old friend, Ian Rhodes."

"He's no friend of mine. You haven't changed much, Colin. Still poaching crocs, I see."

"Oh, but it's not true. I'm afraid I should've put old Winston down, months ago. Naughty boy was harassing local net fishermen. He ate a woman five days ago. We buried what was left of her under that mahogany you're hiding behind. There's not much left of you now, Winston," Colin said to the croc. He sighed and stepped back to admire his skinning job. He sounded like he was eulogizing a close relative.

Poor Colin, you've lived in the bush far too long, thought Rigby.

"I'd shake your hand, but…" Rigby ignored the blood and grabbed his hand.

"It's good to see you, Colin."

"At my age, it's good to be seen."

Colin White was corpselike, a harsh reality born more from alcoholism than old age. His face was framed by scraggly white hair and whiskers. A dark cigar dangling from the corner of his mouth interrupted some missing teeth. His high-pitched cackle could break out for reasons only he understood.

"Bloody shame, what's happened to our country," Colin said in a British accent tainted by forty years in Africa.

"It is, indeed. Say, I need to borrow a rubber raft or any boat, for that matter," said Rigby. The whine of downshifting engines caught their attention. Vehicles appeared at the top of the crest. Everyone jumped out and scrambled down the riverbank.

"Well, if it isn't the Dutchman and Steven— nice to see you two jailbirds." Colin subdued his cackling as he was introduced to the rest of the group. He turned somber as he spoke again. "Heading downriver, are we? It's not safe, you know. Soldiers taking potshots, and robbers trying to…" He stopped midsentence, ran his fingers through his tangled beard and then giggled insanely. "Good God, Croxford, you'll need a bloody cruise ship. Harry Flaxney, is that you I see?"

"What's left of me— this is my new bride, Aggie."

"Well, congratulations. Sorry I can't offer you a brew, Flatty," said Colin.

"No need to. Gave it up, I did," said Harry in response. Agnes smiled approvingly.

[215]

"Pleasure, ma'am. Colin White, at your service," His inquisitive look raked Agnes from head to toe. Colin seemed transfixed by her proportions until Rigby rescued him from his trance.

"About that boat— anything that floats will do." Rigby offered him a cigarette; he declined it, circumcised another cigar with his teeth and then grinned around it.

Colin paddled smoke and squinted as he replied, "Let's see, I've got a rubber raft and two kayaks left. Take what you want." He pulled on his earlobe as he estimated Agnes's weight. "I must warn you, the river's surly this time of year."

"What choice do we have?"

"Probably none, but it's worth mentioning. I'm surprised you weren't ambushed on the roads." He burst out laughing.

After Colin's nervous chuckling subsided, Rigby replied, "We came overland."

"You're bloody lucky. I'd hide the vehicles, if I were you. No sense tipping your hand. I'll have my boys grill some of Winston's tail fillets for your dinner. I'd offer you a sundowner, but I'm down to basics. No ice without petrol. You'll have to settle for warm whi...whisky." He managed a better pronunciation the second time. With teeth missing, some of his words ended in trilling sounds.

"Colin, what's happened to the other camps on the river?"

"They've all been burned," he answered, pointing at the smoldering ruins. "I built this fishing camp twenty years ago with my own hands. Now, look at it. Bloody bastards."

"Why didn't they take your boats?" Dutchy asked.

"Oh, they'll get around to pinching what little I have left. The kayaks may look ratty, but they *do* float. I'm glad you're taking the rubber raft— at least *they* won't get it. Like I said, the kayaks aren't much to look at."

"We're not fussy. I'd like to inspect them, if I could," said Rigby.

"Right you are. Sorry, my social skills are ghastly. Care for a little snort?" he asked, handing Rigby a bottle. "Bottoms up, old chum. Say, that reminds me, I've got a note from your wife."

"She was here?" he asked.

"Two days ago, maybe three. Sometimes, I forget things. God Bless her, she gave me some medicine for my teeth, what's left of them." He held his hand to his cheek and winced to make his point. "She had Dutchy's wife and kids with her." When Dutchy overheard Colin's remark, he gave a fist-pump.

"Was Tim Brooks with her?" asked Rigby.

His manner was somber when he answered this time. "I hate telling you this. Tim has passed on. God knows, I'll miss him."

"I guess he finally drank himself under the ground." Rigby looked downriver and sighed.

Colin's eyes said he was troubled. "I married Tim's second wife, after they got divorced, of course. She turned out to be an absolute toad."

"I forgot you married her."

"I'd like to forget that one, myself. Say, Tim's old game-tracker was with your wife. You know... the old fella who wears the fur cap. I swear, I think he sleeps with that filthy thing on his head."

"Davy Crockett."

"That's him. I think you better read your wife's letter." Colin put his hand on Rigby's shoulder in a consoling manner and then walked away. When Rigby looked into Colin's eyes, he felt the need to sit down.

The Zambezi Vendetta

Dear Rigby,

The news is so dreadful. By now, you know Rhodes has burned the medical clinic and that he is occupying our farm.

I'm afraid I have the worst possible news about Tim Brooks. I'm certain he's dead and I believe Ian Rhodes is responsible. The last time I saw Tim, he confided in me about Steven's being his son. He said you've known all along. I find the longer I live in Africa, the less I know. Somehow, I think he knew he was going to die. I'll fill you in on the details when I see you.

Before we parted company, Tim told me about the pact you made thirty years ago in South Africa. I'm begging you to please let this thing go. After this country gets sorted out, Ian Rhodes will have to answer for his crimes. Let's let others judge him. I need you more than ever. I have not talked to our daughter. I hope you've had better luck with the telephone service. She also needs you. Tell Dutchy that Sadie and his kids are in good health.

Tim's man, Crockett, has gotten us this far. He says our boat is too small to navigate the last ten kilometers. Our plan is to leave the boat and hike on the Zambian side to our rendezvous spot.

All my love,
Helen

He crumbled the letter into a ball as he watched a fish eagle flare and grab a fish in the shallows. The sound of water trickling over rocks merged with the haunting cries of the eagle. The disappearing sun cast long tree-shadows on the water. The Zambezi looked so peaceful, but he knew that beyond the horizon, where the water gathered speed on its way to the Indian Ocean, the river would be unforgiving.

He thought about his friend, Tim Brooks, and the times they'd spent together on the Zambezi. The river usually lifted his spirits, but not this time. When he closed his eyes he saw Ian Rhodes's face.

Agnes walked up behind him and announced, "I hate being such a major pain in the ass, but I need to speak to you about my kids."

He shaded his eyes and looked up. "What's on your mind?"

"There has to be a way of contacting the American Embassy. After all, they *are* American citizens."

"I wish it were that easy."

"But there must be something you can do."

Rigby fidgeted nervously as he responded. "Let's say, for argument's sake, we had a satellite telephone, which we don't. And let's assume your country had a functioning embassy, which by now, I'm sure it doesn't. Do you see what I mean?"

"If you're putting my kids at risk for your wife's sake, I can't say I blame you, but that doesn't make it right."

"Unfortunately, there isn't an easy way of getting all of you out of Zimbabwe. Believe me— I don't need this...this entourage. The Zambezi is our only option. I know what I'm doing."

"First of all, I want you to know this isn't about me. Part of this is my fault. I know you're still angry with me, and rightfully so."

"Agnes, I'm not mad at you. If you'd stayed on, we'd still be in this fix. I must tell you, your travel company will be charged extra for this river excursion."

When she saw him grin, she smiled and asked, "Care if I join you?"

He offered her his hand. She grabbed it, but almost fell over backwards as she sat down. "Oops," she said, straightening herself.

"Agnes, I bet you can't wait to get back home."

He offered her a cigarette; she accepted it and then she said, "Funny you should mention leaving. I haven't told Harry yet, but I'd like to stay here in Africa. That's assuming things return to normal."

"You're quite serious, aren't you? With all this craziness, you want to live here."

"I'm very serious. My life has been so...so antiseptic, for the use of a better term. I could never live the way I used to, even with Harry. I thought you, of all people, would understand. Looking back, I realize I was imprisoned by boredom, but not anymore," she said, grinning.

He started to tell her about Tim's death, but he had second thoughts. Instead, he told her about growing up on a farm in Rhodesia. When he expressed doubts about his future in Africa, she interrupted him.

"Mr. Croxford, you don't strike me as someone who'd be happy living a normal life— whatever normal means."

"Sometimes I think I should have packed it in years ago."

"Oh, come now, you live in one of the most fascinating places on earth. I know it's been challenging, but you've been blessed. I mean, just look at this river. It has to be one of God's most beautiful creations."

"You're seeing Zimbabwe at her absolute worst. Someday, I'd like to show you her best— assuming, like you say, things get sorted out."

"I'm sure the chaos won't last forever. Harry says living in Africa is addictive. I must say, I find it invigorating. I like not knowing what's around the next bend."

"I think Harry found himself a good woman."

"How nice of you, Mr. Croxford. I think they're serving dinner," she said, glancing at the boathouse.

"I'm right behind you." He stubbed out his cigarette butt and then looked back at the river.

*   *   *

Wanker's table manners were greatly improved. He didn't beg for food, nor did he pleasure himself. The monkey appeared jumpy and insisted on clinging to Harry's neck. Dutchy tried to bribe him with table scraps, but he turned up his nose at the offerings. Harry was about to mention Wanker's behavior, when he remembered crocodiles often prey on careless vervet monkeys. He was certain Wanker had escaped a close encounter with a crocodile, and that the main course was evoking bad memories.

As Rigby surveyed his group, he made mental preparations. Dutchy would act as the oarsman for the rubber raft. He would take the lead with Billy in a kayak. Colin would bring up the rear.

[221]

he's that crazy man who lives on the river.' The munts say I'm a reincarnated catfish."

"I heard you married a crocodile once upon a time," said Rigby, laughing.

"Now see here, that particular rumor wasn't true. Although Brook's wife was certainly uglier than any croc I ever saw.

"Let's be serious for a minute. Rhodes has flipped his lid, mate. He's totally insane— he's unpredictable, and he's got the entire army behind him. Some people say he's only a gunshot away from heading up the entire army."

"Colin, were you always so optimistic?"

"I'm just being realistic. There's something else I need to say. I know I'm not the man I used to be, but neither are you. I *do* know the Zambezi better than any man alive— even better than you. Take me with you tomorrow. Tim Brooks was my mate, too. Besides, there's nothing left for me here."

"By nothing left, you mean that was your last bottle of brandy?"

"That's not what I mean, and you know it," Colin countered, seemingly bruised by what was intended as humor.

Rigby moved uneasily at the suggestion. Under most circumstances he would decline the offer. At this point, there was nothing to lose.

"Colin, I'd be honored to have you along."

"You won't be sorry."

"Was there ever a doubt?"

"Jolly good. I'll certainly drink to that. Down the hatch," Colin saluted, taking a nip. "And thanks awfully, old chap."

"For what?"

"Mr. Croxford, this casserole is divine. What kind of meat is it?" Agnes asked.

"It's called anonymous stew. I think he said river terrapins," Rigby answered.

"It tastes more like pork," she said.

Colin reappeared from the galley. His face was unbalanced from inebriation. "Mr. White, did the cook use warthog to make this stew?" Agnes asked.

"If it's pork— it would have to be secondhand pork." Colin winked at Croxford. "A proper name would be Winston's delight." His cackling ended in a coughing jag. He re-swallowed something and smiled. "You see, it's crocodile, ma'am." Rigby tried to dissuade him from a more detailed explanation by frowning. Colin didn't get the hint.

"Aren't crocodiles on the endangered species list?" Agnes asked. Her nose puckered as she swallowed painfully.

"I wouldn't know about that, ma'am. On the Zambezi, it's the natives that are endangered. I reckon crocs take one African everyday on this river. This one ate a...."

Rigby cut him off. "Have any of you ever done any whitewater rafting?" Rigby waited for their responses. His frowning at Colin was answered by unbridled hilarity.

"Don't worry— I'll have you paddling like Tonga oarsmen in no time."

"You were saying, Mr. White?" Agnes pressed Colin.

Colin's memory had escaped him. "I was going to ask if you'd care for a sniffer of brandy. There's nothing like brandy to loosen the bowels and settle the stomach." He drained the last of his, and belched silently.

"How informative," she said. "Mr. White, were you born in Africa?"

"Me? No ma'am, I'm a POM, same as Flatty."

"You mean Harry?" Her beady stare reddened his face.

"Sorry, I meant to say, Harry."

"Do you know the derivation of the term POM?" she asked.

"I guess it means, 'prisoner of mother England', or something like that."

She frowned and shook her head. "The term POM is bastardized from the French word '*pomme*', which means apple. It refers to light-skinned Brits like yourself turning as red as your nose, Mr. White. Come along, Harry," she said, getting up from the table. Her husband jumped to his feet and pulled back her chair.

"*Bonne nuit,* everyone," she announced.

As soon as everyone got settled in for the night, Rigby left the boathouse to stand guard on a hilltop. He sat down next to a giant termite mound and placed his rifle in his lap. A cloudy sky reduced his view of the Zambezi to a darkened void. A hunting leopard's cough carried on the water from the other side of the river. The sound of a match scratching was followed by the illumination of a man's face.

"I thought you could use some company." Colin handed him a bottle of brandy and kept one for himself. Rigby took a long guzzle and shuddered when it hit bottom.

"Bloody bad luck about Tim Brooks," said Colin.

"Bad luck had no part in Tim's death. We both know how news travels on the Zambezi. You might as well give me the details, before I hear it from someone else."

Colin acted like he didn't hear his request. "Flatty's got his hands full with that one." He took another swig of brandy.

"You mean Agnes? She's not so bad. You admit, she *has* improved Flatty's social skills."

Colin throttled his cackle to speak. "You d Rhodes means to kill you."

"It's like that, is it? Someone's got to stop might as well be me," Rigby said, quietly.

"May I offer a bit of advice? Let this thi Rhodes go."

"It's gone too far to let it go."

"In that case, there's something I haven't to Colin confessed. "Rumor has it that Rhodes tortur Tim terribly. Some of Rhodes's men were horrif was always popular with the munts. I think because he kept that black mistress."

"You knew about her?" asked Rigby.

"Everyone in Zimbabwe knew about her. I'm have more grisly news. It's about Leon Campbell family."

Rigby listened to his account of the Campbell massacre. When Colin told him it was Ian Rho orchestrated the attack, Rigby reclaimed the bo stood up. He drained it and hurled the empty river.

Choked with emotion, Rigby stared at the mo long time before he spoke. "Leon's daughter same age as my daughter. I hope God forgives me gonna enjoy killing that maggot."

"You can't do it alone. Let me help you insisted.

"Thanks, but I don't need any help."

"You think I'm a drunken old fool, don't you? what people say about me. 'You remember Colin

"Well, for lots of things, not least of which is being a good mate to me. I wanted you to know in case— well, you know."

"Why, it's been my pleasure, Colin." He added as an afterthought, "Better keep the negative comments to ourselves. God only knows what these kids are in for."

"Mum's the word." Colin placed a finger to his lips. He was silent for awhile and then spoke again, "Can I ask you a question?"

"Sure."

"How often do you dream about the war?"

"Every night."

"Thank God. I thought I was the only one."

They started discussing Zimbabwe politics, but the brandy loosened their recollections about Tim Brooks. When Rigby mentioned one of Tim's favorite war stories, Colin pressed him to retell it.

"Tim loved telling about the time we used him as bait," said Rigby.

"Refresh my memory, will you?" Colin requested.

"As I remember— two black scouts marched Tim into a village under the ploy of turning him over to the chief, who was a known terrorist operating here on the Zambezi. Our primary objective was to kidnap the chief. The trick had worked before, but this fella was cagy. To reassure the headsman, my men tore Tim's clothes off and they proceeded to beat him. Of course they pulled their punches. The village women weren't pleased with the beating and joined in."

"As I recall, Tim said that he knew how the Christians felt being thrown to the lions," added Colin, chuckling.

"Exactly. Anyway, Tim was dragged naked before the howling mob. The village women yelled insults about the size of his maleness. Men smeared ash on their faces to mimic his inferior color. Tim said the children would sneak in and bite his ankles. After a heated discussion, the tribeswomen decided they would settle for nothing less than castration. A woman came forward with a pair of sharpened tin-snips to relieve him of his balls. Tim loved to say, that's when the party really got going. Thankfully, the old chief countermanded the women's demand for Tim's nuts."

Colin laughed so hard, he dislodged his partial bridge. Rigby had to stop speaking to allow Colin time to refit his false teeth.

"Where was I? In desperation my men hustled Tim away from the village to a cave where I was hiding. We fired some shots hoping to convince the villagers that Tim had been executed. The deception would have worked perfectly, but the chief thought it might be fun to cut Tim's head off."

"Probably wanted to use it to scare the be-Jesus out of some poor white farmer," offered Colin.

"Undoubtedly. At any rate, I called in an airstrike to end the fiasco. Twenty minutes later, two Vampire jets strafed the village. The operation was a bust."

"Didn't Tim say that he ran headlong into the old gal with the tin-snips when the firing started?"

"He did indeed. He said he was sure she thought he was a ghost."

Both men remained silent as they reflected on other war memories. After a time, Rigby spoke, "Colin, are you awake?" When he didn't get a response, he took off his jacket and draped it over Colin's shoulders.

Rigby tried to dream about more pleasant things, but his recollection focused on the worst day of his life. It was the day his best friend Willie got killed.

"So, Mister Croxford, did you enjoy your leave in Salisbury?" the colonel asked.

"Yes sir."

"That's good. Now, let's get down to business. I'll not sit here and bore you with politics. In my opinion, politics is the work of pimps. We're soldiers— we fix what the politicians screw up. Having said that, what I'm about to tell you comes from the very highest authority."

"Sir, do you mean the prime minister?"

The colonel defused the query by asking another question. "What do you know about the Johnston farm incident?"

"I grew up on a farm next to the Johnston's place. I attended Plum Tree with Seth Johnston. They were like family to me. Naturally, when I heard about the raid, I was horrified."

"I see. Did you know the devils came over from Mozambique? They raped and killed Johnston's daughters— one was only eleven and her sister was twelve. After they killed his little girls, they cut Johnston's throat."

The colonel was clever. He knew I was boiling inside, but the old man wasn't taking any chances, he kept pouring petrol on the fire.

"Johnston had been a friend to the Afro farmers in his district for over thirty years. His wife looked after their sick. He let them water their cattle at his boreholes during droughts. And this is how they repay him?"

"Sir, it's like I told you— they were like family to me. Mrs. Johnston is a saint. What's the latest on her condition?"

"Good God, Croxford, I thought you knew. Mrs. Johnston committed suicide yesterday morning. Poor woman hanged herself."

His words cut into me like a knife. I couldn't breathe. I got up, walked over to a window and leaned on the windowsill for support.

"Croxford, you take your time. Bloody hard times we find ourselves in— bloody hard times, indeed." He waited for me to say something, but I was speechless. "Are you sure you're all right? Perhaps, you'd care for a whiskey."

"No. Really, I'm fine."

"Now then, as I'm sure you know, farmers are the backbone of our economy. Make no mistake about it, without farming, Rhodesia's finished. This barbaric assault on the Johnstons was meant to intimidate our farmers. Attacks like this one could start a mass exodus. We can't let that happen." The colonel supported his multiple chins with his fists as he waited for me to agree.

"No Sir, I guess we can't."

"Precisely, lad. The people who run this country have ordered me to handle this problem as I see fit. I mean to use extreme measures. I'm calling this one, 'Operation Retaliation.' We will take the fight to the enemy. The terrorists' sanctuaries have been off-limits —not anymore.

"You were chosen to lead this operation because you grew up in the area. The Johnston farm sits right on the border. You will do a high altitude low-opening jump into a drop-zone ten kilometers from the Johnston farm. A well-known terrorist sympathizer lives in this village." He indicated a point on the map spread across his desk. "It's here on the Pungwe River."

[229]

"I've been to that village many times."

"So you know the chief? I believe his name's Morgan Chiritsa."

"I've known Chiritsa for years. Is he the sympathizer?"

"He is. Now, let's talk about the two men going in with you. I take it you have confidence in Willie van Piet?"

"The utmost."

"Now, what about the African scout?"

"I'd trust Sam Mabota under all circumstances."

"Is he a Matabele?"

"Yes. Why is that important?"

"This area is part of the Ngorima Tribal Trust Lands, which is Shona territory," he said, spreading his hands over the map. "As we both know, there's a long standing blood feud between the Matabele and the Shona. I mean to exploit that tribal hatred to the fullest extent. You will be operating in a neutral country. If you're captured in Mozambique, I'm afraid you're on your own." He opened the humidor on his desk and selected a cigar. After rolling the cigar between his lips, he lit it. He brushed away the hanging smoke. "Any questions?" he asked, blowing a smoke ring.

"So, Chiritsa's our objective?"

"This is a little more, shall I say, complicated. We need to send a message to these savages. If you harm our women and children, the price you will pay will be horrific. I want the entire village eradicated."

"By eradicated, you mean burned?" The question almost stuck in my throat.

"I want every goat, cow, even the insects killed."

"What about the villagers?"

"It's been decided, under the present circumstances, they're expendable." He banged a fist on his desk with an emphatic smack. "Son, we're fighting for Rhodesia's

[230]

survival. *If you can't stomach this order, I suggest you should back out now. I wouldn't think any less of you."*

"Colonel, I know the area. To send someone else could put the operation at risk."

"Croxford, you're a damn fine credit to your country. Your father would be proud. You know, I served with your old man, may God rest his soul. We fought the Huns back in forty-two. Your father was a hell of a man and a brilliant soldier."

"Thank you, sir."

He patted his desk and stood up, indicating the briefing had ended. *"I think that about covers everything. You have two objectives. First, we must have accurate intelligence on that village. Make sure they're harboring terrorists before you call in the air-strike. Napalm's bloody expensive— we can't afford to waste it. Second, set charges on the bridge indicated on this map. Hopefully, that'll block a counterattack."*

When the colonel shook hands I sensed he was troubled. *"Now, a bit of advice— take it or leave it, it's your call. Five minutes after the vampires make their strafing runs— a special assault group will arrive by helicopters. All of them are Matabele especially trained for this operation. They've got old scores to settle. I don't know if you've ever witnessed Africans in a killing frenzy. Well, let's just say, it's something you'll never forget. You get out of there. I can tell you from past experiences, the nightmares last forever. I know you'll do your duty, Mr. Croxford. Good luck and God's speed."*

A noise startled Rigby, stopping his dream. After awhile, the rhythm of night returned and he closed his eyes. He wiped the cold sweat from his forehead. His shirt was damp. Colin was sleeping peacefully. Again, he

[231]

tried to dream about pleasant things, but his dreaming returned to the war.

The freezing wind worked into my jumpsuit. We huddled trying to steal each other's warmth. A red light flashed on. The jumpmaster worked his way along the C-47's bulkhead holding up three fingers indicating it was three minutes to the drop-zone.

"All right, mates, last check. Good luck, and all that rubbish. See you back at the watering hole. First drink's on me." He turned to get a signal from the pilot. This time he held up one finger.

As I moved closer to the door, I saw my terror reflected in Willie's eyes. Willie's face was buried under a thick beard. Flying at one hundred knots, I could smell him. The colonel had warned us, "If you're gonna fight Africans, you must smell like them. A bush Afro can smell soap at a thousand meters. This isn't a bloody tea dance."

When the light flashed from red to green we fell into space. My only thought was to pull my rip-chord. The drag-chute deployment was followed by the canopy opening— for the moment I wasn't afraid.

Colin's snoring stirred him. "Wake up Colin. Why don't you go back to the boathouse?"
Colin said in a voice thickened by sleep, "Goodnight, mate. See you at first light." Colin shuffled down the incline. Rigby closed his eyes and resumed his dream.

It was a moonlit night. There was only a split second between seeing the ground and hitting it. We gathered up the chutes and waited for Sam to give us the all clear signal. After burying the chutes, we followed Sam into the night.

We passed so close to a herd of elephants I could hear their stomachs grumbling. That's when I heard a soft metallic click, followed by the ear-splitting bang. After the dust settled, I found Willie lying on the ground. He'd stepped on a toe-topper— a Chinese landmine. Part of his boot was missing.

"How bad is it?" I yelled.

"Huh?" Willie cupped his hand behind his ear indicating that he couldn't hear.

"How does it feel?" I yelled louder.

"My foot's gone, isn't it?" Willie asked, refusing to look.

"Your foot's not gone— only a few toes. Your dream of becoming a ballerina is buggered, but you'll walk. Hold on, I'm gonna give you morphine."

"Promise you won't leave me. I wanna see my wife and kids again, damn it." Willie moaned.

"Tomorrow night we'll have sundowners together. Right now, I need you to stay put."

"I'm not going anywhere," Willie answered, in a voice subdued by pain.

"Pity, you're gonna miss the fireworks."

"Be careful. You're my lift home."

It was the last time I saw Willie alive. The next day we found his naked body hanging from a tree. They'd taken his ears and his genitals as souvenirs. Willie's wife cursed me for not bringing her husband's body home for burial. I could never let her see what they'd done to poor Willie.

Rigby fought to stay awake, but the brandy dampened his will. Soon his head slumped forward. A series of images raced through his mind. *A low-flying aircraft followed by napalm— screaming villagers on fire— the stench of burning flesh— helicopters unloading soldiers. And the moment he knew it was an ambush, his guilt melted into fear. He saw himself running behind Sam, stumbling over dead and dying soldiers. The vision of Willie's corpse reappeared.*

He was wide awake and sweaty from anger. He saw a mental picture of Ian Rhodes's face.

*   *   *

Rigby got up early. He was surprised to find Colin already up and busy directing Steven and Ezekiel's work on the boats.

"Getting things ship-shape, as they say," said Colin, cracking his knuckles.

Rigby watched them for a few minutes before speaking. "Colin, you seem awful chipper this morning."

"Why, I've never felt better." Colin's insane giggling was met by unbelieving stares from the men around him.

"I feel like my head's in a vice. I'd like to borrow Steven for a minute," Rigby said.

"He's all yours," said Colin.

Rigby and Steven walked together without speaking. When they were far enough not to be heard, Rigby sat down on a fallen tree trunk and indicated that Steven should sit next to him.

"There's something I need to say to you. It concerns you and Tim Brooks. I don't know how to tell you this, except by getting right to the point. Sam may have raised you, but he wasn't your biological father."

[234]

"What are you saying?"

"Tim Brooks was your real father."

They remained silent for a few long minutes. Steven's expression revealed that his mind was filled with conflicting emotions. "If that's true, why hasn't someone told me about this before?"

"I guess Sam figured it wasn't necessary. He *did* raise you like his own flesh and blood. He died trying to eke out a living for you and the rest of his family."

Steven looked away as he reflected on what he had just heard. "While I was away at the university, someone kept sending me money. It was him, wasn't it?"

"Probably."

"If I'd known the money came from a rapist, I would never have accepted it."

"*Rapist*? Is that what you think?"

"Europeans brought nothing but misery to Africa."

Rigby collected his thoughts and then he said, "Africans were mistreating Africans for thousands of years before the first white man set foot on this continent."

"So that justifies what the whites have done to us?"

"Of course not. Look, the father who raised you was my best friend— Tim was a close second. Next to Sam, he was the finest man I ever knew. Like it or not, you're half-white."

"I'm African where it counts— in here." He pointed at his heart.

"I can't blame you for being upset. There are two things you should know. Your mother and Tim lived together for years. And Tim has left you everything in his will. Thanks to Tim Brooks, you're a wealthy man."

"Your friend didn't have the common decency to come to my mother's funeral. If I take his money, I'm no

[235]

better than he was." Without saying another word, Steven got up and walked away.

That certainly went well enough, Rigby thought sarcastically.

17

Rhodes used his field glasses to study the boat idling towards him. The African steering the boat was standing. Two women and four children were sitting. The narrow channel between two islands was funneling the boat into a perfect killing zone. He estimated the distance at three hundred meters. Just a little closer, he thought, wetting his lips. He felt his breathing stutter. He cleared his eyes of sweat and made a wind check.

"Sergeant, put the crosshairs on his hat. Light wind's on your left. Fire when you're ready."

The sound of the discharge made him jerk and lose the image. When he refocused his binoculars, he saw the boat heading for the shoreline.

They're getting away. Give me your weapon, you idiot," He grabbed the man's rifle.

It wasn't the first time Davy Crockett had taken gunfire. As an army tracker, he was usually on-point and was accustomed to drawing fire. When he heard the bullet whiz overhead, he instinctively ducked. The shot had been fired from his twelve o'clock. He veered left and headed for the riverbank. The current was stronger in the channel. He tried to avoid the shallows, but without sufficient speed, the boat was made rudderless.

The boat made a loud scraping noise as it ran aground. Helen and Sadie jumped over the side to help him wrestle the boat off the snag. After pushing and pulling, the boat floated free. They cheered and scrambled back over the gunnels. Davy gunned the engine and made for the shoreline.

Rhodes watched them through the rifle scope. He inhaled, held his breath and squeezed the trigger. Davy never heard the bullet that struck him. The others weren't sure what had happened. One second he was there, and then he wasn't. Helen grabbed the steering wheel and circled back around to find him, but the current had moved the boat more than she realized.

After searching up and down the river, she anchored the boat on a reed-fringed island.

The icy water numbed Davy until he had no feeling in his limbs. He wanted to splash to get their attention, but he couldn't risk attracting crocodiles.

He was dogpaddling to the shoreline when he saw the gunboat coming towards him. He held his breath and ducked under a floating island of tiger-lilies. The boat passed very close to him, but he remained submerged and unseen. He stayed in the water for a long time. Hypothermia clouded his mind. Davy knew he would die soon, but not before he completed his destiny. A sorcerer had predicted it and sorcerers were never wrong about such serious matters, he thought.

Helen and Sadie continued shouting for Davy as they waded through the thick sedges at the water's edge. When he didn't answer, the women led the children to higher ground above the riverbank. The early rains had incubated mosquitoes. Their insidious whine rose from the disturbed reeds. Clouds of the insects swarmed them, filling their nostrils and their eyes. They screamed and waded blindly into the elephant grass. Helen emerged from the undergrowth and stopped dead in her tracks.

"Good afternoon, Dr. Croxford. I've been waiting for you." Ian Rhodes's eyes betrayed his smile. "Thank God, you're safe. You'll be relieved to know, you *and* your daughter are now under my full protection."

18

The river's reflections sparkled like diamonds in the sun. Its banks were worm-holed by nesting carmine bee-eaters. Great herds of buffalo and elephant watched the rafters drift by. Their course took them underneath mahogany and ebony trees overhanging the river. The trees' branches were covered with social weaverbird nests. The wailing cry of a trumpeter hornbill carried on the water. At times the river grew wider and benign, but on the narrower stretches it moved more swiftly. A fish-eagle swooped down, snatched a fish in its talons and then landed on a nest where it tore off pieces for its nestlings. Under normal circumstances, the rafting would have been glorious, but not now.

Rigby and Colin coached the teenagers before they reached each set of rapids.

"Ready with the paddles!" Colin ordered. "Remember, the horses have to lead the cart." Their raft bounced tenderly over the gentle drops.

Rigby led them to a sandbar to rest.

"Mr. Croxford, do we have to wear these life preservers?" Agnes shouted.

"It's too hot to wear them," added Jacob.

"You're damn right you have to wear them," said Colin.

"Mr. White has more experience on the Zambezi than any man alive. If he says you must keep the life-preservers on, don't argue," said Rigby. "Colin, tell them what they can expect up ahead."

"Before I get started, I noticed some of you dangling your feet in the water. I wouldn't do that, if I were you. I wasn't joking when I told you Africans are taken by crocs every day on the Zambezi."

"So taking a swim is out of the question?" asked Jacob.

"Most definitely," Colin replied. "What you've seen so far is more like a pond, actually. The Tonga say the next part of the river is Satan's work. We affectionately call it the "Devil's Gorge." Mr. Croxford will take the lead— I'll bring up the rear. By hanging back, I can collect any dead bodies." His remark caused quizzical stares.

"Oh, come on. It was a joke, for heaven's sake. Where's your sense of humor? Tourists used to pay me big bucks for a river outing like this one— you're getting it free of charge," Colin giggled.

"Okay, off you go. And don't stop paddling. And remember, watch out for hippos. If you do fall out, you must get back in the raft as quickly as possible."

"Why?" Billy asked.

[241]

"The crocodiles," Jacob said and then added as an afterthought, "At least he's not charging us for collecting our bodies."

"Such a deal. Hey, what bodies? The crocodiles will eat us," said his brother.

The humor was not missed by the others, but their snickers were short-circuited by Colin's stare. "I hope you're all still laughing an hour from now." Colin frowned carefully around his lack of teeth.

Rigby led them to the middle of the river where there was less chance of running aground. The Devil's Gorge lay around the next bend. At first, they saw the mist and then they heard the ominous low rumble.

"So far, so good," declared Agnes.

"My dear lady, this is nothing," said Colin, shaking his head.

"Everyone pay attention. The next two kilometers are a bit tricky. The island up ahead splits the river in two. We must stay to the left of that island, near the Zambian shore. The river's quite a bit tamer on the left."

"What's it like on the right?" Henry asked.

"Someone named the last set of rapids, "the Ladder to Hell." Remember, people, we stay to the left. Let's get on with it."

Rigby's back-paddling allowed the raft to pull ahead. Dutchy pulled hard on his left oar and loafed with his right one to counteract the current. Rigby eased his kayak into position behind them. Colin hung back.

The current was flowing much faster now. The low hiss from the rapids grew louder. Tall illala palms on the island appeared out of a watery mist as promontories.

"He leadeth me beside still waters," yelled Jacob.

"Shut up and paddle," shouted his brother.

Their passage around the island was uneventful and then Dutchy saw the gunboats. He pointed just as the lead gunboat fired a short burst of machine gun fire. The bullets ricocheted on the water. Without hesitating, Rigby yelled, "Follow me!" He paddled straight for the mouth of the Devil's Gorge.

The gorge appeared like a jagged wound cut into the earth's crust. White-barked fever trees clung to the black canyon walls. Yellow mossy lichens and red aloes filled the cracks and crevices. The sheer magnitude of what lay before them lulled the gawking paddlers into complacency.

"People, this isn't the time to stop paddling," Colin shouted.

The first cataract was composed of gradually declining steps. Cheering erupted as their raft bucked gently over each drop. It looked like they might make it, but the gorge narrowed and the Zambezi turned into an angry beast. Their boats were sucked into the turbulence. Within seconds, they were battered and tossed about by giant waves.

Rigby screamed at Billy to paddle, but Billy was paralyzed with fear. Their kayak vaulted over a mountainous swell, buried its bow into the next wave and then was it jettisoned backwards like a missile. Rigby used his paddle to steady the kayak for the next set of rapids, but they were swept over and shot straight to the bottom. The sucking undertow held them under. When he couldn't hold his breath any longer, Rigby pushed hard against his paddle to right the kayak; it came over easily and popped to the surface. Billy had lost his paddle, but somehow he'd managed to hold on. Both came up gasping for air.

There wasn't time to relax; the next set of rapids was already mauling their kayak. "Hold on, Billy!" Rigby shouted above the roar.

Dutchy heaved on the oars to gather enough speed to stay in control, but the overloaded raft was sluggish. The first waterfall was so steep it jackknifed the rubber boat, which launched two paddlers over the bow. Dutchy pulled hard enough to snap an oar. Without steerage, the raft dropped helplessly stern first over a vertical cataract. It flipped over at the bottom, throwing the rest of the paddlers overboard. Their screams were consumed by the river's deafening roar.

Colin eased his kayak into position and then back-paddled, waiting for that split- second when the river was vulnerable. He used a massive wave to propel his tiny boat into the first set of cataracts. It looked like he might smash against some rocks, but, at the last second, he heeled over and missed them. The kayak had seen better days, but never a better oarsman. He surfed down giant waves, pirouetted and then vaulted over each waterfall. It was as if his boat had sprouted wings. Colin didn't fight the river, he tamed it. When it was over, he drifted out of a misty halo at the bottom of the chasm.

Time seemed to standstill, but their run down the ravine was over in minutes. Rigby paddled into a quiet lagoon to wait for the others. When he saw the capsized raft float by, his heart sank.

Ezekiel, Steven and Wanker had managed to stay with the overturned raft. Both men were dazed, but unharmed. Wanker clung to Steven's neck. Rigby chased down the rubber boat, and towed it back to the lagoon. Seconds later, Agnes and Harry floated out of the gorge. They were followed by Dutchy and the Goldman brothers. Colin was counting heads as he back-sculled into the lagoon.

"Did you see Henry and Tish?" Rigby yelled. Colin shook his head no and looked back at the gorge.

Rigby waded out to help Agnes, but she pushed him away. "My God, I never understood the fascination with whitewater rafting. That was thrilling. Someday, I'd like to run those rapids in a kayak. Of course, I'd want Mr. Colin at the helm. No offense, Mr. Croxford," Agnes said. She used her pith-helmet to cover her nipples as she waded ashore.

"Any sign of them?" Rigby hollered again. When Colin shook his head, no, he added, "Well, isn't this just so fucking brilliant."

"What's brilliant?" Agnes asked.

"The rafting, of course," responded Rigby, improvising.

*   *   *

Two scenarios crossed Rigby's mind. That part of the river was too swift for crocodiles, which meant, either they drowned or they managed to climb out of the gorge.

As they waited for Henry and Latisha, Agnes went ballistic. "May I say something?"

"Please do."

"It seems your little river excursion has backfired. They're dead, aren't they?" Her look impaled Rigby.

"Sweetheart, you don't mean what you're saying," said Harry. "Nobody's dead. They probably climbed out of the gorge. Rigby will find them."

"Why didn't we turn ourselves over to those soldiers? They only fired when we refused to stop. We're Americans, for God's sake," stated Agnes. Harry tried to console his wife with a hug, but she untangled herself.

"I haven't got time for this. Harry, tell her," Rigby demanded.

"Aggie, it was the same man who tried to— well, you know. They forced us into the gorge 'oping the river would kill us."

The teenagers were wide-eyed. Agnes pulled away from her husband again and faced Croxford. "This can't be happening to us," she said to him.

"It's happening, all right. Those soldiers will be looking for us. Let's hide the boats."

After camouflaging the boats with papyrus reeds, they split up into two groups. Rigby and Ezekiel would search the gorge for Henry and Latisha. Colin would stay with the boats.

Rigby cornered Colin away from the others. "Think you could run the river at night?"

"I've done it before, but that was when I was young and foolish. It would be risky with greenhorns. Traveling during the day has gotten so dangerous, we may have to give it a go."

"If we're not back by nightfall, you'll know what to do. I'm counting on you, Colin."

Colin smiled and said, "Good luck."

[246]

*   *   *

Rigby and Ezekiel climbed to the top of the ravine. The steep ascent winded them. They stopped to catch their breath.

"Do you think they're still alive?" Ezekiel asked Rigby, peering over the edge.

"The odds aren't good. I reckon their bodies are jammed under a ledge."

"If they're already dead, why are we looking for them?" Ezekiel shivered and looked fearful. Rigby didn't reply because he knew Ezekiel believed the serpent-headed river God, Nyami, had swallowed Henry and Latisha. To search for the bodies was a waste of time.

*   *   *

Henry pulled Latisha over the sandstone rim with his good arm. His other arm appeared broken and hung at his side. He was ashen. He held the wrist of his crippled arm, and hobbled away from the edge. He struggled for balance as he sat down on the ground.

When Latisha saw the others floating downstream, she screamed, "Don't leave us!" Her shouting was consumed by the river.

"Henry, they're leaving us. What are we gonna do?" She wiped her nose on her wrist. "Well, why don't you say something?"

Even breathing added to his misery. Muscle contractions sent shooting spasms into his shoulder.

"What's wrong with you?"

"My shoulder's dislocated. It's an old football injury. Take the zip-lock out of my pocket and roll me one." A muscle twinge made him gasp. She fumbled with the marijuana, but managed to roll him a joint and light it.

"It'll relax me," he murmured, before sucking in a lungful of smoke. "You're gonna have to reset my shoulder. We'll need your shirt. I swear to God, I won't look," he said. His face was contorted by pain. He looked like he was about to faint.

"I'm not taking my shirt off."

"Do it before I pass out." After she struggled out of her soggy shirt, he told her to tie it around his elbow joint and to lie down at a right angle to him on the ground. He had her place one foot on his neck and her other foot under his armpit.

"Wrap your hands around the sleeves and pull as hard as you can."

She did what he asked her to do but his moaning stopped her. "I can't do this, Henry. I want to help you, but I can't."

"You have to." His voice was almost inaudible.

This time, she took a deep breath, closed her eyes and pulled so hard her arms shook. Henry gritted his teeth and groaned. There was a hideous pop as his shoulder snapped back into place. He closed his eyes and sighed. She cradled his head in her lap and used her shirt to daub the sweat from his eyes.

It wasn't fate that had brought them together. Henry saw himself as Latisha's protector. When the raft capsized, he had grabbed her hand as they were tossed overboard. At the risk of drowning, he had pushed her to the surface. The truth was Henry had been infatuated with her for a long time. Now, he found Latisha's doting on him intoxicating.

[248]

He opened his eyes and looked up at her bronze breasts beaded with perspiration. When she looked into his eyes, she saw a reflection of her own thoughts. She pushed him away and turned to hide her nakedness. She put on her shirt, and then turned back to face him. "How does it feel?"

"Sore," he said, massaging his shoulder.

"What're we gonna do?"

"Follow the river, I guess."

"You guess? If you didn't *save* me, I could have floated downriver with the others. Now, I'm stuck in the middle of Africa with a—"

"Oh yeah, as I remember, you were drowning. I just wish you were..."

"Aha. What were you gonna say?" She waggled her finger at him.

"What do you mean, aha?"

"I know what you were gonna say."

"But I didn't say anything."

"You didn't have to. Henry, I wish you looked like Denzel Washington, but you don't. Oh, did I mention, you're dumb."

"Why do you have to be such a bitch?" His eyes revealed pain.

*　　*　　*

They walked without speaking. The soft sand made them weary. The only sound was the insidious buzzing of cicadas. Razor-edged grass shredded their clothes. Henry had to remove embedded thorns from Latisha's feet and his own. Their progress was slowed by the oxbows that criss-crossed their path. Henry used the setting sun as a compass, but the river's life-giving water was like a magnet. They had no means of carrying water and had to continuously backtrack to the river to drink. They drank until their bellies were extended.

The disappearing sun gave urgency to their walking. They stopped on the eroded bank of a wide tributary. The fading light lengthened the shadows. It was silent and windless. They could go no further.

Both of them were frightened by the prospect of sleeping in the bush. Henry acted unconcerned by whistling as he carefully used his last match to start a fire. They sat on opposite sides of the campfire looking into the flames. The fire attracted insects, which attracted feeding bats. Latisha sobbed quietly and brushed her runny nose on the back of her hand.

He tried to comfort her by saying, "I'll bet lots of Africans sleep under the stars."

"Oh, shut up, Henry," she said, sniffling.

He jumped up, walked over to the tree and leaned his forehead against its trunk. His voice sounded wounded. "You hate me, don't you?" He waited for her answer. When he didn't get one, he continued. "Before, when I said, I wish you were—. You didn't know what I was gonna say, did you?"

"Finish it, Henry. You wish I was what."

He looked over at her with an unfamiliar expression. "Nicer. I wish you were nicer. That's all I was gonna say. I wish you were nicer to me."

"Oh come on, Henry. You can do better than that. You wish I was *nicer*?" Her laughter was tainted with suspicion, but when she looked into his eyes, her heart sank. Now what do I say, she asked herself.

"My feet hurt," she blurted out.

"Stop whining. I should have let you drown in the river."

"I'm sorry, Henry. What more can I say?"

He heard her apology, but he took his time acknowledging it. "Oh, it's all right. There was a sheepish grin locked on his dirty face. "I *did* get you to take your shirt off."

"I bet you can't wait to tell your buddies."

"I'll never tell them."

"We'll see about that." The tiny evidence of a grin pinched the corners of her mouth.

She tried to relieve the awkwardness by saying, "So, Henry, tell me about your family."

"I was raised by a bunch of foster parents. I got into a few scraps with the police, nothing serious, mind you, but it was an excuse for them to dump me. I was always good at sports— that's why our school wanted me. What about you?"

She started to answer him, but the sound of rustling leaves stopped her. "What was that?"

"It's nothing. You were saying," he said, acting blasé to reassure her.

She continued to stare into the night as she spoke. "My parents are divorced. I *was* living with my mother and her latest live-in. He was getting a little too friendly, if you know what I mean. That's when she sent me off to boarding school."

A lion's roaring quieted her. "Whatever that is— it sounds close." She hugged her knees under her chin and shivered. Suddenly the night was filled with the booming growls of a dominant lion and his would-be successor. The bellowing ended with a series of deep grunts.

"I think it's safe as long as we keep the fire going. Let's try to get some sleep."

Henry yawned and closed his eyes. "Goodnight, Tish."

Latisha was too petrified to close her eyes. The night sounds were terrifying. It started with a growl and a squealing warthog. Glowing eyes stared back at her. She thought she saw silhouettes moving. Her whisper was followed by a wet sniffle. "Henry, I know you're awake. If I come over there, it doesn't mean anything."

He faked a yawn, nodded acceptance and raised his arm as an invitation. She walked around and sat down next to him. She ended up falling asleep with her head in his lap.

During the night, she was awakened by stomach cramps. "I'm gonna be sick," she groaned. She jumped up, ran into the bushes and vomited. Henry followed her. When she tried to push him away, he insisted on holding her. Dry-heaving weakened her so much; he had to carry her back to the campfire. After a few minutes, she fell into a twitchy sleep.

Tending the fire kept Henry up for most of the night. As the cruelty of the African night abated, he catnapped.

Twittering river birds signaled sunrise. Henry's stomach grumbles woke him up. "I wish there was a way to boil our water." He ran behind a tree clutching his stomach. He threw up loudly.

They started walking as sunlight gave form to the land. The blood-streaked sky was a stage for cauliflower clouds on the horizon. Some of the darker clouds had slanted rain underneath them. The morning air, freshened by night dew, made their walking tolerable, but soon the sun became unbearable. They were so exhausted they collapsed under an ancient teak tree. Almost immediately, both of them dozed off.

Henry was shocked when he opened his eyes. An old man stood over him. The African wore nothing but a fur hat. His body bore the telltale signs of a life in the bush. Among his glossy scars were those of a failed leopard attack and a healed knife wound delivered by a jealous husband.

Henry nudged Latisha with his foot. "Wake up, we've got company."

When she saw the old African, she screamed, which shocked the man. He jumped back and brushed the flies away from his face.

"He's gonna kill us," she yelled, cowering behind Henry.

"We don't have any money," declared Henry. The old man smiled, but gave no reply. There was something calming, almost grandfatherly about him.

"We're both sick. It's from the river water," Henry explained, pointing at his stomach and pretending to regurgitate. The man seemed to understand, but remained silent.

The African started a fire and boiled some water in a charred pot he took from his knapsack. He added dried leaves and seeds to the water and handed a tin can of the contents to Henry, who sniffed it and turned up his nose.

"He's trying to poison you," Latisha warned in a low voice. The concoction attracted a cloud of gnats.

"I'm so sick, I don't give a shit." Henry shooed the bugs away, downed the contents and gagged. The man helped Latisha up into a sitting position and held the cup to her lips. She tried to push the cup away, but he persisted until she drained it.

"I wish you could speak English." Henry said.

"But I do speak English, my son," stated Davy Crockett.

Latisha and Henry's lethargy made even talking difficult. Davy knew he needed to feed them. They looked too weak to walk more than a few steps, let alone make it to the island where he hoped to find Helen, Sadie and the children.

Earlier, he'd borrowed a cooking pot and some matches from a fishing village near the river. Food was so scarce he was hard-pressed to ask the villagers for any. He left Henry and Latisha and set out to scavenge for food. The crocodile nests he discovered had already been invaded by monitor lizards— the eggs were reduced to punctured ping-pong shells. The guinea fowl he encountered were too wary to be hit with stones. If he had more time, he could have set snares. In desperation, he climbed a tree to gather the mopani grubs that hadn't morphed into the emperor moths they would become. The wiggly grubs were as thick and long as a man's finger. He plucked them from the lower dead branches and dropped them to the ground. With his pot brimming with squirming grubs, he started back.

Davy found them awake, but they were too weak to sit up. He sat down on a log next to the campfire and prepared the grubs for cooking. He squeezed each one like a tube of toothpaste; it squirted a bright green gooey liquid. The sight was enough to make Latisha gag. "I'm not eating worms," she insisted.

Davy giggled and said, "To my people, mopani grubs are a gift from God." He plopped one into his mouth and smacked his lips. "My children, you are too weak to walk. You must eat and regain your strength, or I'll be forced to leave you." Telling the lie made Davy uneasy. "The man who did this to me will be looking for us," he said, showing them his bullet wound that was oozing yellow pus.

"I'll try one," Henry said. "Me too," added Tish. As they chewed, their scowls curled up into guarded smiles. "They taste like peanut butter crackers," acknowledged Henry.

Davy knew they were the missing American tourists he'd heard rumors about. He decided to let them find out who he was. When he mentioned the name Croxford, a light of recognition switched on. Sometimes, it's better to let strangers figure out things on their own, Davy thought. He laughed inwardly at how one minute they were sure he meant to kill them and now they treated him like he was their father.

Fortified by mopani grubs and Davy's secret potion, Henry and Latisha showed marked improvement. Davy's wound had turned septic, but he gave no sign of discomfort. As soon as they were able to walk, he led them to where he'd hidden the boat.

As they rested in the shade before casting off, Davy heard a noise. He left them to investigate. When he returned, he was accompanied by a young boy. Davy and the boy carried on a heated discussion in Shona that ended with Davy's looking troubled. After the boy gave them some milk, he left them to tend to his father's goats. Henry questioned Davy about what the boy said, but the old man was evasive.

Davy glanced downriver and sighed. In his heart was a sharp regret. Tim had asked him to look after Helen and the others and he'd failed. The Shona boy had told him Helen, Sadie and the children were now prisoners of Ian Rhodes.

*   *   *

19

Heat waves rose like gas fumes from the tarmac. The road dissected a leafless khaki colored forest. An antique bus spewing black smoke struggled up a steep hill on the outskirts of Victoria Falls. The bus was stuffed with passengers. Some women riders had babies lashed to their stomachs in dirty-white crocheted shawls. A few men rode precariously on the roof.

A black Mercedes wedged between two olive-green Land Rovers, drew guarded stares from the bus passengers as the convoy sped pass them.

Dr. Jeremiah Hitler Seke, the new president of Zimbabwe, stared back indifferently at the bus travelers. Ian Rhodes sat next to Seke in the chauffeur-driven Benz.

Seke was a Polish educated African doctor who had been the head of Mugabe's secret police before becoming president. Next to Mugabe, he was the most feared man in all of Zimbabwe. His private torture chamber was infamous. The man who supplied Seke with political prisoners was Ian Rhodes.

When rebels ousted Robert Mugabe, Seke used the distraction to seize power for himself. Seke smiled inwardly reflecting on the criticism he received when he included Rhodes in his coup. Rhodes was white, which made him an outsider, but by giving Rhodes absolute authority over all of Matabeleland, he was putting the most ruthless man he had ever known in charge of a potentially problematic region.

The United Nations had condemned Seke's takeover. What he needed was a game-changer to soften world condemnation. If he could legitimize his presidency, the foreign aid spigot would reopen. Without money to pay off his accomplices, all was lost. Time was running out.

When President Seke learned that five American teenagers and their chaperone were lost somewhere on the Zambezi, he was mildly interested. When the foreign press called the tourists' disappearances politically motivated kidnappings, he was horrified. To make things worse, the American government was holding him personally responsible. His surprise visit was intended to show that he was taking charge of the rescue effort.

At a private meeting, Rhodes had presented an interesting stratagem. He suggested killing the American tourists and then blaming their deaths on Seke's political opponents. As he explained, initially there might be criticism, but in the end, the move would legitimize

Seke's absolute authority over Zimbabwe. Seke accepted the plan without reservations.

Seke glanced over at Rhodes and realized, having you around me, is like sleeping with a cobra. I must move cautiously.

Seke's convoy turned at a side road leading to the airport. After driving through the security gate, they stopped at the foot of a gangway to a Boeing 737.

He grabbed Rhodes's arm. "Before I go, I want to make sure you understand how dangerous our situation has become. If these deaths are linked to me or anyone in my administration, it would be disastrous. There can be no witnesses."

Seke's eyes were so disturbing few men could withstand his gaze. Rhodes was no exception. "Mr. President, it shall be done as you ordered," he said, looking down.

"Good. I have confidence in you, comrade. There's one more thing. We must have photographs as evidence." He grabbed Rhodes's hand and looked into his eyes. "Your success will be rewarded beyond your wildest dreams. And failure— well, let's not talk about failure." His smile made the hair on Rhodes's neck stand up.

Seke was ushered up the air-stairs by two soldiers. Rhodes stood at attention and saluted as the Boeing taxied away from the ramp.

As soon as the aircraft lifted off, he was escorted to a Chinese attack helicopter that would fly him back to his encampment on the Zambezi River.

*   *   *

The Z-10 helicopter swooped down the river below treetop level. Rhodes stared blindly at the landscape passing beneath him. The pilot pointed at a Cape buffalo, but Rhodes showed no interest. The solitary bull shuffled up the riverbank, spun around to face the noisy intruder and then lost his nerve and disappeared into a thicket. Submerged boulders that had been polished by the tireless current looked like hippos. Flocks of open-billed storks took to the air. Crocodiles exploded into the water as the copter passed overhead.

Two native fishermen in a dugout canoe shaded their eyes to look up at the helicopter as it flew by. Rhodes ordered the pilot to turn around and make another low pass over the fishermen. The helicopter flew so low, the rotor-wash from its twin turbo-shaft engines beat its wake into white foam. The fishermen waved as the helicopter raced towards them. Without warning, Rhodes unlocked the thirty-millimeter cannon on the helicopter's nose and opened fire. A steady stream of bullets kicked up water as the helicopter bore down on the helpless men. At the last second, the fishermen jumped overboard. Rhodes burst out laughing as he glanced over his shoulder at the bullet riddled canoe. The bobbing fishermen hurled obscene gestures.

Up ahead, a herd of elephants browsed leisurely on reeds at the river's edge. The matriarch of the herd used her trunk to vacuum up muddy water and spray it over her calf. Alerted by the sound of the approaching helicopter, she rumbled a warning. The elephants shuffled away from the river as the sound grew louder.

Rhodes's blood lust wasn't satisfied. When he saw the elephants, he ordered his pilot to fly directly at them. The elephants charged into a jesse thicket and disappeared. Bullets shredded the leaves, narrowly missing the cowherd. Rhodes threw up his hands in frustration. He twirled his finger, indicating he wanted to try another strafing run. The pilot obliged him by flying at the herd from a different direction. The elephants burst into a clearing just as Rhodes opened fire. The thirty-caliber projectiles ripped into a young female's back, severing her spine. Her mother abandoned the safety of the canopy and raced back to defend her. The old matriarch used her tusks to try to lift her daughter, but the elephant was paralyzed. The herd surrounded the downed elephant as the helicopter raced away.

Rhodes was exhausted. He rubbed his temples and closed his eyes. Almost immediately, his head drooped forward. A long sting of drool hung from his lower lip. Seconds later, a bad dream caused a convulsive jerk, and he was awake.

The pilot decreased the copter's airspeed, banked sharply into the wind, hovered briefly and then landed in a clearing encircled by tents. Rhodes stooped below the spinning rotor and emerged from the swirling dust cloud. He walked to the mess-tent where his subordinates were having afternoon tea and biscuits.

Even though Rhodes had been sober for three days, his hands shook so violently he needed both hands to calm his teacup. He took a sip before speaking. "Gentlemen, you'll be pleased to hear my meeting with the president went well." He told them about his plan to murder the American tourists and blame the political opposition for the killings. As they listened, some of his men looked distressed.

"How far upriver are the Americans?" Rhodes asked.

The soldier answering had not healed from the injuries inflicted by Agnes Flaxney. His mouth was so swollen his words were garbled. Rhodes leaned forward to better understand him. He seemed distracted when he learned his quarry had split-up into two groups. "So, Croxford's no longer with the main party?"

"Our spies say he's following the main group in a kayak. Two Americans may have already drowned."

"It seems the Zambezi is doing our work. Mr. Chitoa, tell me what you know about Steven Mabota?" Joseph Chitoa was sitting at the opposite end of the table and was so preoccupied with stuffing cookies into his mouth he didn't hear the question. When Rhodes didn't get an answer, he jumped up and threw his teacup at Chitoa. The cup ricocheted off of Chitoa's forehead.

"Stop filling your face and pay attention," Rhodes hissed.

Before Chitoa could answer, Rhodes held up his hand to stop him. He was distracted by a waiter serving tea. "Does this hideous creature have a security clearance?"

Moses tried to smile, but his deformity twisted his face into an idiotic grin. Rhodes continued his tirade. "I've never seen this man before. I'm surrounded by idiots. If we're not careful, we'll all face a firing squad. You may think you're immune, but you don't know Seke like I do. I hate to think about how many people we killed during..." Rhodes never finished the sentence.

Chitoa came to attention and rubbed the lump on his forehead as he spoke. "This man was maimed by Croxford in a prison fight. I'll vouch for him."

The information appeased Rhodes. He waved at Chitoa to continue. "Sir, Mabota spent the last two years in Hwange prison. He was sentenced for violating the Sedition Act."

"If we make Mabota the ringleader, I must know more about the man. Who were his friends in prison?"

"Rigby Croxford was Mabota's protector. Croxford and Mabota's father served together in the bush war." Chitoa's dry mouth impaired his speech.

"Comrade Chitoa stays, the rest of you get out!" Rhodes screamed at the soldiers.

"Perhaps, you don't understand what's at stake here," Rhodes yelled, after they were alone. "If this government fails, you and I will share the same fate, my friend. And I can assure you, it won't be pretty." To emphasize the point, he imitated the cutting of his throat.

"What does any of this have to do with me? I was only a warden."

"A warden who starved prisoners by selling their food on the black market?" Rhodes asserted.

Chitoa buried his face in his hands. "My children were starving," he sobbed. "Tell me what you want me to do?"

"How do I know I can trust you?" Rhodes asked. He leaned forward, unsheathed a pistol hidden under the table and pointed it at Chitoa's belly.

"You wanted Croxford's daughter and I delivered her." This man is crazy, Chitoa thought, looking at Rhodes.

Chitoa's reminder satisfied Rhodes; he leaned back and uncocked his revolver. "Go to Croxford. Tell him I have his wife *and* his daughter. And take *that* with you." He glared at Moses who was standing outside of the tent.

"Croxford's more cunning than a leopard. He may not come to the bait."

"You let me worry about Croxford. Just do as you're told."

Chitoa nodded his acceptance. Rhodes motioned, indicating Chitoa should leave him. After Rhodes was

[263]

alone, he resumed his sulking over the map on his field-desk.

*   *   *

Later that night, Chitoa stared at the star-studded sky as he reflected on his dilemma. The men sleeping around him were snoring peacefully, but he was too conflicted to sleep. When Rhodes described the plan to kill Rigby Croxford and his family and the Americans, Chitoa was horror-struck. He found himself entrapped in a plot to kill the man who spared his life during the war. To make things worse, he had led Croxford's daughter, a woman who had shown him great kindness, to what would surely be her death. I am a gazelle sleeping with a hungry lion, he surmised. I can do nothing but wait for the lion to eat me. He pulled the blanket over his face and closed his mind.

The next morning, Joseph Chitoa and Moses left in a gunboat accompanied by four armed soldiers. Their orders were to proceed upriver and intercept Croxford. Rhodes chose Moses to accompany Chitoa, because he knew Moses possessed a deep-seated hatred for the man who disfigured him. Rhodes's last order was to spare only one person, Rigby Croxford.

*   *   *

The slanted trees along the shoreline were burdened by flowered creepers and ropy vines. Native women washing clothes and fishermen mending nets waved at Colin's group as they floated by. Colin navigated the Zambezi around the clock. Few men could have taken them downriver in darkness, but he was sober now and led them without incident to a spot ten kilometers upriver from where Rhodes waited in ambush.

A few times Colin came ashore to leave telltale signs for Rigby. An oddly broken limb or an overturned rock would be overlooked by most men, but to Rigby and Ezekiel, they stood out like road signs.

Despite Harry's encouragements, Agnes turned inward as she considered Henry and Latisha's fate. More than once, Harry caught his wife sobbing and tried to console her. Agnes's mood dampened the group's collective spirit. Their paddling in silence pleased Colin who warned, "Sound travels on water like a telegraph wire."

*   *   *

Colin's group waited for Rigby at their predetermined rendezvous island. They didn't have to wait long; Rigby arrived two days later.

Colin stood with his hands on his hips watching Rigby's kayak bump up against the shoreline. Dutchy and the rest of the group gathered around.

"Well done, mate. What took you so long?" asked Colin.

"Any luck?" inquired Dutchy.

Rigby gave them thumbs down. "Odds are they climbed out," he replied, prevaricating.

Agnes twisted free from Harry and ran away.

20

Rhodes set his snare. His men dragged two fifty-caliber machine guns into position. Five hundred meters upriver, thirty men armed with AK-47s manned the top of the gorge.

He'd ordered Joseph Chitoa to offer Croxford a chance to be reunited with his wife and daughter. If Croxford declined his offer, it would be his death warrant. There was nothing left to do but wait for his quarry to take the bait.

The hours passed slowly, and then a lookout spotted a kayak entering the gorge. Rhodes focused his binoculars, but the setting sun distorted his view. He thought he recognized Joseph Chitoa and Moses as the paddlers. The blindfolded man between them was hunched over in a dejected slouch. As the kayak got closer, Rhodes recognized Rigby Croxford.

"Hold your fire. Let them pass," Rhodes yelled, refocusing his field glasses. From his vantage point one hundred meters above the river, he could see Croxford had been beaten. His clothes were shredded and his blindfold was blood-stained. Rhodes grinned as he imagined Croxford suffering. It will be my distinct pleasure watching you die, he thought.

He was about to walk down to meet the beached kayak, when he saw one of his men pointing at something else floating in the river. Clouds blocking the sun made it hard to see, but when his eyes adjusted he saw bodies floating face down around a semi-submerged rubber boat. There was a body clad in a clinging dress hanging over the stern. The body's head bobbed in the water. The bottom of the raft was awash in bloody foam. As the raft got closer, Rhodes was sure it was Harry's wife. He rubbed his genitals as he recollected their brief encounter.

"Sergeant, have the men commence firing at will. And get those photographs."

The crack and whistle of gunshots echoed in the gorge. The soldiers riddled the bodies with continuous gunfire until their magazines were empty. Bullets hitting flesh made meaty thumps. The raft was now totally deflated and slid over the rapids like a flattened slinky. Gunfire decapitated the woman. Agnes's pith-helmet floated nearby. Rhodes started to order his men to retrieve the bodies, but the rumbling hiss of Victoria Falls changed his mind. Let the crocodiles do their dirty work. Besides, I've got the photographs.

*   *   *

[267]

Johannesburg, South Africa

The American ambassador to South Africa pushed back his tortoiseshell half-rounds and squinted through a magnifying glass at a grainy photograph; it was one of several photos strewn helter-skelter across his desk. A deep worry-wrinkle erupted between his eyes. He washed his face with his hands and shook his head. The men around his desk also shook their heads as they examined the pictures.

The director of the South African security police, sitting in a chair facing the ambassador, spoke. "They had no business in Zimbabwe," His English was tainted by Afrikaans.

"You're positive it's them?" the ambassador asked the director without opening his eyes. "God help us if we've made a mistake."

The director used a ballpoint pen to direct the group's attention to the woman lying face-down in the overturned raft. "We're certain this one's the Flaherty woman. These bodies floating around the rubber raft are her students. Look, I wish it weren't true, but these photographs are conclusive evidence. They're all dead."

"So what happened to their bodies?" asked the ambassador.

"I guess they were swept over Victoria Falls. This *is* Africa. I would imagine the crocs took them."

"Is that what you want me to tell their parents? Sorry, no bodies for burial. Crocodiles ate your children?"

"Mr. Ambassador, have a look," another man said, pointing at the television monitor. The CNN headlines running across the bottom of the screen read: *Death on the Zambezi River. Six American tourists killed by terrorists in Zimbabwe.*

President Seke appeared on camera with a microphone stuck in his face. He made the following statement in a compassionate tone of voice:

> "I send my heartfelt condolences to the families of the murdered American tourists. We Zimbabweans have suffered during our long struggle to free ourselves from the yokes of our oppressors, Great Britain and the United States. Those governments must shoulder the blame for this atrocity, because they supported the rebels. We share a special bond with the grieving families, because, like them, we have also lost sons and daughters.
>
> "I have captured the criminals responsible for this vile act. We have obtained written confessions. Rest assured— I will deal with these

perpetrators by the harshest measures imaginable."

Seke pushed the reporters aside, walked offstage and disappeared behind a black curtain.

The ambassador muted the television's volume before responding, "Seke never misses an opportunity to bash the United States. He knows we had no part in this."

"Mr. Ambassador, will you hold a press conference?" a man asked.

"It's too late for that."

"For the life of me, I can't imagine what it's like for their parents." He pushed the intercom button on his desk.

"Ms Johnson, I need two aspirin."

*   *   *

Connecticut
Saint Paul's Academy

The headmaster was middle-aged with a paunch and duplicated chins. His hair was a shade too dark to be natural. He held Agnes Flaherty's letter of resignation to the light to examine his backdating for imperfections. He rechecked the date to make sure it coincided with a date before her departure. His forgery wouldn't absolve the school, but it might save his job. Is it my fault she took her students on an unauthorized side-trip to Zimbabwe? No, of course not, he thought, optimistically.

He had allowed Agnes to make the school's first overseas fieldtrip because he was afraid she might tell his wife about their affair. One trip led to another, and before he knew it, students were lining up to make the summer excursions. The school awarded the students with academic credits for the trips, which according to the school's attorney, made them legally responsible for the students. The parents had signed indemnity forms, but

[271]

the students had been killed in Zimbabwe, a country that was under a restrictive travel advisory issued by the State Department.

A commotion outside snapped him out of his daydream. He pulled back the curtain and peeked. A television crew and a reporter were interviewing someone he didn't recognize at first, and then it dawned on him. Oh no, it's Jacob and Joshua Goldman's father, the New York attorney.

*　　*　　*

21

72 hours earlier

Joseph Chitoa feigned loose bowels as an excuse to go ashore. He needed to talk to Moses in private. As the gunboat pushed up against the shoreline, Chitoa turned to Moses. "You come with me. The rest of you stay put. Take this," he said, handing Moses a pistol.

After they were alone, he confronted Moses. "Do you know we've been sent to kill the Americans?" When he didn't see the revulsion he had hoped for, he pressed Moses with another question. "Rhodes means to kill Croxford's family." Moses's lack of trepidation evoked an even more pointed question. "His daughter treated your wound. Don't you care what happens to her?"

"Croxford has marked me," Moses said, pointing at his mouth. "His women mean nothing to me." He was ugly-faced with hatred.

"It's too bad you feel that way. I'm afraid I must leave you here," he said to Moses. Upon hearing this, Moses fired his pistol point-blank at Chitoa's face. The click from the empty chamber startled him. He continued pulling the trigger and then stopped to inspect the revolver as if it were somehow defective.

The bullet hitting Moses hardly staggered him. He stared momentarily at the smoke curling from Chitoa's pistol, and then fell to his knees before falling face-down in the sand. He began to shake violently. A death rattle sounded from the depths of his lungs. Moses's eyes were unmoving and his mouth lay open.

The gunshot brought the soldiers. "Bandits tried to rob us," Chitoa gasped. After the soldiers carried Moses's body back to the boat, they set out to search the island. As soon as they disappeared, Chitoa started the outboard, backed the gunboat out into the river and headed upstream.

*   *   *

*I*n Harry's haste to escape from Rhodes, he neglected to grab some ammunition. Rigby had one round in the chamber and two more in reserve. Colin White was down to six shells. Rigby hated to waste rounds, but he needed to feed his group. He set off with Ezekiel to find an animal to shoot. Not far from the river, they came upon a herd of grazing impalas intermixed with foraging baboons. A sentinel baboon barked a warning, but not soon enough. Rigby killed a ram with a perfect heart shot. As they were field-dressing the antelope, Ezekiel froze and whispered, "*Baba*, we're not alone. Someone is watching ."

Joseph Chitoa walked into the clearing with his hands raised.

"Well, I'll be damned. You're the last person I ever expected to see," Rigby exclaimed.

"I...I've... come to warn you." Chitoa stuttered and his hands trembled.

"Shit, warden, what happened to your teeth?"

Chitoa ignored the question. Without hesitating, he told him about Rhodes's ambush. As Rigby listened, his eyes expressed suspicion. When Chitoa stated that Rhodes was holding Helen *and* his daughter, it was as if someone stabbed Rigby in the gut with a dull knife. Pain flooded his face as he spoke. "My daughter was supposed to be in Cape Town."

"I met your daughter at the Kasane border crossing. I led her to Rhodes," admitted Chitoa. "I didn't think he would hurt her. I'm sorry."

"You're sorry?" Rigby walked over and leaned his head against a tree trunk. With his back turned, he asked, "Did Rhodes send you?"

"Yes, but that's not why I came."

It was awhile before Rigby spoke. When he did, he turned and gave Chitoa a disbelieving look. "Why should I trust you?"

When Chitoa didn't reply, Ezekiel intervened in his behalf, "In my heart, I trust him."

"Now that I've disobeyed Rhodes, he will kill me," added Chitoa in his own defense.

"If you're telling me the truth, Rhodes would have killed you anyway. He can't afford witnesses."

Chitoa's eyes revealed that he was frightened.

Rigby wrapped the dead impala around his neck and motioned for Chitoa to lead the way. They followed him to a lagoon where he'd hidden the gunboat. As Ezekiel climbed onboard he was startled by Moses's corpse.

Rigby waved the blowflies away from the dead man's face. He's done for," he said, feeling his pulse.

"Who killed him?"

"I did," Chitoa answered.

"Well done," said Ezekiel, devoid of sympathy.

*   *   *

*D*utchy alerted the group that a gunboat was coming into view. As soon as he recognized Joseph Chitoa, Rigby and Ezekiel, he directed Colin White's attention on Chitoa. Colin took a bead on Chitoa's head with his .300 Mag.

"Why, it's my old friend, the warden. This ought to be bloody interesting," Dutchy remarked. "I'll walk down and meet them. If Chitoa makes a move, shoot him straight away."

"With pleasure, sir," replied Colin, saluting.

Chitoa came ashore with his hands raised. Dutchy motioned for everyone to come forward, which they did with caution. Rigby asked the group to listen to Chitoa's account of Rhodes's ambush plan. When Chitoa finished speaking, Rigby held up his hand to stop their questions.

"I believe this man's telling the truth, because basically, he has no reason to lie. Here's the way I see it. If we stay put, Rhodes will eventually send his men to sort us out. And if we head downriver, they'll ambush us. I believe there *is* a way to get all of you out of Zimbabwe."

Agnes's voice was choked by grief. "Mr. Croxford, this can't be happening."

"Agnes, you keep saying the same thing." He waited for her delayed reaction.

[276]

"It's just that..." She was too choked up to finish her rebuttal.

"Now, where was I? We used a similar hoax during the war, and rather effectively I might add. We affectionately called it the 'Tethered Goat Deception.' If we can pull it off, you could all be headed home in a few days."

"Your last little misadventure killed Henry and Latisha. For God's sake, you can gamble with my life, but they're only children."

Rigby retorted by saying, "God has no role in this. Ian Rhodes has done some despicable things in his life— killing children means nothing to him. Henry and Latisha are tough kids— I wouldn't write them off, at least not yet. If you've got a better idea, let's hear it."

She nodded for him to continue. "Agnes, I'll need one of your dresses and your boots. I want each of you kids to bring me a set of your clothing. Hats would be brilliant. I must have your pith helmet, Agnes. Oh, and I need one of your brassieres. And cold cream, any kind will do. Face powder, if you have it."

"What on earth do you want with my bra?"

"You'll see."

Rigby sent Dutchy and Colin on a baboon hunt. One hour later, they dragged four dead baboons into the clearing. Ezekiel cut off their tails. Steven helped him dress the apes in the teenagers' clothes. The teenagers were mortified, as was Agnes, but not as much as Wanker— the monkey clung to Harry's neck and refused to watch their gruesome work.

Rigby and Colin dressed Moses's corpse in Agnes's dress. They stuffed her bra with grass and fastened it around the corpse's chest. Colin smeared the dead man's face with cold cream and then dusted it with baby powder.

Rigby stepped back to admire the makeover. "You have to admit, the lipstick and the bra are nice touches. You know something, Colin, she, or rather he, does look a little like your last wife."

"Nonsense, my wife was much uglier." Colin chuckled and then turned serious. "Think it will fool them?"

"Chitoa says Rhodes's men are hiding above the gorge. If we enter at sundown, the fading light might do the trick."

"And if it doesn't?" Colin asked Rigby.

"God help us."

Rigby reviewed his plan as he watched the teenagers gorge themselves on impala fillets. He couldn't help but think that this might be their last meal. He would pose as a captive in the lead kayak with Chitoa and Steven Mabota pretending to be his guards. The only assurance that Rhodes wouldn't open fire was that Chitoa said Rhodes wanted him alive. Part of the deception was the rubber-raft and the corpse dressed like Agnes, and the floating baboons made to look like the teenagers. Colin and Dutchy would wait for nightfall before drifting through the gorge in the stolen gunboat. The island where Rigby had hidden the weapons cache was five kilometers downriver from Rhodes's encampment. Dutchy, Steven and Colin could use those weapons to rescue Rigby and the others. Harry would use the diversion to get his wife and the teenagers safely across the border into Zambia.

*   *   *

*C*olin towed the partially deflated rubber raft into position. Rigby's kayak remained lashed to the gunboat. As Rigby pushed off, Agnes asked, "Are you sure this is necessary?"

"You've met Ian Rhodes— what's your opinion?"

"He's a psychopathic sadist."

"I rest my case." He paused, daring her to disagree.

"Please tell me you'll be safe," she said at last.

"Don't worry about me— worry about them," he said, smiling at the teenagers. "All right then, let's get cracking." A split second later, he was gone.

Colin and Dutchy arranged the body and baboons in the rubber raft and set it adrift. As they waited for nightfall, they heard distant gunfire. When it ended there was only the low purring growl of the rapids.

*   *   *

*A*fter paddling through the ambush unharmed, Chitoa, Steven and their make-believe prisoner, Rigby, came ashore at Rhodes's campsite. Steven, who was unknown to Rhodes, mingled into the crowd as Rigby was taken into custody.

Right on schedule, Colin's group drifted silently past the camp undetected a few hours later.

*   *   *

*D*avy Crockett's septic gunshot wound poisoned his blood. He'd watched men die from bullet wounds before and he knew he would die soon. Only his will to find Helen, Sadie and the children was keeping him alive.

[279]

Davy rambled to himself as he guided Henry and Latisha through the torturous razor grass. During his more lucid moments, he asked them questions to divert their attention from the misery.

With their new protector sleeping near them, the nights were not as terrifying for the young couple. They fell asleep talking to each other about what they would do and what they would eat when they got home. The days bore on as endlessly as the river. On the third day of hiking, they emerged from a grassy riverbank with a view of Livingstone Island.

The green speck on the watery horizon made them duck for cover. As soon as they realized it was Colin White paddling a kayak, Henry and Latisha started jumping up and down and yelling at the top of their lungs. Colin saw them and changed course immediately.

Latisha threw her arms around Colin as he came ashore. Henry and Davy were more reserved. As Davy listened to Colin, he was so shocked by what he heard, he had to lean on Henry for support. Exultation evaporated into despondency.

*   *   *

*J*ust before dawn, Chitoa was awakened and escorted by two armed soldiers back to the river. When he got there, he saw Rhodes and some of his men gathered around something floating in the shallows.

"Care to explain this?" asked Rhodes. He used a flashlight to illuminate a dead baboon dressed in a red Harvard jersey and blue jeans.

"What's wrong, cat got your tongue?" Chitoa was too petrified to speak. He shook his head no, but he was unconvincing.

"Lock him up with Croxford."

It didn't take the soldiers long to recover the remaining dead baboons and what was left of Moses. As Rhodes surveyed the bodies, fear overwhelmed him. A time-bomb was ticking. He'd radioed Seke and told him that all of the American tourists were dead, and that the photographs of the dead bodies were being delivered by helicopter. Now he knew it was all a hoax. If he could kill the Americans within the next twenty-four hours, it might save his life.

*   *   *

*R*igby was afraid that Joseph Chitoa would break under interrogation. He had prepared Chitoa by telling him, "You must fake terrible pain *before* they hurt you." He hoped Rhodes wouldn't use members of the Shona tribe to torture Chitoa, who was Matabele. Rhodes had used tribal racism before in interrogating prisoners. The handpicked Shona tormentors showed no mercy. After beating Chitoa senseless, they dragged him feet-first to a bamboo cage that held Rigby.

Rigby had also been beaten. His eyes were almost swollen shut, but his injuries weren't as severe. For some reason, his assailants allowed him to stuff bits of cotton cloth into his nostrils and around his teeth to prevent any real damage. One soldier even gave him water.

After they were alone, he whispered to Chitoa, "The soldiers are pulling their punches. They have no stomach for torture. Steven Mabota will rescue us."

Chitoa's response was barely audible. "Maybe they have no stomach for torturing you, but they seem to enjoy hurting me. If you're counting on Mabota to save us, we're in big trouble. He told me he didn't care what happened to you or your family."

"Steven said that?"

"Yes. I can't last much longer."

"If you give up, he'll kill us both," Rigby warned.

"I'm curious," mumbled Chitoa, spitting up blood. "Do I look as bad as you do?"

Rigby squinted painfully and said, "I reckon we probably look about the same."

"Now I am very afraid," Chitoa whispered.

Rigby and Chitoa were marched to Rhodes's command tent. A soldier removed their blindfolds, but not their manacles. As their eyes adjusted to the light, they saw Rhodes sitting with his feet propped up on the back of a chair fondling a revolver. His eyes looked more reptilian than human. He picked a scab on his chin as he spoke. "My men are on their way here with your wife and daughter. You have no idea what I'm prepared to do to them if you don't cooperate. I need the whereabouts of those Americans and I need it now."

"Do you have any idea how fucking stupid you are? How long do you think Seke will keep you around?"

"If I'm so stupid, why is your life in my hands?"

When Rigby didn't reply, he turned to Chitoa. "Warden, for the life of me, I can't understand why you're protecting these criminals. It's simple — talk to me and you're free to go. You describe yourself as a son of the revolution, but when your country needs help, you refuse. I should have let your inmates kill you."

Rigby spoke for Chitoa, "You must think he's as crazy as you are. You mean to kill us, no matter what we do. So, let's dispense with the formalities and get on with it." His boldness made Chitoa gasp.

Rhodes walked around from behind his desk. He jerked Rigby to his feet and yelled in his face, "I've waited a long time for this, and so help me God, I mean to enjoy it. Sergeant, put these two dogs back in their cage."

Rigby got the last word in and said, "Those American kids you were so eager to murder are in Zambia by now. By tomorrow, Seke will know the truth. So you see— your prospects are no better than mine."

"Croxford, your time on this earth is very limited. I'm going to enjoy your daughter." Rhodes stepped back anticipating his reaction. Rigby lunged at him, but the legs irons dropped him to his knees.

"Rhodes, you weren't born— you were hatched like a shit-eating maggot."

Rigby readied himself for Rhodes's violent reaction and he got it. The beating stopped when Rhodes was too exhausted to continue.

As Rigby was being dragged back to his holding pen, he noticed a guard armed with an AK-47 lurking in the shadows. He cocked his head to get a better view. What he saw was so upsetting, he dry-heaved. It was Steven Mabota.

22

Helen, Christine and Sadie objected when the guards tried to bind their hands. Helen goaded the soldiers by saying, "What are you so frightened of— three unarmed women?"

"But, *Amai*, these are my orders," the man in charge, explained.

Helen stood with her hands on her hips and announced defiantly, "I don't care what Rhodes ordered you to do. You're not trussing us up like three goats for the butchery. Someday, your Mr. Rhodes will pay for his crimes. I'd be careful if I were you. Let's hope you don't share his fate."

"Yes *Amai*," the soldier said, looking embarrassed. The soldiers motioned for them to start walking. Helen and Sadie followed Christine down the footpath.

As they marched, Helen asked the guards about their political leanings, but they ignored her. When she switched to medical issues, they seemed more interested.

At first, Christine couldn't fathom why her mother seemed so intent on engaging the guards with small talk and then it dawned on her— her mother's intention was to become more than a nameless victim.

Helen stopped abruptly and asked a guard, "Don't I know you?"

"You treated my wife at your clinic, *Amai*."

"How is your wife doing?"

"She died six months ago."

"I'm sorry for your loss. What caused her death?"

"It was the slow puncture," he answered, comparing her body to a deflating tire.

"So it was AIDS that took her life," Christine interjected. The man nodded his head affirmatively.

"How many wives do you have?"

"Right now, only three."

"Are they healthy?"

"Yes. They're all pregnant."

"You must be very proud," said Christine, sardonically.

The guards stopped talking as they entered the thorn-bush gate to the encampment. Helen protested when she learned they were to be separated. This time, her captors wouldn't relent. The women were escorted by armed guards to opposite ends of the encampment.

Later that night, Rhodes paid a visit to Helen. He folded back the tent flap and stuck his head in, announcing, "Good evening, Dr. Croxford. Sorry about the ungodly hour. I need your signature on this." He held up some papers.

Helen felt his eyes exploring her body. She instinctively pinched her collar together and grabbed the

[285]

document. She held it up to the light and took her time reading the first page.

"This says I've conspired to lead a coup against the government, which is total bullshit. I'm not signing this." She flung the papers in his face.

"Make no mistake about it— one way or another, you'll sign."

"Where's my daughter?"

"You needn't worry about your daughter. I'm taking good care of Christine." His face twisted into a suggestive sneer. The intimate ring of his words made Helen nauseous.

"Like you took care of Tim Brooks?"

"I don't know what you're talking about." His expression was riddled with nervous twitches.

"What about the Campbells? I suppose you don't know what happened to them, either. I'm sure my husband will be keen to hear you explain their deaths."

"Your husband has been arrested for subversive activities against the new government. He's being held here in protective custody."

"I don't believe you."

"Now you see — that's a real shame."

"If you're holding my husband, I want to see him."

"Very well— follow me."

His consent shocked her.

Rhodes and two armed guards escorted Helen to the bamboo holding pen. Helen glanced at Rhodes as he opened the gate and motioned for her to go inside. Why are you so full of yourself, she asked herself.

It was almost too dark to see. The air was saturated with the sweet metallic smell of fresh blood. Helen stumbled over something balled up in a corner of the cage. Her husband groaned. She stooped down and put her arms around Rigby and Joseph Chitoa.

"Rhodes, what have you done to my husband and this man? If you have a speck of human decency— you'll let me treat them."

"My dear lady, I'm not a barbarian. Of course you can treat your husband, but before you do, I want the confession signed."

"Don't sign it," her husband said in weak voice.

Helen hesitated and then said, "All right, give me the papers. Now, have someone bring me my medical bag."

Rhodes whispered to his moon-faced subordinate, "As soon as she signs, I want both of them executed. Pick men you can trust and do it away from the camp. Dump their bodies in the river."

"What about the daughter?"

Rhodes smiled and didn't answer.

*   *   *

23

Livingstone Island's shoreline was interrupted by a weathered shack. The men waded through thick elephant grass to reach it. When Dutchy kicked in the front door, bats exploded in every direction. Agnes and Latisha held torches as the men pried up the floor boards. The survival cache was exactly where Rigby said it would be. Each weapon had been carefully wrapped in oily rags and sealed in plastic wrappings. There were crates of ammunition, boxes of outdated K-rations and even a supply of black camouflage cream. Colin remarked that they had enough equipment to start a war.

The plan called for Harry, Agnes and the teenagers to escape downriver in the gunboat. Steven was supposed to steal a boat and rendezvous with Dutchy and the others. When Steven didn't show up, it became apparent that something had gone wrong.

Agnes asked Dutchy, "How long will it take you to march back to where they're holding Rigby and the others."

"Three to four hours."

"And by boat?"

"Fifteen minutes."

Colin intervened, "Ma'am, there's a chance Rhodes has found out we're not dead. You can bet you'll see that helicopter at first light. You and Harry need to take these kids and get out of here."

"Mr. White, I'm not a fool. We both know the boat gives you a better chance of getting away."

"We're wasting time, Mrs. Flaxney. Take the boat and go, before I change my mind."

"Harry can watch over my students. I'm going back with you."

"Sweetheart, you're talking rubbish." Harry said to Agnes.

"Part of this is my fault. Don't you see — I can't leave them."

"If something should 'appen to you, why, I reckon I wouldn't wanna go on living," Harry said. Agnes kissed him on his cheek.

Henry and Latisha stepped forward and raised their hands to speak. "We think we should have a voice in this," said Henry. Latisha nodded in agreement.

Jacob spoke up before Agnes could disagree, "I say, we all go back."

"Jacob's right, we should all go back," added Billy.

Agnes tried to argue, but the teenagers weren't listening. As she prepared to counter, Colin whispered to her, "Don't worry— I'll keep them out of harm's way. Truth be known, they're safer with us."

Colin gave the kids a quick weapons demonstration. Joshua joked that Henry already knew about firearms because he'd used them in armed robberies. Henry took the ribbing good-naturedly.

They all piled into the gunboat and pushed off. Dutchy smiled, looking at Jacob and Joshua huddled in the gunboat. Their faces were blackened with the camouflage cream. They had ammunition bandoliers crisscrossing their chests. They *were* afraid of their own shadows and now look at them. My children's army of overnight men, he thought.

As they neared the campsite, Colin cut the outboard engine and let the gunboat snuggle up against the riverbank. Everyone climbed out and disappeared silently into the torpedo grass.

Away from the river, Dutchy suggested that Agnes stay behind with the teenagers. Initially, she complained, but relented when Harry supported Dutchy. Davy also agreed to stay behind, but without warning he vanished into the night.

The men got close enough to hear the soldiers' voices. Dutchy whispered to Ezekiel, "Get closer and find out where they're holding our women." Ezekiel crawled away.

*   *   *

24

Helen scribbled her signature on the confession and handed it to Rhodes. He refused to hand her the medical bag. He handed it to a man standing behind him.

"Dr. Croxford, surely you can't expect me to waste precious medicine on condemned criminals."

"You despicable bastard," Helen tried to slap him, but he grabbed her hand.

"Sergeant, do your duty."

The sergeant came to attention and pointed his weapon at Rigby.

Rhodes grabbed Rigby and yelled in his face, "Croxford, I hope your last thought is of me shagging your daughter."

Rigby tried to head butt him, but Rhodes expected it and stepped back.

They blindfolded Helen, Rigby, Chitoa and Sadie and led them down a darkened path. Rigby knew they were to be executed. He sensed they were being marched to the river.

"Helen, listen to me. When I charge, you make for the water. It's our only option. Remember how much I love you."

"If you love me, don't resist. Do you understand me?"

"Yes, but…"

"Please, just do as I say."

The soldiers lined up the condemned prisoners with their backs to the river's edge. Chitoa had to be helped to his feet. Rigby asked to have his blindfold removed, but his request was denied. There was no granting of last requests. Rigby's thinking was numbed by fear and then he heard a familiar voice shout, "Ready… aim…fire!" The blast stunned Chitoa— he fell to his knees. The rest of the prisoners stood fast.

Ezekiel had crawled within a few meters of the clearing where the execution was being staged, but his view was obscured. The boom of multiple rifle shots fired simultaneously startled him. He'd heard the sound of a firing squad before. He knew someone had been executed.

25

Sulfur fused smoke made it hard to see. Rigby held his breath and waited for the pain. When it didn't come, he exhaled. Chitoa, realizing that he was still alive, giggled. He searched his body for a bullet wound and when he didn't find one, he laughed hysterically.

Steven Mabota pulled Rigby's blindfold off and cut his bindings. The executioners, having mock-fired their weapons, were gone.

"Bloody hell, Steven, I thought we were finished. Why didn't you say something?" he said, looking at his wife. "Look what you've done to poor Chitoa." Chitoa was sobbing with his hands locked in prayer.

"It happened so fast I didn't have time. I never thought Rhodes would go through with it," Steven replied.

Ezekiel walked out of the underbrush. "I see you, my brother," he said, greeting Rigby.

"Where's Dutchy?"

"Not far," Ezekiel said, pointing.

"Did you find the weapons?"

"*Yebo*, where you said we would."

The sound of gunfire brought Dutchy and the others. It also brought Rhodes's men. Steven had been working behind the scenes to turn Rhodes's men against him. Their allegiance was based only on fear. They willingly turned against their leader.

Dutchy grabbed his wife and hoisted her in the air. A soldier had escorted Dutchy's children to the clearing—when they saw their father they ran to him. The jubilation ended with Helen's shrieking, "Where's Christine?"

Rigby demanded that everyone stay put, except Steven, who led him back to Rhodes's command tent.

Darkness made the illuminated tent transparent. A lone silhouette moved on the inside. Rigby ducked underneath the tent flap, and stood there undetected. Rhodes was talking to someone only he could see in his demented mind. Rigby's daughter had been tied facedown to an army cot. Rhodes smiled maniacally as he knelt down and stroked her hair. When he playfully spanked her bare buttocks, she began to cry. Her sobbing enraged Rigby, but he kept quiet and moved closer. The forearm smash delivered to the base of Rhodes's skull dropped him like he'd taken a bullet to the brain.

Rigby wrapped his daughter in a blanket and held her for a long time without speaking. She tried to say something, but he stopped her. He brushed away her tears and then his. "Christine, did he...?"

"No." she answered.

Rhodes was conscious, but disoriented. When he saw Rigby, he gasped. His eyes said he knew he was about to die.

"Before I kill you, I want some questions answered."

"I've devoted my life to this country. Someday, Zimbabweans will erect a statue in my memory."

"Good God, you really are insane. Unfortunately, we're not accepting insanity as a plea. So tell me, did you spy for the Russians in the war or not?"

Before Rhodes could deny the accusation, everyone rushed into the tent. Helen ran to her daughter and cradled her. The women cried. Agnes motioned for the men to leave.

As soon as Rigby dragged Rhodes outside, his soldiers turned on him like a pack of feeding hyenas. He begged, but they wouldn't stop beating him. Rigby ended it by firing a warning shot.

"This man has wronged me and I *will* have my revenge."

The mob cheered. Rigby held a pistol to Rhodes's head. The crowd chanted, "Do it— do it."

Helen's reappearance silenced them. "Hasn't there been enough killing? I'm begging you, don't do this. Let others judge him. One way or another, he'll pay for his crimes."

"This man's responsible for the deaths of innocent people. I signed a blood oath to avenge their deaths." He cocked his pistol and pressed the barrel against Rhodes's temple.

"Don't you see, if you kill him, we're the ones who'll suffer."

"You may suffer, but I won't."

"And that doesn't matter to you?"

Her words defused him. His eyes softened. He stood there for what seemed like an eternity before tossing the pistol aside. She wrapped her arms around him. They reentered the tent together. The mob dispersed quietly.

Steven ordered the soldiers to lock Rhodes up in his bamboo cage. Without hesitation they complied.

*   *   *

A blanket of predawn fog settled over the camp. Fatigue had pounded the survivors into submission. The soldiers were also exhausted. The camp was silent as everyone slept.

Davy Crockett and Ezekiel slipped into the encampment unseen. They unlocked the bamboo cage that imprisoned Rhodes, who was now babbling to himself. After tying a rope around Rhodes's neck they tiptoed between some sleeping soldiers and disappeared down the path leading to the river. After they reached the riverbank, they helped Rhodes into one of the boats.

As Ezekiel fended the boat off, Davy yelled to his friend, "Go well, my friend." Ezekiel waved goodbye and then disappeared behind in the fog.

Davy and Rhodes idled downriver in silence for a long time before Rhodes spoke, "I don't know who you are, but I'm gonna make you very rich. Can you understand me?"

Davy acted like he didn't understand. His smile unnerved Rhodes and he asked, "Why did you save my life?" Again, Davy pretended ignorance. He grinned, picked up his honey badger cap and put it on. Instantly, Rhodes recognized him.

"I'll give you anything you want— anything, just name it." Davy ignored him and pressed on downriver.

As they approached the eastern cataract of Victoria Falls the current became stronger. A deafening thunderous rumble echoed from the bowels of the gorge. Beyond the waterfall, the horizon vanished into infinity.

Rhodes wiped the mist from his eyes and shouted over the roar, "Why are you doing this to me?"

The old Tonga ignored him. Rhodes cried out, "You crazy bastard, you're gonna kill us both." Davy's gap-toothed smile broadened.

Rhodes knocked him aside and grabbed the steering wheel. Davy had disconnected the fuel hose from the outboard. The engine sputtered a few times and quit. Rhodes pulled on the rope starter, but the engine wouldn't fire. The powerless boat drifted towards the abyss.

Davy laughed and slapped his thigh as Rhodes tried to paddle with his hands. At the last minute, Rhodes struggled into a lifejacket and jumped overboard. Swimming against the current was a waste of time. He teetered for a few moments by clinging to a rock, and then fell kicking and screaming over the rim.

Davy made no effort to save himself as he was sucked over the falls. Time slowed down into a dreamlike unreality. As he fell he saw a vision of Tim Brooks in the mist and then everything went black.

*   *   *

26

Ian Rhodes's head was alive. A broken neck had severed the nerves to his extremities. The life preserver supporting his head allowed him to breathe. He screamed, but his voice was soundless. As he floated downriver, placid eddies and gentle whirlpools rotated his lifeless body in circles giving him panoramic vision. The lazy current drifted him until he came to rest on a sandbar. He bobbed there motionless for hours.

His mind wandered in and out of consciousness. Suddenly, he felt an evil presence. Fear like he had never known consumed him. He cried out, but again it was a wasted effort. When he blinked away the water, what he saw made his heart race. He was looking at scaly monsters with snaggle-tooth grins and yellow-sickle eyes blinking behind transparent lids.

The crocodiles were impatient, but cautious. When they bumped Rhodes's body with their snouts he didn't resist, which bolstered their curiosity. They surrounded him and slowly tightened the circle.

Without warning, an emboldened female turned on her side and latched on to Rhodes's right arm as another man-eater grabbed his left arm. Both crocs started their death rolls in opposite directions. He felt no pain as he was being torn apart. His last thought was that he was witnessing someone else's death. Smaller crocs took turns twisting off chunks from his armless torso. The same big female made off with what was left of Rhodes to store him in her underwater den. Catfish devoured the bits of flesh suspended in the blood boil. Within minutes, only the life preserver remained. It was like what had happened never occurred.

The air was sweet and cool. The setting sun dusted the cliffs in shades of gold and red. The Zambezi was serene once again.

Victoria Falls Hotel
Two years later

The political speeches droned on. Intermittent shafts of sunlight shining through the limbs of mango trees drenched the attendees. Unable to endure the heat, men shed their coats and women used colorful parasols as sun-blockers. The light breeze wasn't strong enough to rustle the leaves. The resident baboon troop succumbed to the unrelenting heat. A juvenile ape started a ruckus, but it was short-lived.

Looking westward, the Zambezi disappeared behind bluish hills that had been thrust upward from the center of the earth by volcanic eruptions. Far away, the same river emptied into the Indian Ocean.

Steven Timothy Mabota let his mind wander from the rehearsal of his speech. Was his elation misplaced? He had felt this way before, only to be disappointed. Of course, there would be challenges, but maybe this really was a new beginning.

Suddenly Steven realized everyone was standing and applauding, and it was directed at him. After locating Rigby, he stepped forward to the podium. The crowd pressed forward to hear him. When he raised his arms, the audience hushed.

"Fellow Zimbabweans— we are here today to write a new chapter in African politics. The newly elected president must convey to the world— come to Zimbabwe— invest in our future and you will be rewarded beyond your wildest dreams. Give us the opportunity to show you what we can do. Be assured, there will be no meddlesome politicians looking for bribes.

"The new president seeks no personal gain from this election and will grant no special favors. I think we have elected the right person at the right moment in our history. I give you the new president of Zimbabwe— the Honorable Dr. Helen Croxford."

EPILOGUE

*J*eremiah Seke was forced into exile after the plot to kill the Americans was foiled.

*T*he American government sent a private aircraft to Zimbabwe to transport the teenagers back to the United States. The last thing Agnes said to her students was, "Someday, when you're old like me, you'll reminisce about what you endured here and you'll know that you handled yourselves with great courage. I am so very proud to know each one of you."

*R*igby Croxford and Dutchy Bosshart returned to their respective farms. Rigby gave some land to Ezekiel to farm. He lives there with his three wives and fourteen children.

*C*hristine Croxford rebuilt her mother's medical clinic.

*A*gnes and Harry Flaxney moved to Bulawayo. Agnes teaches African children in a rural school. Harry works as a game warden.

*J*oseph Chitoa resumed his position as the warden of Hwange Prison.

*C*olin White reopened his fishing camp.

*W*ith Rigby's blessings, Steven Mabota and Helen Croxford were flown to Harare to help form an interim government.

*P*art of the plan to rebuild Zimbabwe was that farmers whose land had been confiscated could lease back their farms for ninety-nine years at a cost of one dollar. The only stipulation was that a portion of their profits would be used to send black students to agricultural colleges in Europe and the United States. The International Monetary Fund guaranteed the farm loans. Hospitals and schools reopened. Slowly, the transformation of Zimbabwe began to take shape.

*W*hat happened on the Zambezi changed all of them.

COMING AUGUST 2011
PENNINGTON
PUBLISHERS

In Book Three of James Gardner's Dark Continent Chronicles trilogy, Rigby Croxford leaves Africa and travels to America where he helps protect his brother-in-law, a newscaster/journalist from a foreign government trying to silence him.

The conspiring government's ultimate goal is the complete destruction of the American economy. Their flawless strategy is as real as it is sinister. Their fanaticism is unwavering.

One man will try to stop them...

Read more about James Gardner and
The *Dark Continent Chronicles* at:

JamesGardnerNow@blogspot.com

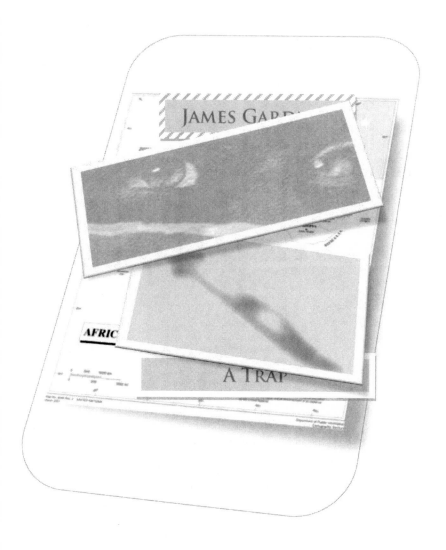

THE THRILL RIDE THAT STARTED IT ALL
THE LION KILLER
BOOK ONE OF *THE DARK CONTINENT CHRONICLES*

THE LION KILLER

DARK CONTINENT CHRONICLES BOOK I

"*A riveting thriller...with twists and turns galore.*"
Robert Halmi, Jr. President, RHI Entertainment. Executive Producer of
the Award Winning series, *Lonesome Dove*

"*Few really good books come out of Africa, but James
Gardner's The Lion Killer is one of them. His powerful writing
illuminates The Dark Continent.*"
Nelson DeMille, New York Times Best-Selling Author

JAMES GARDNER

"*I highly recommend The Lion Killer. I have
seldom come across such fine descriptive writing
in a thriller* "

—James Patterson, America's
Best Selling Author